MONSTER EDITION #1

Look for more Goosebumps books
by R.L. STINE:

MONSTER EDITION #1

R.L. STINE

Three scary Goosebumps novels to make you scream!

#1 *Welcome to Dead House*
#2 *Stay Out of the Basement*
#4 *Say Cheese and Die!*

Scholastic Inc.
New York

A PARACHUTE PRESS BOOK

ISBN 0-590-50995-0

Compilation copyright © 1995 by Parachute Press, Inc.
All rights reserved. Published by Scholastic Inc.
GOOSEBUMPS is a registered trademark of Parachute Press, Inc.

12 11 10 9 8 7 6 5 4 3   5 6 7 8 9/9 0/0

Printed in the U.S.A.   37

First Scholastic printing, October 1995

CONTENTS

MONSTER EDITION #1

Welcome to Dead House

GOOSEBUMPS #1

Josh and I hated our new house.

Sure, it was big. It looked like a mansion compared to our old house. It was a tall redbrick house with a sloping black roof and rows of windows framed by black shutters.

It's so dark, I thought, studying it from the street. The whole house was covered in darkness, as if it were hiding in the shadows of the gnarled, old trees that bent over it.

It was the middle of July, but dead brown leaves blanketed the front yard. Our sneakers crunched over them as we trudged up the gravel driveway.

Tall weeds poked up everywhere through the dead leaves. Thick clumps of weeds had completely overgrown an old flower bed beside the front porch.

This house is creepy, I thought unhappily.

Josh must have been thinking the same thing. Looking up at the old house, we both groaned loudly.

Mr. Dawes, the friendly young man from the local real estate office, stopped near the front walk and turned around.

"Everything okay?" he asked, staring first at Josh, then at me, with his crinkly blue eyes.

"Josh and Amanda aren't happy about moving," Dad explained, tucking his shirttail in. Dad is a little overweight, and his shirts always seem to be coming untucked.

"It's hard for kids," my mother added, smiling at Mr. Dawes, her hands shoved into her jeans pockets as she continued up to the front door. "You know. Leaving all of their friends behind. Moving to a strange new place."

"Strange is right," Josh said, shaking his head. "This house is gross."

Mr. Dawes chuckled. "It's an old house, that's for sure," he said, patting Josh on the shoulder.

"It just needs some work, Josh," Dad said, smiling at Mr. Dawes. "No one has lived in it for a while, so it'll take some fixing up."

"Look how big it is," Mom added, smoothing back her straight black hair and smiling at Josh. "We'll have room for a den and maybe a rec room, too. You'd like that — wouldn't you, Amanda?"

I shrugged. A cold breeze made me shiver. It was actually a beautiful, hot summer day. But the closer we got to the house, the colder I felt.

I guessed it was because of all the tall, old trees.

I was wearing white tennis shorts and a sleeveless blue T-shirt. It had been hot in the car. But now I was freezing. Maybe it'll be warmer in the house, I thought.

"How old are they?" Mr. Dawes asked Mom, stepping onto the front porch.

"Amanda is twelve," Mom answered. "And Josh turned eleven last month."

"They look so much alike," Mr. Dawes told Mom.

I couldn't decide if that was a compliment or not. I guess it's true. Josh and I are both tall and thin and have curly brown hair like Dad's, and dark brown eyes. Everyone says we have "serious" faces.

"I really want to go home," Josh said, his voice cracking. "I hate this place."

My brother is the most impatient kid in the world. And when he makes up his mind about something, that's it. He's a little spoiled. At least, I think so. Whenever he makes a big fuss about something, he usually gets his way.

We may look alike, but we're really not that similar. I'm a lot more patient than Josh is. A lot more sensible. Probably because I'm older and because I'm a girl.

Josh had hold of Dad's hand and was trying to pull him back to the car. "Let's go. Come on, Dad. Let's go."

I knew this was one time Josh wouldn't get his way. We were moving to this house. No doubt about it. After all, the house was absolutely free. A great-uncle of Dad's, a man we didn't even know, had died and left the house to Dad in his will.

I'll never forget the look on Dad's face when he got the letter from the lawyer. He let out a loud whoop and began dancing around the living room. Josh and I thought he'd flipped or something.

"My Great-Uncle Charles has left us a house in his will," Dad explained, reading and rereading the letter. "It's in a town called Dark Falls."

"Huh?" Josh and I cried. "Where's Dark Falls?"

Dad shrugged.

"I don't remember your Uncle Charles," Mom said, moving behind Dad to read the letter over his shoulder.

"Neither do I," admitted Dad. "But he must've been a great guy! Wow! This sounds like an incredible house!" He grabbed Mom's hands and began dancing happily with her across the living room.

Dad sure was excited. He'd been looking for an excuse to quit his boring office job and devote all of his time to his writing career. This house — absolutely free — would be just the excuse he needed.

And now, a week later, here we were in Dark Falls, a four-hour drive from our home, seeing our new house for the first time. We hadn't even gone inside, and Josh was trying to drag Dad back to the car.

"Josh — stop pulling me," Dad snapped impatiently, trying to tug his hand out of Josh's grasp.

Dad glanced helplessly at Mr. Dawes. I could see that he was embarrassed by how Josh was carrying on. I decided maybe I could help.

"Let go, Josh," I said quietly, grabbing Josh by the shoulder. "We promised we'd give Dark Falls a chance — remember?"

"I already gave it a chance," Josh whined, not letting go of Dad's hand. "This house is old and ugly and I hate it."

"You haven't even gone inside," Dad said angrily.

"Yes. Let's go in," Mr. Dawes urged, staring at Josh.

"I'm staying outside," Josh insisted.

He can be really stubborn sometimes. I felt just as unhappy as Josh looking at this dark, old house. But I'd never carry on the way Josh was.

"Josh, don't you want to pick out your own room?" Mom asked.

"No," Josh muttered.

He and I both glanced up to the second floor. There were two large bay windows side by side up there. They looked like two dark eyes staring back at us.

"How long have you lived in your present house?" Mr. Dawes asked Dad.

Dad had to think for a second. "About fourteen years," he answered. "The kids have lived there for their whole lives."

"Moving is always hard," Mr. Dawes said sympathetically, turning his gaze on me. "You know, Amanda, I moved here to Dark Falls just a few months ago. I didn't like it much either, at first. But now I wouldn't live anywhere else." He winked at me. He had a cute dimple in his chin when he smiled. "Let's go inside. It's really quite nice. You'll be surprised."

All of us followed Mr. Dawes, except Josh. "Are there other kids on this block?" Josh demanded. He made it sound more like a challenge than a question.

Mr. Dawes nodded. "The school's just two blocks away," he said, pointing up the street.

"See?" Mom quickly cut in. "A short walk to school. No more long bus rides every morning."

"I *liked* the bus," Josh insisted.

His mind was made up. He wasn't going to give my parents a break, even though we'd both promised to be open-minded about this move.

I don't know what Josh thought he had to gain by being such a pain. I mean, Dad already had plenty to worry about. For one thing, he hadn't been able to sell our old house yet.

I didn't like the idea of moving. But I knew that inheriting this big house was a great opportunity for us. We were so cramped in our little house.

10

And once Dad managed to sell the old place, we wouldn't have to worry at all about money anymore.

Josh should at least give it a chance. That's what I thought.

Suddenly, from our car at the foot of the driveway, we heard Petey barking and howling and making a fuss.

Petey is our dog, a white, curly-haired terrier, cute as a button, and usually well-behaved. He never minded being left in the car. But now he was yowling and yapping at full volume and scratching at the car window, desperate to get out.

"Petey — quiet! Quiet!" I shouted. Petey usually listened to me.

But not this time.

"I'm going to let him out!" Josh declared, and took off down the driveway toward the car.

"No. Wait — " Dad called.

But I don't think Josh could hear him over Petey's wails.

"Might as well let the dog explore," Mr. Dawes said. "It's going to be his house, too."

A few seconds later, Petey came charging across the lawn, kicking up brown leaves, yipping excitedly as he ran up to us. He jumped on all of us as if he hadn't seen us in weeks and then, to our surprise, he started growling menacingly and barking at Mr. Dawes.

"Petey — stop!" Mom yelled.

"He's never done this," Dad said apologetically. "Really. He's usually very friendly."

"He probably smells something on me. Another dog, maybe," Mr. Dawes said, loosening his striped tie, looking warily at our growling dog.

Finally, Josh grabbed Petey around the middle and lifted him away from Mr. Dawes. "Stop it, Petey," Josh scolded, holding the dog up close to his face so that they were nose-to-nose. "Mr. Dawes is our friend."

Petey whimpered and licked Josh's face. After a short while, Josh set him back down on the ground. Petey looked up at Mr. Dawes, then at me, then decided to go sniffing around the yard, letting his nose lead the way.

"Let's go inside," Mr. Dawes urged, moving a hand through his short blond hair. He unlocked the front door and pushed it open.

Mr. Dawes held the screen door open for us. I started to follow my parents into the house.

"I'll stay out here with Petey," Josh insisted from the walk.

Dad started to protest, but changed his mind. "Okay. Fine," he said, sighing and shaking his head. "I'm not going to argue with you. Don't come in. You can *live* outside if you want." He sounded really exasperated.

"I want to stay with Petey," Josh said again,

watching Petey nose his way through the dead flower bed.

Mr. Dawes followed us into the hallway, gently closing the screen door behind him, giving Josh a final glance. "He'll be fine," he said softly, smiling at Mom.

"He can be so stubborn sometimes," Mom said apologetically. She peeked into the living room. "I'm really sorry about Petey. I don't know what got into that dog."

"No problem. Let's start in the living room," Mr. Dawes said, leading the way. "I think you'll be pleasantly surprised by how spacious it is. Of course, it needs work."

He took us on a tour of every room in the house. I was beginning to get excited. The house was really kind of neat. There were so many rooms and so many closets. And my room was huge and had its own bathroom and an old-fashioned window seat where I could sit at the window and look down at the street.

I wished Josh had come inside with us. If he could see how great the house was inside, I knew he'd start to cheer up.

I couldn't believe how many rooms there were. Even a finished attic filled with old furniture and stacks of old, mysterious cartons we could explore.

We must have been inside for at least half an

hour. I didn't really keep track of the time. I think all three of us were feeling cheered up.

"Well, I think I've shown you everything," Mr. Dawes said, glancing at his watch. He led the way to the front door.

"Wait — I want to take one more look at my room," I told them excitedly. I started up the stairs, taking them two at a time. "I'll be down in a second."

"Hurry, dear. I'm sure Mr. Dawes has other appointments," Mom called after me.

I reached the second-floor landing and hurried down the narrow hallway and into my new room. "Wow!" I said aloud, and the word echoed faintly against the empty walls.

It was so big. And I loved the bay window with the window seat. I walked over to it and peered out. Through the trees, I could see our car in the driveway and, beyond it, a house that looked a lot like ours across the street.

I'm going to put my bed against that wall across from the window, I thought happily. And my desk can go over there. I'll have room for a computer now!

I took one more look at my closet, a long, walk-in closet with a light in the ceiling, and wide shelves against the back wall.

I was heading to the door, thinking about which of my posters I wanted to bring with me, when I saw the boy.

14

He stood in the doorway for just a second. And then he turned and disappeared down the hall.

"Josh?" I cried. "Hey — come look!"

With a shock, I realized it wasn't Josh.

For one thing, the boy had blond hair.

"Hey!" I called and ran to the hallway, stopping just outside my bedroom door, looking both ways. "Who's here?"

But the long hall was empty. All of the doors were closed.

"Whoa, Amanda," I said aloud.

Was I seeing things?

Mom and Dad were calling from downstairs. I took one last look down the dark corridor, then hurried to rejoin them.

"Hey, Mr. Dawes," I called as I ran down the stairs, "is this house haunted?"

He chuckled. The question seemed to strike him funny. "No. Sorry," he said, looking at me with those crinkly blue eyes. "No ghost included. A lot of old houses around here are said to be haunted. But I'm afraid this isn't one of them."

"I — I thought I saw something," I said, feeling a little foolish.

"Probably just shadows," Mom said. "With all the trees, this house is so dark."

"Why don't you run outside and tell Josh about the house," Dad suggested, tucking in the front of his shirt. "Your Mom and I have some things to talk over with Mr. Dawes."

15

"Yes, master," I said with a little bow, and obediently ran out to tell Josh all about what he had missed. "Hey, Josh," I called, eagerly searching the yard. "Josh?"

My heart sank.

Josh and Petey were gone.

2

"Josh! Josh!"

First I called Josh. Then I called Petey. But there was no sign of either of them.

I ran down to the bottom of the driveway and peered into the car, but they weren't there. Mom and Dad were still inside talking with Mr. Dawes. I looked along the street in both directions, but there was no sign of them.

"Josh! Hey, Josh!"

Finally, Mom and Dad came hurrying out the front door, looking alarmed. I guess they heard my shouts. "I can't find Josh or Petey!" I yelled up to them from the street.

"Maybe they're around back," Dad shouted down to me.

I headed up the driveway, kicking away dead leaves as I ran. It was sunny down on the street, but as soon as I entered our yard, I was back in the shade, and it was immediately cool again.

"Hey, Josh! Josh — where are you?"

Why did I feel so scared? It was perfectly natural for Josh to wander off. He did it all the time.

I ran full speed along the side of the house. Tall trees leaned over the house on this side, blocking out nearly all of the sunlight.

The backyard was bigger than I'd expected, a long rectangle that sloped gradually down to a wooden fence at the back. Just like the front, this yard was a mass of tall weeds, poking up through a thick covering of brown leaves. A stone birdbath had toppled onto its side. Beyond it, I could see the side of the garage, a dark, brick building that matched the house.

"Hey — Josh!"

He wasn't back here. I stopped and searched the ground for footprints or a sign that he had run through the thick leaves.

"Well?" Out of breath, Dad came jogging up to me.

"No sign of him," I said, surprised at how worried I felt.

"Did you check the car?" He sounded more angry than worried.

"Yes. It's the first place I looked." I gave the backyard a last quick search. "I don't believe Josh would just take off."

"I do," Dad said, rolling his eyes. "You know your brother when he doesn't get his way. Maybe he wants us to think he's run away from home." He frowned.

"Where is he?" Mom asked as we returned to the front of the house.

Dad and I both shrugged. "Maybe he made a friend and wandered off," Dad said. He raised a hand and scratched his curly brown hair. I could tell that he was starting to worry, too.

"We've *got* to find him," Mom said, gazing down to the street. "He doesn't know this neighborhood at all. He probably wandered off and got lost."

Mr. Dawes locked the front door and stepped down off the porch, pocketing the keys. "He couldn't have gotten far," he said, giving Mom a reassuring smile. "Let's drive around the block. I'm sure we'll find him."

Mom shook her head and glanced nervously at Dad. "I'll kill him," she muttered. Dad patted her on the shoulder.

Mr. Dawes opened the trunk of the small Honda, pulled off his dark blazer, and tossed it inside. Then he took out a wide-brimmed, black cowboy hat and put it on his head.

"Hey — that's quite a hat," Dad said, climbing into the front passenger seat.

"Keeps the sun away," Mr. Dawes said, sliding behind the wheel and slamming the car door.

Mom and I got in back. Glancing over at her, I saw that Mom was as worried as I was.

We headed down the block in silence, all four of us staring out the car windows. The houses we passed all seemed old. Most of them were even bigger than our house. All of them seemed to be in better condition, nicely painted with neat, well-trimmed lawns.

I didn't see any people in the houses or yards, and there was no one on the street.

It certainly is a *quiet* neighborhood, I thought. And shady. The houses all seemed to be sur-rounded by tall, leafy trees. The front yards we drove slowly past all seemed to be bathed in shade. The street was the only sunny place, a narrow gold ribbon that ran through the shadows on both sides.

Maybe that's why it's called Dark Falls, I thought.

"Where is that son of mine?" Dad asked, staring hard out the windshield.

"I'll kill him. I really will," Mom muttered. It wasn't the first time she had said that about Josh.

We had gone around the block twice. No sign of him.

Mr. Dawes suggested we drive around the next few blocks, and Dad quickly agreed. "Hope I don't get lost. I'm new here, too," Mr. Dawes said, turning a corner. "Hey, there's the school," he announced, pointing out the window at a tall red-brick building. It looked very old-fashioned, with white columns on both sides of the double front doors. "Of course, it's closed now," Mr. Dawes added.

My eyes searched the fenced-in playground behind the school. It was empty. No one there.

"Could Josh have walked this far?" Mom asked, her voice tight and higher than usual.

"Josh doesn't walk," Dad said, rolling his eyes. "He runs."

"We'll find him," Mr. Dawes said confidently, tapping his fingers on the wheel as he steered.

We turned a corner onto another shady block. A street sign read "Cemetery Drive," and sure enough, a large cemetery rose up in front of us. Granite gravestones rolled along a low hill, which sloped down and then up again onto a large flat stretch, also marked with rows of low grave markers and monuments.

A few shrubs dotted the cemetery, but there weren't many trees. As we drove slowly past, the gravestones passing by in a blur on the left, I realized that this was the sunniest spot I had seen in the whole town.

"There's your son." Mr. Dawes, pointing out the window, stopped the car suddenly.

"Oh, thank goodness!" Mom exclaimed, leaning down to see out the window on my side of the car.

Sure enough, there was Josh, running wildly along a crooked row of low, white gravestones. "What's he doing *here*?" I asked, pushing open my car door.

I stepped down from the car, took a few steps onto the grass, and called to him. At first, he didn't react to my shouts. He seemed to be ducking and

21

dodging through the tombstones. He would run in one direction, then cut to the side, then head in another direction.

Why was he doing that?

I took another few steps — and then stopped, gripped with fear.

I suddenly realized why Josh was darting and ducking like that, running so wildly through the tombstones. He was being chased.

Someone — or something — was after him.

Then, as I took a few reluctant steps toward Josh, watching him bend low, then change directions, his arms outstretched as he ran, I realized I had it completely backward.

Josh wasn't being chased. Josh was *chasing*.

He was chasing after Petey.

Okay, okay. So sometimes my imagination runs away with me. Running through an old graveyard like this — even in bright daylight — it's only natural that a person might start to have weird thoughts.

I called to Josh again, and this time he heard me and turned around. He looked worried. "Amanda — come help me!" he cried.

"Josh, what's the matter?" I ran as fast as I could to catch up with him, but he kept darting through the gravestones, moving from row to row.

"Help!"

"Josh — what's wrong?" I turned and saw that

Mom and Dad were right behind me.

"It's Petey," Josh explained, out of breath. "I can't get him to stop. I caught him once, but he pulled away from me."

"Petey! Petey!" Dad started calling the dog. But Petey was moving from stone to stone, sniffing each one, then running to the next.

"How did you get all the way over here?" Dad asked as he caught up with my brother.

"I had to follow Petey," Josh explained, still looking very worried. "He just took off. One second he was sniffing around that dead flower bed in our front yard. The next second, he just started to run. He wouldn't stop when I called. Wouldn't even look back. He kept running till he got here. I had to follow. I was afraid he'd get lost."

Josh stopped and gratefully let Dad take over the chase. "I don't know what that dumb dog's problem is," he said to me. "He's just *weird*."

It took Dad a few tries, but he finally managed to grab Petey and pick him up off the ground. Our little terrier gave a halfhearted yelp of protest, then allowed himself to be carried away.

We all trooped back to the car on the side of the road. Mr. Dawes was waiting by the car. "Maybe you'd better get a leash for that dog," he said, looking very concerned.

"Petey's never been on a leash," Josh protested, wearily climbing into the backseat.

"Well, we might have to try one for a while,"

Dad said quietly. "Especially if he keeps running away." Dad tossed Petey into the backseat. The dog eagerly curled up in Josh's arms.

The rest of us piled into the car, and Mr. Dawes drove us back to his office, a tiny, white, flat-roofed building at the end of a row of small offices. As we rode, I reached over and stroked the back of Petey's head.

Why did the dog run away like that? I wondered. Petey had never done that before.

I guessed that Petey was also upset about our moving. After all, Petey had spent his whole life in our old house. He probably felt a lot like Josh and I did about having to pack up and move and never see the old neighborhood again.

The new house, the new streets, and all the new smells must have freaked the poor dog out. Josh wanted to run away from the whole idea. And so did Petey.

Anyway, that was my theory.

Mr. Dawes parked the car in front of his tiny office, shook Dad's hand, and gave him a business card. "You can come by next week," he told Mom and Dad. "I'll have all the legal work done by then. After you sign the papers, you can move in anytime."

He pushed open the car door and, giving us all a final smile, prepared to climb out.

"Compton Dawes," Mom said, reading the white business card over Dad's shoulder. "That's an unusual name. Is Compton an old family name?"

Mr. Dawes shook his head. "No," he said, "I'm the only Compton in my family. I have no idea where the name comes from. No idea at all. Maybe my parents didn't know how to spell Charlie!"

Chuckling at his terrible joke, he climbed out of the car, lowered the wide black Stetson hat on his head, pulled his blazer from the trunk, and disappeared into the small white building.

Dad climbed behind the wheel, moving the seat back to make room for his big stomach. Mom got up front, and we started the long drive home. "I guess you and Petey had quite an adventure today," Mom said to Josh, rolling up her window because Dad had turned on the air conditioner.

"I guess," Josh said without enthusiasm. Petey was sound asleep in his lap, snoring quietly.

"You're going to love your room," I told Josh. "The whole house is great. Really."

Josh stared at me thoughtfully, but didn't answer.

I poked him in the ribs with my elbow. "Say something. Did you hear what I said?"

But the weird, thoughtful look didn't fade from Josh's face.

The next couple of weeks seemed to crawl by. I walked around the house thinking about how I'd never see my room again, how I'd never eat breakfast in this kitchen again, how I'd never watch TV in the living room again. Morbid stuff like that.

I had this sick feeling when the movers came one afternoon and delivered a tall stack of cartons. Time to pack up. It was really happening. Even though it was the middle of the afternoon, I went up to my room and flopped down on my bed. I didn't nap or anything. I just stared at the ceiling for more than an hour, and all these wild, unconnected thoughts ran through my head, like a dream, only I was awake.

I wasn't the only one who was nervous about the move. Mom and Dad were snapping at each other over nothing at all. One morning they had a big fight over whether the bacon was too crispy or not.

In a way, it was funny to see them being so childish. Josh was acting really sullen all the time. He hardly spoke a word to anyone. And Petey sulked, too. That dumb dog wouldn't even pick himself up and come over to me when I had some table scraps for him.

I guess the hardest part about moving was saying good-bye to my friends. Carol and Amy were away at camp, so I had to write to them. But Kathy was home, and she was my oldest and best friend, and the hardest to say good-bye to.

I think some people were surprised that Kathy and I had stayed such good friends. For one thing, we look so different. I'm tall and thin and dark, and she's fair-skinned, with long blonde hair, and a little chubby. But we've been friends since pre-school, and best best friends since fourth grade.

When she came over the night before the move, we were both terribly awkward. "Kathy, you shouldn't be nervous," I told her. "You're not the one who's moving away forever."

"It's not like you're moving to China or something," she answered, chewing hard on her bubble gum. "Dark Falls is only four hours away, Amanda. We'll see each other a lot."

"Yeah, I guess," I said. But I didn't believe it. Four hours away was as bad as being in China, as far as I was concerned. "I guess we can still talk on the phone," I said glumly.

She blew a small green bubble, then sucked it back into her mouth. "Yeah. Sure," she said, pretending to be enthusiastic. "You're lucky, you know. Moving out of this crummy neighborhood to a big house."

"It's *not* a crummy neighborhood," I insisted. I don't know why I was defending the neighborhood. I never had before. One of our favorite pastimes was thinking of places we'd rather be growing up.

"School won't be the same without you," she sighed, curling her legs under her on the chair. "Who's going to slip me the answers in math?"

I laughed. "I always slipped you the *wrong* answers."

"But it was the thought that counted," Kathy said. And then she groaned. "Ugh. Junior high. Is your new junior high part of the high school or part of the elementary school?"

I made a disgusted face. "Everything's in one building. It's a small town, remember? There's no separate high school. At least, I didn't see one."

"Bummer," she said.

Bummer was right.

We chatted for hours. Until Kathy's mom called and said it was time for her to come home.

Then we hugged. I had made up my mind that I wouldn't cry, but I could feel the big, hot tears forming in the corners of my eyes. And then they were running down my cheeks.

"I'm so miserable!" I wailed.

I had planned to be really controlled and mature. But Kathy was my best friend, after all, and what could I do?

We made a promise that we'd always be together on our birthdays — no matter what. We'd force our parents to make sure we didn't miss each other's birthdays.

And then we hugged again. And Kathy said, "Don't worry. We'll see each other a lot. Really." And she had tears in her eyes, too.

She turned and ran out the door. The screen door slammed hard behind her. I stood there staring out into the darkness until Petey came scampering in, his toenails clicking across the linoleum, and started to lick my hand.

The next morning, moving day, was a rainy Saturday. Not a downpour. No thunder or lightning. But just enough rain and wind to make the long drive slow and unpleasant.

The sky seemed to get darker as we neared the new neighborhood. The heavy trees bent low over the street. "Slow down, Jack," Mom warned shrilly. "The street is really slick."

But Dad was in a hurry to get to the house before the moving van did. "They'll just put the stuff anywhere if we're not there to supervise," he explained.

Josh, beside me in the backseat, was being a real pain, as usual. He kept complaining that he was thirsty. When that didn't get results, he started whining that he was starving. But we had all had a big breakfast, so that didn't get any reaction, either.

He just wanted attention, of course. I kept trying to cheer him up by telling him how great the house was inside and how big his room was. He still hadn't seen it.

But he didn't want to be cheered up. He started wrestling with Petey, getting the poor dog all worked up, until Dad had to shout at him to stop.

"Let's all try really hard not to get on each other's nerves," Mom suggested.

Dad laughed. "Good idea, dear."

"Don't make fun of me," she snapped.

They started to argue about who was more exhausted from all the packing. Petey stood up on his hind legs and started to howl at the back window.

"Can't you shut him up?" Mom screamed.

I pulled Petey down, but he struggled back up and started howling again. "He's never done this before," I said.

"Just get him quiet!" Mom insisted.

I pulled Petey down by his hind legs, and Josh started to howl. Mom turned around and gave him a dirty look. Josh didn't stop howling, though. He thought he was a riot.

Finally, Dad pulled the car up the driveway of the new house. The tires crunched over the wet gravel. Rain pounded on the roof.

"Home sweet home," Mom said. I couldn't tell if she was being sarcastic or not. I think she was really glad the long car ride was over.

"At least we beat the movers," Dad said, glancing at his watch. Then his expression changed. "Hope they're not lost."

"It's as dark as night out there," Josh complained.

Petey was jumping up and down in my lap, desperate to get out of the car. He was usually a good traveler. But once the car stopped, he wanted out immediately.

I opened my car door and he leaped onto the driveway with a splash and started to run in a wild zigzag across the front yard.

"At least *someone's* glad to be here," Josh said quietly.

Dad ran up to the porch and, fumbling with the unfamiliar keys, managed to get the front door open. Then he motioned for us to come into the house.

Mom and Josh ran across the walk, eager to get in out of the rain. I closed the car door behind me and started to jog after them.

But something caught my eye. I stopped and looked up to the twin bay windows above the porch.

I held a hand over my eyebrows to shield my eyes and squinted through the rain.

Yes. I saw it.

A face. In the window on the left.

The boy.

The same boy was up there, staring down at me.

4

"Wipe your feet! Don't track mud on the nice clean floors!" Mom called. Her voice echoed against the bare walls of the empty living room.

I stepped into the hallway. The house smelled of paint. The painters had just finished on Thursday. It was hot in the house, much hotter than outside.

"This kitchen light won't go on," Dad called from the back. "Did the painters turn off the electricity or something?"

"How should I know?" Mom shouted back.

Their voices sounded so loud in the big, empty house.

"Mom — there's someone upstairs!" I cried, wiping my feet on the new welcome mat and hurrying into the living room.

She was at the window, staring out at the rain, looking for the movers probably. She spun around as I came in. "What?"

"There's a boy upstairs. I saw him in the window," I said, struggling to catch my breath.

Josh entered the room from the back hallway. He'd probably been with Dad. He laughed. "Is someone already living here?"

"There's no one upstairs," Mom said, rolling her eyes. "Are you two going to give me a break today, or what?"

"What did *I* do?" Josh whined.

"Listen, Amanda, we're all a little on edge today — " Mom started.

But I interrupted her. "I saw his face, Mom. In the window. I'm not crazy, you know."

"Says who?" Josh cracked.

"Amanda!" Mom bit her lower lip, the way she always did when she was really exasperated. "You saw a reflection of something. Of a tree probably." She turned back to the window. The rain was coming down in sheets now, the wind driving it noisily against the large picture window.

I ran to the stairway, cupped my hands over my mouth, and shouted up to the second floor, "Who's up there?"

No answer.

"Who's up there?" I called, a little louder.

Mom had her hands over her ears. "Amanda — please!"

Josh had disappeared through the dining room. He was finally exploring the house.

"There's someone up there," I insisted and, impulsively, I started up the wooden stairway, my sneakers thudding loudly on the bare steps.

"Amanda — " I heard Mom call after me.

But I was too angry to stop. Why didn't she believe me? Why did she have to say it was a reflection of a tree I saw up there?

I was curious. I had to know who was upstairs. I had to prove Mom wrong. I had to show her I hadn't seen a stupid reflection. I guess I can be pretty stubborn, too. Maybe it's a family trait.

The stairs squeaked and creaked under me as I climbed. I didn't feel at all scared until I reached the second-floor landing. Then I suddenly had this heavy feeling in the pit of my stomach.

I stopped, breathing hard, leaning on the banister.

Who could it be? A burglar? A bored neighborhood kid who had broken into an empty house for a thrill?

Maybe I shouldn't be up here alone, I realized.

Maybe the boy in the window was dangerous.

"Anybody up here?" I called, my voice suddenly trembly and weak.

Still leaning against the banister, I listened.

And I could hear footsteps scampering across the hallway.

No.

Not footsteps.

The rain. That's what it was. The patter of rain against the slate-shingled roof.

For some reason, the sound made me feel a little

calmer. I let go of the banister and stepped into the long, narrow hallway. It was dark up here, except for a rectangle of gray light from a small window at the other end.

I took a few steps, the old wooden floorboards creaking noisily beneath me. "Anybody up here?"

Again no answer.

I stepped up to the first doorway on my left. The door was closed. The smell of fresh paint was suffocating. There was a light switch on the wall near the door. Maybe it's for the hall light, I thought. I clicked it on. But nothing happened.

"Anybody here?"

My hand was trembling as I grabbed the doorknob. It felt warm in my hand. And damp.

I turned it and, taking a deep breath, pushed open the door.

I peered into the room. Gray light filtered in through the bay window. A flash of lightning made me jump back. The thunder that followed was a dull, distant roar.

Slowly, carefully, I took a step into the room. Then another.

No sign of anyone.

This was a guest bedroom. Or it could be Josh's room if he decided he liked it.

Another flash of lightning. The sky seemed to be darkening. It was pitch-black out there even though it was just after lunchtime.

I backed into the hall. The next room down was

going to be mine. It also had a bay window that looked down on the front yard.

Was the boy I saw staring down at me in *my* room?

I crept down the hall, letting my hand run along the wall for some reason, and stopped outside my door, which was also closed.

Taking a deep breath, I knocked on the door. "Who's in there?" I called.

I listened.

Silence.

Then a clap of thunder, closer than the last. I froze as if I were paralyzed, holding my breath. It was so hot up here, hot and damp. And the smell of paint was making me dizzy.

I grabbed the doorknob. "Anybody in there?"

I started to turn the knob — when the boy crept up from behind and grabbed my shoulder.

5

I couldn't breathe. I couldn't cry out.

My heart seemed to stop. My chest felt as if it were about to explode.

With a desperate, terrified effort, I spun around.

"Josh!" I shrieked. "You scared me to death! I thought — "

He let go of me and took a step back. "Gotcha!" he declared, and then started to laugh, a high-pitched laugh that echoed down the long, bare hallway.

My heart was pounding hard now. My forehead throbbed. "You're not funny," I said angrily. I shoved him against the wall. "You really scared me."

He laughed and rolled around on the floor. He's really a sicko. I tried to shove him again but missed.

Angrily, I turned away from him — just in time to see my bedroom door slowly swinging open.

I gasped in disbelief. And froze, gaping at the moving door.

Josh stopped laughing and stood up, immediately serious, his dark eyes wide with fright.

I could hear someone moving inside the room.

I could hear whispering.

Excited giggles.

"Who — who's there?" I managed to stammer in a high little voice I didn't recognize.

The door, creaking loudly, opened a bit more, then started to close.

"Who's there?" I demanded, a bit more forcefully.

Again, I could hear whispering, someone moving about.

Josh had backed up against the wall and was edging away, toward the stairs. He had an expression on his face I'd never seen before — sheer terror.

The door, creaking like a door in a movie haunted house, closed a little more.

Josh was nearly to the stairway. He was staring at me, violently motioning with his hand for me to follow.

But instead, I stepped forward, grabbed the doorknob, and pushed the door open hard.

It didn't resist.

I let go of the doorknob and stood blocking the doorway. "Who's there?"

The room was empty.

Thunder crashed.

It took me a few seconds to realize what was making the door move. The window on the opposite wall had been left open several inches. The gusting wind through the open window must have been opening and closing the door. I guessed that also explained the other sounds I heard inside the room, the sounds I thought were whispers.

Who had left the window open? The painters, probably.

I took a deep breath and let it out slowly, waiting for my pounding heart to settle down to normal.

Feeling a little foolish, I walked quickly to the window and pushed it shut.

"Amanda — are you all right?" Josh whispered from the hallway.

I started to answer him. But then I had a better idea.

He had practically scared me to death a few minutes before. Why not give *him* a little scare? He deserved it.

So I didn't answer him.

I could hear him take a few timid steps closer to my room. "Amanda? Amanda? You okay?"

I tiptoed over to my closet, pulled the door open a third of the way. Then I laid down flat on the floor, on my back, with my head and shoulders hidden inside the closet and the rest of me out in the room.

"Amanda?" Josh sounded very scared.

"Ohhhhh," I moaned loudly.

I knew when he saw me sprawled on the floor like this, he'd totally freak out!

"Amanda — what's happening?"

He was in the doorway now. He'd see me any second now, lying in the dark room, my head hidden from view, the lightning flashing impressively and the thunder cracking outside the old window.

I took a deep breath and held it to keep from giggling.

"Amanda?" he whispered. And then he must have seen me, because he uttered a loud "Huh?!" And I heard him gasp.

And then he screamed at the top of his lungs. I heard him running down the hall to the stairway, shrieking, "Mom! Dad!" And I heard his sneakers thudding down the wooden stairs, with him screaming and calling all the way down.

I snickered to myself. Then, before I could pull myself up, I felt a rough, warm tongue licking my face.

"Petey!"

He was licking my cheeks, licking my eyelids, licking me frantically, as if he were trying to revive me, or as if to let me know that everything was okay.

"Oh, Petey! Petey!" I cried, laughing and throwing my arms around the sweet dog. "Stop! You're getting me all sticky!"

But he wouldn't stop. He kept on licking fiercely.

The poor dog is nervous, too, I thought.

"Come on, Petey, shape up," I told him, holding his panting face away with both my hands. "There's nothing to be nervous about. This new place is going to be fun. You'll see."

6

That night, I was smiling to myself as I fluffed up my pillow and slid into bed. I was thinking about how terrified Josh had been that afternoon, how frightened he looked even after I came prancing down the stairs, perfectly okay. How angry he was that I'd fooled him.

Of course, Mom and Dad didn't think it was funny. They were both nervous and upset because the moving van had just arrived, an hour late. They forced Josh and me to call a truce. No more scaring each other.

"It's hard *not* to get scared in this creepy old place," Josh muttered. But we reluctantly agreed not to play any more jokes on each other, if we could possibly help it.

The men, complaining about the rain, started carrying in all of our furniture. Josh and I helped show them where we wanted stuff in our rooms. They dropped my dresser on the stairs, but it only got a small scratch.

The furniture looked strange and small in this big house. Josh and I tried to stay out of the way while Mom and Dad worked all day, arranging things, emptying cartons, putting clothes away. Mom even managed to get the curtains hung in my room.

What a day!

Now, a little after ten o'clock, trying to get to sleep for the first time in my new room, I turned onto my side, then onto my back. Even though this was my old bed, I couldn't get comfortable.

Everything seemed so different, so wrong. The bed didn't face the same direction as in my old bedroom. The walls were bare. I hadn't had time to hang any of my posters. The room seemed so large and empty. The shadows seemed so much darker.

My back started to itch, and then I suddenly felt itchy all over. The bed is filled with bugs! I thought, sitting up. But of course that was ridiculous. It was my same old bed with clean sheets.

I forced myself to settle back down and closed my eyes. Sometimes when I can't get to sleep, I count silently by twos, picturing each number in my mind as I think it. It usually helps to clear my mind so that I can drift off to sleep.

I tried it now, burying my face in the pillow, picturing the numbers rolling past . . . 4 . . . 6 . . . 8 . . .

I yawned loudly, still wide awake at two-twenty.

I'm going to be awake forever, I thought. I'm never going to be able to sleep in this new room.

But then I must have drifted off without realizing it. I don't know how long I slept. An hour or two at the most. It was a light, uncomfortable sleep. Then something woke me. I sat straight up, startled.

Despite the heat of the room, I felt cold all over. Looking down to the end of the bed, I saw that I had kicked off the sheet and light blanket. With a groan, I reached down for them, but then froze.

I heard whispers.

Someone was whispering across the room.

"Who — who's there?" My voice was a whisper, too, tiny and frightened.

I grabbed my covers and pulled them up to my chin.

I heard more whispers. The room came into focus as my eyes adjusted to the dim light.

The curtains. The long, sheer curtains from my old room that my mother had hung that afternoon were fluttering at the window.

So. That explained the whispers. The billowing curtains must have woken me up.

A soft, gray light floated in from outside. The curtains cast moving shadows onto the foot of my bed.

Yawning, I stretched and climbed out of bed. I felt chilled all over as I crept across the wooden floor to close the window.

As I came near, the curtains stopped billowing and floated back into place. I pushed them aside and reached out to close the window.

"Oh!"

I uttered a soft cry when I realized that the window *was* closed.

But how could the curtains flutter like that with the window closed? I stood there for a while, staring out at the grays of the night. There wasn't much of a draft. The window seemed pretty airtight.

Had I imagined the curtains billowing? Were my eyes playing tricks on me?

Yawning, I hurried back through the strange shadows to my bed and pulled the covers up as high as they would go. "Amanda, stop scaring yourself," I scolded.

When I fell back to sleep a few minutes later, I had the ugliest, most terrifying dream.

I dreamed that we were all dead. Mom, Dad, Josh, and me.

At first, I saw us sitting around the dinner table in the new dining room. The room was very bright, so bright I couldn't see our faces very well. They were just a bright, white blur.

But, then, slowly, slowly, everything came into focus, and I could see that beneath our hair, we had no faces. Our skin was gone, and only our gray-green skulls were left. Bits of flesh clung to my bony cheeks. There were only deep, black sockets where my eyes had been.

The four of us, all dead, sat eating in silence. Our dinner plates, I saw, were filled with small bones. A big platter in the center of the table was piled high with gray-green bones, human-looking bones.

And then, in this dream, our disgusting meal was interrupted by a loud knocking on the door, an insistent pounding that grew louder and louder. It was Kathy, my friend from back home. I could see her at our front door, pounding on it with both fists.

I wanted to go answer the door. I wanted to run from the dining room and pull open the door and greet Kathy. I wanted to talk to Kathy. I wanted to tell her what had happened to me, to explain that I was dead and that my face had fallen away.

I wanted to see Kathy *so* badly.

But I couldn't get up from the table. I tried and tried, but I couldn't get up.

The pounding on the door grew louder and louder, until it was deafening. But I just sat there with my gruesome family, picking up bones from my dinner plate and eating them.

I woke up with a start, the horror of the dream still with me. I could still hear the pounding in

47

my ears. I shook my head, trying to chase the dream away.

It was morning. I could tell from the blue of the sky outside the window.

"Oh, no."

The curtains. They were billowing again, flapping noisily as they blew into the room.

I sat up and stared.

The window was still closed.

7

"I'll take a look at the window. There must be a draft or a leak or something," Dad said at breakfast. He shoveled in another mouthful of scrambled eggs and ham.

"But, Dad — it's so weird!" I insisted, still feeling scared. "The curtains were blowing like crazy, and the window was *closed*!"

"There might be a pane missing," Dad suggested.

"Amanda is a pain!" Josh cracked. His idea of a really witty joke.

"Don't start with your sister," Mom said, putting her plate down on the table and dropping into her chair. She looked tired. Her black hair, usually carefully pulled back, was disheveled. She tugged at the belt on her bathrobe. "Whew. I don't think I slept two hours last night."

"Neither did I," I said, sighing. "I kept thinking that boy would show up in my room again."

"Amanda — you've really got to stop this,"

Mom said sharply. "Boys in your room. Curtains blowing. You have to realize that you're nervous, and your imagination is working overtime."

"But, Mom — " I started.

"Maybe a ghost was behind the curtains," Josh said, teasing. He raised up his hands and made a ghostly "oooooooh" wail.

"Whoa." Mom put a hand on Josh's shoulder. "Remember what you promised about scaring each other?"

"It's going to be hard for all of us to adjust to this place," Dad said. "You may have dreamed about the curtains blowing, Amanda. You said you had bad dreams, right?"

The terrifying nightmare flashed back into my mind. Once again I saw the big platter of bones on the table. I shivered.

"It's so damp in here," Mom said.

"A little sunshine will help dry the place out," Dad said.

I peered out the window. The sky had turned solid gray. Trees seemed to spread darkness over our backyard. "Where's Petey?" I asked.

"Out back," Mom replied, swallowing a mouthful of eggs. "He got up early, too. Couldn't sleep, I guess. So I let him out."

"What are we doing today?" Josh asked. He always needed to know the plan for the day. Every detail. Mainly so he could argue about it.

"Your father and I still have a lot of unpacking

to do," Mom said, glancing to the back hallway, which was cluttered with unopened cartons. "You two can explore the neighborhood. See what you can find out. See if there are any other kids your age around."

"In other words, you want us to get lost!" I said.

Mom and Dad both laughed. "You're very smart, Amanda."

"But I want to help unpack *my* stuff," Josh whined. I knew he'd argue with the plan, just like always.

"Go get dressed and take a long walk," Dad said. "Take Petey with you, okay? And take a leash for him. I left one by the front stairs."

"What about our bikes? Why can't we ride our bikes?" Josh asked.

"They're buried in the back of the garage," Dad told him. "You'll never be able to get to them. Besides, you have a flat tire."

"If I can't ride my bike, I'm not going out," Josh insisted, crossing his arms in front of his chest.

Mom and Dad had to argue with him. Then threaten him. Finally, he agreed to go for "a short walk."

I finished my breakfast, thinking about Kathy and my other friends back home. I wondered what the kids were like in Dark Falls. I wondered if I'd be able to find new friends, real friends.

I volunteered to do the breakfast dishes since

Mom and Dad had so much work to do. The warm water felt soothing on my hands as I sponged the dishes clean. I guess maybe I'm weird. I like washing dishes.

Behind me, from somewhere in the front of the house, I could hear Josh arguing with Dad. I could just barely make out the words over the trickle of the tap water.

"Your basketball is packed in one of these cartons," Dad was saying. Then Josh said something. Then Dad said, "How should *I* know which one?" Then Josh said something. Then Dad said, "No, I don't have time to look now. Believe it or not, your basketball isn't at the top of my list."

I stacked the last dish onto the counter to drain, and looked for a dish towel to dry my hands. There was none in sight. I guess they hadn't been unpacked yet.

Wiping off my hands on the front of my robe, I headed for the stairs. "I'll be dressed in five minutes," I called to Josh, who was still arguing with Dad in the living room. "Then we can go out."

I started up the front stairs, and then stopped.

Above me on the landing stood a strange girl, about my age, with short black hair. She was smiling down at me, not a warm smile, not a friendly smile, but the coldest, most frightening smile I had ever seen.

8

A hand touched my shoulder.

I spun around.

It was Josh. "I'm not going for a walk unless I can take my basketball," he said.

"Josh — please!" I looked back up to the landing, and the girl was gone.

I felt cold all over. My legs were all trembly. I grabbed the banister.

"Dad! Come here — please!" I called.

Josh's face filled with alarm. "Hey, I didn't do anything!" he shouted.

"No — it's — it's not you," I said, and called Dad again.

"Amanda, I'm kind of busy," Dad said, appearing below at the foot of the stairs, already perspiring from uncrating living room stuff.

"Dad, I saw somebody," I told him. "Up there. A girl." I pointed.

"Amanda, please," he replied, making a face.

53

"Stop seeing things — okay? There's no one in this house except the four of us . . . . and maybe a few mice."

"Mice?" Josh asked with sudden interest. "Really? Where?"

"Dad, I didn't imagine it," I said, my voice cracking. I was really hurt that he didn't believe me.

"Amanda, look up there," Dad said, gazing up to the landing. "What do you see?"

I followed his gaze. There was a pile of my clothes on the landing. Mom must have just unpacked them.

"It's just clothes," Dad said impatiently. "It's not a girl. It's clothes." He rolled his eyes.

"Sorry," I said quietly. I repeated it as I started up the stairs. "Sorry."

But I didn't really feel sorry. I felt confused.

And still scared.

Was it possible that I thought a pile of clothes was a smiling girl?

No. I didn't think so.

I'm not crazy. And I have really good eyesight.

So then, what was going on?

I opened the door to my room, turned on the ceiling light, and saw the curtains billowing in front of the bay window.

Oh, no. Not again, I thought.

I hurried over to them. This time, the window was open.

Who opened it?

Mom, I guessed.

Warm, wet air blew into the room. The sky was heavy and gray. It smelled like rain.

Turning to my bed, I had another shock.

Someone had laid out an outfit for me. A pair of faded jeans and a pale blue, sleeveless T-shirt. They were spread out side by side at the foot of the bed.

Who had put them there? Mom?

I stood at the doorway and called to her. "Mom? Mom? Did you pick out clothes for me?"

I could hear her shout something from downstairs, but I couldn't make out the words.

Calm down, Amanda, I told myself. Calm down.

Of *course* Mom pulled the clothes out. Of *course* Mom put them there.

From the doorway, I heard whispering in my closet.

Whispering and hushed giggling behind the closet door.

This was the last straw. "What's going on here?" I yelled at the top of my lungs.

I stormed over to the closet and pulled open the door.

Frantically, I pushed clothes out of the way. No one in there.

Mice? I thought. Had I heard the mice that Dad was talking about?

"I've got to get out of here," I said aloud.

The room, I realized, was driving me crazy.

No. I was driving *myself* crazy. Imagining all of these weird things.

There was a logical explanation for everything. Everything.

As I pulled up my jeans and fastened them, I said the word "logical" over and over in my mind. I said it so many times that it didn't sound like a real word anymore.

Calm down, Amanda. Calm down.

I took a deep breath and held it to ten.

"Boo!"

"Josh — cut it out. You didn't scare me," I told him, sounding more cross than I had meant to.

"Let's get out of here," he said, staring at me from the doorway. "This place gives me the creeps."

"Huh? You, too?" I exclaimed. "What's *your* problem?"

He started to say something, then stopped. He suddenly looked embarrassed. "Forget it," he muttered.

"No, tell me," I insisted. "What were you going to say?"

He kicked at the floor molding. "I had a really creepy dream last night," he finally admitted, looking past me to the fluttering curtains at the window.

"A dream?" I remembered my horrible dream.

"Yeah. There were these two boys in my room. And they were mean."

"What did they do?" I asked.

"I don't remember," Josh said, avoiding my eyes. "I just remember they were scary."

"And what happened?" I asked, turning to the mirror to brush my hair.

"I woke up," he said. And then added impatiently, "Come *on*. Let's go."

"Did the boys say anything to you?" I asked.

"No. I don't think so," he answered thoughtfully. "They just laughed."

"Laughed?"

"Well, giggled, sort of," Josh said. "I don't want to talk about it anymore," he snapped. "Are we going for this dumb walk, or not?"

"Okay. I'm ready," I said, putting down my brush, taking one last look in the mirror. "Let's go on this dumb walk."

I followed him down the hall. As we passed the stack of clothes on the landing, I thought about the girl I had seen standing there. And I thought about the boy in the window when we first arrived. And the two boys Josh had seen in his dream.

I decided it proved that Josh and I were both

really nervous about moving to this new place. Maybe Mom and Dad were right. We were letting our imaginations run away with us.

It had to be our imaginations.

I mean, what *else* could it be?

9

A few seconds later, we stepped into the backyard to get Petey. He was as glad to see us as ever, leaping on us with his muddy paws, yapping excitedly, running in frantic circles through the leaves. It cheered me up just to see him.

It was hot and muggy even though the sky was gray. There was no wind at all. The heavy, old trees stood as still as statues.

We headed down the gravel driveway toward the street, our sneakers kicking at the dead, brown leaves, Petey running in zigzags at our sides, first in front of us, then behind. "At least Dad hasn't asked us to rake all these old leaves," Josh said.

"He will," I warned. "I don't think he's unpacked the rake yet."

Josh made a face. We stood at the curb, looking up at our house, the two second-floor bay windows staring back at us like eyes.

The house next door, I noticed for the first time,

was about the same size as ours, except it was shingle instead of brick. The curtains in the living room were drawn shut. Some of the upstairs windows were shuttered. Tall trees cast the neighbors' house in darkness, too.

"Which way?" Josh asked, tossing a stick for Petey to chase.

I pointed up the street. "The school is up that way," I said. "Let's check it out."

The road sloped uphill. Josh picked up a small tree branch from the side of the road and used it as a walking stick. Petey kept trying to chew on it while Josh walked.

We didn't see anyone on the street or in any of the front yards we passed. No cars went by.

I was beginning to think the whole town was deserted, until the boy stepped out from behind the low ledge.

He popped out so suddenly, both Josh and I stopped in our tracks. "Hi," he said shyly, giving us a little wave.

"Hi," Josh and I answered at the same time.

Then, before we could pull him back, Petey ran up to the boy, sniffed his sneakers, and began snarling and barking. The boy stepped back and raised his hands as if he were protecting himself. He looked really frightened.

"Petey — stop!" I cried.

Josh grabbed the dog and picked him up, but he kept growling.

"He doesn't bite," I told the boy. "He usually doesn't bark, either. I'm sorry."

"That's okay," the boy said, staring at Petey, who was squirming to get out of Josh's arms. "He probably smells something on me."

"Petey, stop!" I shouted. The dog wouldn't stop squirming. "You don't want the leash — do you?"

The boy had short, wavy blond hair and very pale blue eyes. He had a funny turned-up nose that seemed out of place on his serious-looking face. He was wearing a maroon long-sleeved sweatshirt despite the mugginess of the day, and black straight-legged jeans. He had a blue baseball cap stuffed into the back pocket of his jeans.

"I'm Amanda Benson," I said. "And this is my brother Josh."

Josh hesitantly put Petey back on the ground. The dog yipped once, stared up at the boy, whimpered softly, then sat down on the street and began to scratch himself.

"I'm Ray Thurston," the boy said, stuffing his hands into his jeans pockets, still staring warily at Petey. He seemed to relax a little, though, seeing that the dog had lost interest in barking and growling at him.

I suddenly realized that Ray looked familiar. Where had I seen him before? Where? I stared hard at him until I remembered.

And then I gasped in sudden fright.

Ray was the boy, the boy in my room. The boy in the window.

"You — " I stammered accusingly. "You were in our house!"

He looked confused. "Huh?"

"You were in my room — right?" I insisted.

He laughed. "I don't get it," he said. "In your room?"

Petey raised his head and gave a low growl in Ray's direction. Then he went back to his serious scratching.

"I thought I saw you," I said, beginning to feel a little doubtful. Maybe it wasn't him. Maybe. . . .

"I haven't been in your house in a long time," Ray said, looking down warily at Petey.

"A long time?"

"Yeah. I used to live in your house," he replied.

"Huh?" Josh and I stared at him in surprise. "Our house?"

Ray nodded. "When we first moved here," he said. He picked up a flat pebble and heaved it down the street.

Petey growled, started to chase it, changed his mind, and plopped back down on the street, his stub of a tail wagging excitedly.

Heavy clouds lowered across the sky. It seemed to grow darker. "Where do you live now?" I asked.

Ray tossed another stone, then pointed up the road.

"Did you like our house?" Josh asked Ray.

"Yeah, it was okay," Ray told him. "Nice and shady."

"You liked it?" Josh cried. "I think it's gross. It's so dark and — "

Petey interrupted. He decided to start barking at Ray again, running up till he was a few inches in front of Ray, then backing away. Ray took a few cautious steps back to the edge of the curb.

Josh pulled the leash from the pocket of his shorts. "Sorry, Petey," he said. I held the growling dog while Josh attached the leash to his collar.

"He's never done this before. Really," I said, apologizing to Ray.

The leash seemed to confuse Petey. He tugged against it, pulling Josh across the street. But at least he stopped barking.

"Let's do something," Josh said impatiently.

"Like what?" Ray asked, relaxing again now that Petey was on the leash.

We all thought for a while.

"Maybe we could go to your house," Josh suggested to Ray.

Ray shook his head. "No. I don't think so," he said. "Not now anyway."

"Where is everyone?" I asked, looking up and down the empty street. "It's really dead around here, huh?"

He chuckled. "Yeah. I guess you could say

that," he said. "Want to go to the playground behind the school?"

"Yeah. Okay," I agreed.

The three of us headed up the street, Ray leading the way, me walking a few feet behind him, Josh holding his tree branch in one hand, the leash in the other, Petey running this way, then that, giving Josh a really hard time.

We didn't see the gang of kids till we turned the corner.

There were ten or twelve of them, mostly boys but a few girls, too. They were laughing and shouting, shoving each other playfully as they came toward us down the center of the street. Some of them, I saw, were about my age. The rest were teenagers. They were wearing jeans and dark T-shirts. One of the girls stood out because she had long, straight blonde hair and was wearing green spandex tights.

"Hey, look!" a tall boy with slicked-back black hair cried, pointing at us.

Seeing Ray, Josh, and me, they grew quiet but didn't stop moving toward us. A few of them giggled, as if they were enjoying some kind of private joke.

The three of us stopped and watched them approach. I smiled and waited to say hi. Petey was pulling at his leash and barking his head off.

"Hi, guys," the tall boy with the black hair said, grinning. The others thought this was very funny for some reason. They laughed. The girl in the green tights gave a short, red-haired boy a shove that almost sent him sprawling into me.

"How's it going, Ray?" a girl with short black hair asked, smiling at Ray.

"Not bad. Hi, guys," Ray answered. He turned to Josh and me. "These are some of my friends. They're all from the neighborhood."

"Hi," I said, feeling awkward. I wished Petey would stop barking and pulling at his leash like that. Poor Josh was having a terrible time holding onto him.

"This is George Carpenter," Ray said, pointing to the short, red-haired boy, who nodded. "And Jerry Franklin, Karen Somerset, Bill Gregory . . ." He went around the circle, naming each kid. I tried to remember all the names but, of course it was impossible.

"How do you like Dark Falls?" one of the girls asked me.

"I don't really know," I told her. "It's my first day here, really. It seems nice."

Some of the kids laughed at my answer, for some reason.

"What kind of dog is that?" George Carpenter asked Josh.

Josh, holding tight to the leash handle, told him. George stared hard at Petey, studying him, as if he had never seen a dog like Petey before.

Karen Somerset, a tall, pretty girl with short

blonde hair, came up to me while some of the other kids were admiring Petey. "You know, I used to live in your house," she said softly.

"What?" I wasn't sure I'd heard her correctly.

"Let's go to the playground," Ray said, interrupting.

No one responded to Ray's suggestion.

They grew quiet. Even Petey stopped barking.

Had Karen really said that she used to live in our house? I wanted to ask her, but she had stepped back into the circle of kids.

The circle.

My mouth dropped open as I realized they had formed a circle around Josh and me.

I felt a stab of fear. Was I imagining it? Was something going on?

They all suddenly looked different to me. They were smiling, but their faces were tense, watchful, as if they expected trouble.

Two of them, I noticed, were carrying baseball bats. The girl with the green tights stared at me, looking me up and down, checking me out.

No one said a word. The street was silent except for Petey, who was now whimpering softly.

I suddenly felt very afraid.

Why were they staring at us like that?

Or was my imagination running away with me again?

I turned to Ray, who was still beside me. He

didn't seem at all troubled. But he didn't return my gaze.

"Hey, guys — " I said. "What's going on?" I tried to keep it light, but my voice was a little shaky.

I looked over at Josh. He was busy soothing Petey and hadn't noticed that things had changed.

The two boys with baseball bats held them up waist high and moved forward.

I glanced around the circle, feeling the fear tighten my chest.

The circle tightened. The kids were closing in on us.

10

The black clouds overhead seemed to lower. The air felt heavy and damp.

Josh was fussing with Petey's collar and still didn't see what was happening. I wondered if Ray was going to say anything, if he was going to do anything to stop them. But he stayed frozen and expressionless beside me.

The circle grew smaller as the kids closed in.

I realized I'd been holding my breath. I took a deep breath and opened my mouth to cry out.

"Hey, kids — what's going on?"

It was a man's voice, calling from outside the circle.

Everyone turned to see Mr. Dawes coming quickly toward us, taking long strides as he crossed the street, his open blazer flapping behind him. He had a friendly smile on his face. "What's going on?" he asked again.

He didn't seem to realize that the gang of kids had been closing in on Josh and me.

"We're heading to the playground," George Carpenter told him, twirling the bat in his hand. "You know. To play softball."

"Good deal," Mr. Dawes said, pulling down his striped tie, which had blown over his shoulder. He looked up at the darkening sky. "Hope you don't get rained out."

Several of the kids had backed up. They were standing in small groups of two and three now. The circle had completely broken up.

"Is that bat for softball or hardball?" Mr. Dawes asked George.

"George doesn't know," another kid replied quickly. "He's never hit anything with it!"

The kids all laughed. George playfully menaced the kid, pretending to come at him with the bat.

Mr. Dawes gave a little wave and started to leave. But then he stopped, and his eyes opened wide with surprise. "Hey," he said, flashing me a friendly smile. "Josh. Amanda. I didn't see you there."

"Good morning," I muttered. I was feeling very confused. A moment ago, I'd felt terribly scared. Now everyone was laughing and kidding around.

Had I imagined that the kids were moving in on us? Ray and Josh hadn't seemed to notice anything peculiar. Was it just me and my overactive imagination?

What would have happened if Mr. Dawes hadn't come along?

"How are you two getting along in the new house?" Mr. Dawes asked, smoothing back his wavy blond hair.

"Okay," Josh and I answered together. Looking up at Mr. Dawes, Petey began to bark and pull at the leash.

Mr. Dawes put an exaggerated hurt expression on his face. "I'm crushed," he said. "Your dog still doesn't like me." He bent over Petey. "Hey, dog — lighten up."

Petey barked back angrily.

"He doesn't seem to like *anybody* today," I told Mr. Dawes apologetically.

Mr. Dawes stood back up and shrugged. "Can't win 'em all." He started back to his car, parked a few yards down the street. "I'm heading over to your house," he told Josh and me. "Just want to see if there's anything I can do to help your parents. Have fun, kids."

I watched him climb into his car and drive away.

"He's a nice guy," Ray said.

"Yeah," I agreed. I was still feeling uncomfortable, wondering what the kids would do now that Mr. Dawes was gone.

Would they form that frightening circle again?

No. Everyone started walking, heading down the block to the playground behind the school. They were kidding each other and talking normally, and pretty much ignored Josh and me.

70

I was starting to feel a little silly. It was obvious that they hadn't been trying to scare Josh and me. I must have made the whole thing up in my mind.

I must have.

At least, I told myself, I hadn't screamed or made a scene. At least I hadn't made a total fool of myself.

The playground was completely empty. I guessed that most kids had stayed inside because of the threatening sky. The playground was a large, flat grassy field, surrounded on all four sides by a tall metal fence. There were swings and slides at the end nearest the school building. There were two baseball diamonds on the other end. Beyond the fence, I could see a row of tennis courts, also deserted.

Josh tied Petey to the fence, then came running over to join the rest of us. The boy named Jerry Franklin made up the teams. Ray and I were on the same team. Josh was on the other.

As our team took the field, I felt excited and a little nervous. I'm not the best softball player in the world. I can hit the ball pretty well. But in the field, I'm a complete klutz. Luckily, Jerry sent me out to right field where not many balls are hit.

The clouds began to part a little and the sky got lighter. We played two full innings. The other team was winning, eight to two. I was having fun.

I had only messed up on one play. And I hit a double my first time at bat.

It was fun being with a whole new group of kids. They seemed really nice, especially the girl named Karen Somerset, who talked with me while we waited for our turn at bat. Karen had a great smile, even though she wore braces on all her teeth, up and down. She seemed very eager to be friends.

The sun was coming out as my team started to take the field for the beginning of the third inning. Suddenly, I heard a loud, shrill whistle. I looked around until I saw that it was Jerry Franklin, blowing a silver whistle.

Everyone came running up to him. "We'd better quit," he said, looking up at the brightening sky. "We promised our folks, remember, that we'd be home for lunch."

I glanced at my watch. It was only eleven-thirty. Still early.

But to my surprise, no one protested.

They all waved to each other and called out farewells, and then began to run. I couldn't believe how fast everyone left. It was as if they were racing or something.

Karen ran past me like the others, her head down, a serious expression on her pretty face. Then she stopped suddenly and turned around. "Nice meeting you, Amanda," she called back. "We should get together sometime."

"Great!" I called to her. "Do you know where I live?"

I couldn't hear her answer very well. She nodded, and I thought she said, "Yes. I know it. I used to live in your house."

But that *couldn't* have been what she said.

11

Several days went by. Josh and I were getting used to our new house and our new friends.

The kids we met every day at the playground weren't exactly friends yet. They talked with Josh and me, and let us on their teams. But it was really hard to get to know them.

In my room, I kept hearing whispers late at night, and soft giggling, but I forced myself to ignore it. One night, I thought I saw a girl dressed all in white at the end of the upstairs hall. But when I walked over to investigate, there was just a pile of dirty sheets and other bedclothes against the wall.

Josh and I were adjusting, but Petey was still acting really strange. We took him with us to the playground every day, but we had to leash him to the fence. Otherwise, he'd bark and snap at all the kids.

"He's still nervous being in a new place," I told Josh. "He'll calm down."

But Petey didn't calm down. And about two weeks later, we were finishing up a softball game with Ray, and Karen Somerset, and Jerry Franklin, and George Carpenter, and a bunch of other kids, when I looked over to the fence and saw that Petey was gone.

Somehow he had broken out of his leash and run away.

We looked for hours, calling "Petey!" wandering from block to block, searching front yards and backyards, empty lots and woods. Then, after circling the neighborhood twice, Josh and I suddenly realized we had no idea where we were.

The streets of Dark Falls looked the same. They were all lined with sprawling old brick or shingle houses, all filled with shady old trees.

"I don't believe it. We're lost," Josh said, leaning against a tree trunk, trying to catch his breath.

"That stupid dog," I muttered, my eyes searching up the street. "Why did he do this? He's never run away before."

"I don't know how he got loose," Josh said, shaking his head, then wiping his sweaty forehead with the sleeve of his T-shirt. "I tied him up really well."

"Hey — maybe he ran home," I said. The idea immediately cheered me up.

"Yeah!" Josh stepped away from the tree and headed back over to me. "I'll bet you're right,

Amanda. He's probably been home for hours. Wow. We've been stupid. We should've checked home first. Let's go!"

"Well," I said, looking around at the empty yards, "we just have to figure out which way is home."

I looked up and down the street, trying to figure out which way we'd turned when we left the school playground. I couldn't remember, so we just started walking.

Luckily, as we reached the next corner, the school came into sight. We had made a full circle. It was easy to find our way from there.

Passing the playground, I stared at the spot on the fence where Petey had been tied. That troublemaking dog. He'd been acting so badly ever since we came to Dark Falls.

Would he be home when we got there? I hoped so.

A few minutes later, Josh and I were running up the gravel driveway, calling the dog's name at the top of our lungs. The front door burst open and Mom, her hair tied in a red bandanna, the knees of her jeans covered with dust, leaned out. She and Dad had been painting the back porch. "Where have you two been? Lunchtime was two hours ago!"

Josh and I both answered at the same time. "Is Petey here?"

"We've been looking for Petey!"

"Is he here?"

Mom's face filled with confusion. "Petey? I thought he was with you."

My heart sank. Josh slumped to the driveway with a loud sigh, sprawling flat on his back in the gravel and leaves.

"You haven't seen him?" I asked, my trembling voice showing my disappointment. "He *was* with us. But he ran away."

"Oh. I'm sorry," Mom said, motioning for Josh to get up from the driveway. "He ran away? I thought you've been keeping him on a leash."

"You've got to help us find him," Josh pleaded, not budging from the ground. "Get the car. We've got to find him — right now!"

"I'm sure he hasn't gotten far," Mom said. "You must be starving. Come in and have some lunch and then we'll — "

"No. Right *now!*" Josh screamed.

"What's going on?" Dad, his face and hair covered with tiny flecks of white paint, joined Mom on the front porch. "Josh — what's all the yelling?"

We explained to Dad what had happened. He said he was too busy to drive around looking for Petey. Mom said she'd do it, but only after we had some lunch. I pulled Josh up by both arms and dragged him into the house.

We washed up and gulped down some peanut butter and jelly sandwiches. Then Mom took the car out of the garage, and we drove around and around the neighborhood searching for our lost pet.

With no luck.

No sign of him.

Josh and I were miserable. Heartbroken. Mom and Dad called the local police. Dad kept saying that Petey had a good sense of direction, that he'd show up any minute.

But we didn't really believe it.

Where was he?

The four of us ate dinner in silence. It was the longest, most horrible evening of my life. "I tied him up really good," Josh repeated, close to tears, his dinner plate still full.

"Dogs are great escape artists," Dad said, "Don't worry. He'll show up."

"Some night for a party," Mom said glumly.

I'd completely forgotten that they were going out. Some neighbors on the next block had invited them to a big potluck dinner party.

"I sure don't feel like partying, either," Dad said with a sigh. "I'm beat from painting all day. But I guess we have to be neighborly. Sure you kids will be okay here?"

"Yeah, I guess," I said, thinking about Petey. I kept listening for his bark, listening for scratching at the door.

But no. The hours dragged by. Petey still hadn't shown up by bedtime.

Josh and I both slinked upstairs. I felt really tired, weary from all the worrying, and the running around and searching for Petey, I guess. But I knew I'd never be able to get to sleep.

In the hall outside my bedroom door, I heard whispering from inside my room and quiet footsteps. The usual sounds my room made. I wasn't at all scared of them or surprised by them anymore.

Without hesitating, I stepped into my room and clicked on the light. The room was empty, as I knew it would be. The mysterious sounds disappeared. I glanced at the curtains, which lay straight and still.

Then I saw the clothes strewn all over my bed.

Several pairs of jeans. Several T-shirts. A couple of sweatshirts. My only dress-up skirt.

That's strange, I thought. Mom was such a neat freak. If she had washed these things, she surely would have hung them up or put them into dresser drawers.

Sighing wearily, I started to gather up the clothes and put them away. I figured that Mom simply had too much to do to be bothered. She had probably washed the stuff and then left it here for me to put away. Or she had put it all down, planning to come back later and put it away, and then got busy with other chores.

Half an hour later, I was tucked into my bed wide awake, staring at the shadows on the ceiling.

Some time after that — I lost track of the time — I was still wide awake, still thinking about Petey, thinking about the new kids I'd met, thinking about the new neighborhood, when I heard my bedroom door creak and swing open.

Footsteps on the creaking floorboards.

I sat up in the darkness as someone crept into my room.

"Amanda — ssshh — it's me."

Alarmed, it took me a few seconds to recognize the hushed whisper. "Josh! What do you want? What are you doing in here?"

I gasped as a blinding light forced me to cover my eyes. "Oops. Sorry," Josh said. "My flashlight. I didn't mean to — "

"Ow, that's bright," I said, blinking. He aimed the powerful beam of white light up at the ceiling.

"Yeah. It's a halogen flashlight," he said.

"Well, what do you want?" I asked irritably. I still couldn't see well. I rubbed my eyes, but it didn't help.

"I know where Petey is," Josh whispered, "and I'm going to go get him. Come with me?"

"Huh?" I looked at the little clock on my bed table. "It's after midnight, Josh."

"So? It won't take long. Really."

My eyes were nearly normal by now. Staring at Josh in the light from the halogen flashlight, I noticed for the first time that he was fully dressed in jeans and a long-sleeved T-shirt.

"I don't get it, Josh," I said, swinging around and putting my feet on the floor. "We looked everywhere. Where do you think Petey is?"

"In the cemetery," Josh answered. His eyes looked big and dark and serious in the white light.

"Huh?"

"That's where he ran the first time, remember? When we first came to Dark Falls? He ran to that cemetery just past the school."

"Now, wait a minute — " I started.

"We drove past it this afternoon, but we didn't look inside. He's there, Amanda. I know he is. And I'm going to go get him whether you come or not."

"Josh, calm down," I said, putting my hands on his narrow shoulders. I was surprised to discover that he was trembling. "There's no reason for Petey to be in that cemetery."

"That's where he went the first time," Josh insisted. "He was looking for something there that day. I could tell. I know he's there again, Amanda." He pulled away from me. "Are you coming or not?"

My brother has to be the stubbornest, most headstrong person in the world.

"Josh, you're really going to walk into a strange

cemetery so late at night?" I asked.

"I'm not afraid," he said, shining the bright light around my room.

For a brief second, I thought the light caught someone, lurking behind the curtains. I opened my mouth to cry out. But there was no one there.

"You coming or not?" he repeated impatiently.

I was going to say no. But then, glancing at the curtains, I thought, it's probably no more spooky out there in that cemetery than it is here in my own bedroom!

"Yeah. Okay," I said grudgingly. "Get out of here and let me get dressed."

"Okay," he whispered, turning off the flashlight, plunging us into blackness. "Meet me down at the end of the driveway."

"Josh — one quick look at the cemetery, then we hurry home. Got it?" I told him.

"Yeah. Right. We'll be home before Mom and Dad get back from that party." He crept out. I could hear him making his way quickly down the stairs.

This is the craziest idea ever, I told myself as I searched in the darkness for some clothes to pull on.

And it was also kind of exciting.

Josh was wrong. No doubt about it. Petey wouldn't be hanging around in that cemetery now. Why on earth should he?

But at least it wasn't a long walk. And it was an adventure. Something to write about to Kathy back home.

And if Josh happened to be right, and we did manage to find poor, lost Petey, well, that would be great, too.

A few minutes later, dressed in jeans and a sweatshirt, I crept out of the house and joined Josh at the bottom of the driveway. The night was still warm. A heavy blanket of clouds covered the moon. I realized for the first time that there were no streetlights on our block.

Josh had the halogen flashlight on, aimed down at our feet. "You ready?" he asked.

Dumb question. Would I be standing there if I weren't ready?

We crunched over dead leaves as we headed up the block, toward the school. From there, it was just two blocks to the cemetery.

"It's so dark," I whispered. The houses were black and silent. There was no breeze at all. It was as if we were all alone in the world.

"It's too quiet," I said, hurrying to keep up with Josh. "No crickets or anything. Are you sure you really want to go to the cemetery?"

"I'm sure," he said, his eyes following the circle of light from the flashlight as it bumped over the ground. "I really think Petey is there."

We walked in the street, keeping close to the curb. We had gone nearly two blocks. The school was just coming into sight on the next block when we heard the scraping steps behind us on the pavement.

Josh and I both stopped. He lowered the light.

We both heard the sounds. I wasn't imagining them.

Someone was following us.

12

Josh was so startled, the flashlight tumbled from his hand and clattered onto the street. The light flickered but didn't go out.

By the time Josh had managed to pick it up, our pursuer had caught up to us. I spun around to face him, my heart pounding in my chest.

"Ray! What are *you* doing here?"

Josh aimed the light at Ray's face, but Ray shot his arms up to shield his face and ducked back into the darkness. "What are *you two* doing here?" he cried, sounding almost as startled as I did.

"You — you scared us," Josh said angrily, aiming the flashlight back down at our feet.

"Sorry," Ray said, "I would've called out, but I wasn't sure it was you."

"Josh has this crazy idea about where Petey might be," I told him, still struggling to catch my breath. "That's why we're out here."

"What about you?" Josh asked Ray.

"Well, sometimes I have trouble sleeping," Ray said softly.

"Don't your parents mind you being out so late?" I asked.

In the glow from the flashlight, I could see a wicked smile cross his face. "They don't know."

"Are we going to the cemetery or not?" Josh asked impatiently. Without waiting for an answer, he started jogging up the road, the light bobbing on the pavement in front of him. I turned and followed, wanting to stay close to the light.

"Where are you going?" Ray called, hurrying to catch up.

"The cemetery," I called back.

"No," Ray said. "You're not."

His voice was so low, so threatening, that I stopped. "What?"

"You're not going there," Ray repeated. I couldn't see his face. It was hidden in darkness. But his words sounded menacing.

"Hurry!" Josh called back to us. He hadn't slowed down. He didn't seem to notice the threat in Ray's words.

"Stop, Josh!" Ray called. It sounded more like an order than a request. "You can't go there!"

"Why not?" I demanded, suddenly afraid. Was Ray threatening Josh and me? Did he know something we didn't? Or was I making a big deal out of nothing once again?

I stared into the darkness, trying to see his face.

"You'd be nuts to go there at night!" he declared.

I began to think I had misjudged him. He was afraid to go there. That's why he was trying to stop us.

"Are you coming or not?" Josh demanded, getting farther and farther ahead of us.

"I don't think we should," Ray warned.

Yes, he's afraid, I decided. I only imagined that he was threatening us.

"You don't have to. But *we* do," Josh insisted, picking up his speed.

"No. Really," Ray said. "This is a bad idea." But now he and I were running side by side to catch up with Josh.

"Petey's there," Josh said, "I know he is."

We passed the dark, silent school. It seemed much bigger at night. Josh's light flashed through the low tree branches as we turned the corner onto Cemetery Drive.

"Wait — please," Ray pleaded. But Josh didn't slow down. Neither did I. I was eager to get there and get it over with.

I wiped my forehead with my sleeve. The air was hot and still. I wished I hadn't worn long sleeves. I felt my hair. It was dripping wet.

The clouds still covered the moon as we reached

the cemetery. We stepped through a gate in the low wall. In the darkness, I could see the crooked rows of gravestones.

Josh's light traveled from stone to stone, jumping up and down as he walked. "Petey!" he called suddenly, interrupting the silence.

He's disturbing the sleep of the dead, I thought, feeling a sudden chill of fear.

Don't be silly, Amanda. "Petey!" I called, too, forcing away my morbid thoughts.

"This is a very bad idea," Ray said, standing very close to me.

"Petey! Petey!" Josh called.

"I know it's a bad idea," I admitted to Ray. "But I didn't want Josh to come here by himself."

"But we shouldn't *be* here," Ray insisted.

I was beginning to wish he'd go away. No one had forced him to come. Why was he giving us such a hard time?

"Hey — look at this!" Josh called from several yards up ahead.

My sneakers crunching over the soft ground, I hurried between the rows of graves. I hadn't realized that we had already walked the entire length of the graveyard.

"Look," Josh said again, his flashlight playing over a strange structure built at the edge of the cemetery.

It took me a little while to figure out what it was in the small circle of light. It was so unexpected. It was some kind of theater. An amphitheater, I guess you'd call it, circular rows of bench seats dug into the ground, descending like stairs to a low stagelike platform at the bottom.

"What on earth!" I exclaimed.

I started forward to get a closer look.

"Amanda — wait. Let's go home," Ray called. He grabbed at my arm, but I hurried away, and he grabbed only air.

"Weird! Who would build an outdoor theater at the edge of a cemetery?" I asked.

I looked back to see if Josh and Ray were following me, and my sneaker caught against something. I stumbled to the ground, hitting my knee hard.

"Ow. What was that?"

Josh shone the light on it as I climbed slowly, painfully, to my feet. I had tripped over an enormous, upraised tree root.

In the flickering light, I followed the gnarled root over to a wide, old tree several yards away. The huge tree was bent over the strange belowground theater, leaning at such a low angle that it looked likely to topple over at any second. Big clumps of roots were raised up from the ground. Overhead, the tree's branches, heavy with leaves, seemed to lean to the ground.

"Timberrr!" Josh yelled.

"How weird!" I exclaimed. "Hey, Ray — what is this place?"

"It's a meeting place," Ray said quietly, standing close beside me, staring straight ahead at the leaning tree. "They use it sort of like a town hall. They have town meetings here."

"In the cemetery?" I cried, finding it hard to believe.

"Let's go," Ray urged, looking very nervous.

All three of us heard the footsteps. They were behind us, somewhere in the rows of graves. We turned around. Josh's light swept over the ground.

"Petey!"

There he was, standing between the nearest row of low, stone grave markers. I turned happily to Josh. "I don't believe it!" I cried. "You were right!"

"Petey! Petey!" Josh and I both started running toward our dog.

But Petey arched back on his hind legs as if he were getting ready to run away. He stared at us, his eyes red as jewels in the light of the flashlight.

"Petey! We found you!" I cried.

The dog lowered his head and started to trot away.

"Petey! Hey — come back! Don't you recognize us?"

With a burst of speed, Josh caught up with him

and grabbed him up off the ground. "Hey, Petey, what's the matter, fella?"

As I hurried over, Josh dropped Petey back to the ground and stepped back. "Ooh — he stinks!"

"What?" I cried.

"Petey — he stinks. He smells like a dead rat!" Josh held his nose.

Petey started to walk slowly away.

"Josh, he isn't glad to see us," I wailed. "He doesn't even seem to recognize us. Look at him!"

It was true. Petey walked to the next row of gravestones, then turned and glared at us.

I suddenly felt sick. What had happened to Petey? Why was he acting so differently? Why wasn't he glad to see us?

"I don't get it," Josh said, still making a face from the odor the dog gave off. "Usually, if we leave the room for thirty seconds, he goes nuts when we come back."

"We'd better go!" Ray called. He was still at the edge of the cemetery near the leaning tree.

"Petey — what's wrong with you?" I called to the dog. He didn't respond. "Don't you remember your name? Petey? Petey?"

"Yuck! What a stink!" Josh exclaimed.

"We've got to get him home and give him a bath," I said. My voice was shaking. I felt really sad. And frightened.

"Maybe this isn't Petey," Josh said thoughtfully. The dog's eyes again glared red in the beam of light.

"It's him all right," I said quietly. "Look. He's dragging the leash. Go get him, Josh — and let's go home."

"*You* get him!" Josh cried. "He smells too bad!"

"Just grab his leash. You don't have to pick him up," I said.

"No. *You.*"

Josh was being stubborn again. I could see that I had no choice. "Okay," I said. "I'll get him. But I'll need the light." I grabbed the flashlight from Josh's hand and started to run toward Petey.

"Sit, Petey. Sit!" I ordered. It was the only command Petey ever obeyed.

But he didn't obey it this time. Instead, he turned and trotted away, holding his head down low.

"Petey — stop! Petey, come on!" I yelled, exasperated. "Don't make me chase you."

"Don't let him get away!" Josh yelled, running up behind me.

I moved the flashlight from side to side along the ground. "Where is he?"

"Petey! Petey!" Josh called, sounding shrill and desperate.

I couldn't see him.

"Oh, no. Don't tell me we've lost him again!" I said.

We both started to call him. "What's *wrong* with that mutt?" I cried.

I moved the beam of light down one long row of gravestones, then, moving quickly, down the next. No sign of him. We both kept calling his name.

And then the circle of light came to rest on the front of a granite tombstone.

Reading the name on the stone, I stopped short.

And gasped.

"Josh — look!" I grabbed Josh's sleeve. I held on tight.

"Huh? What's wrong?" His face filled with confusion.

"Look! The name on the gravestone."

It was Karen Somerset.

Josh read the name. He stared at me, still confused.

"That's my new friend Karen. The one I talk to on the playground every day," I said.

"Huh? It must be her grandmother or some- thing," Josh said, and then added impatiently, "Come on. Look for Petey."

"No. Look at the dates," I said to him.

We both read the dates under Karen Somerset's name. 1960–1972.

"It can't be her mother or grandmother," I said, keeping the beam of light on the stone despite my trembling hand. "This girl died when she was twelve. My age. And Karen is twelve, too. She told me."

"Amanda — " Josh scowled and looked away.

But I took a few steps and beamed the light onto the next gravestone. There was a name on it I'd never heard before. I moved on to the next stone. Another name I'd never heard.

"Amanda, come on!" Josh whined.

The next gravestone had the name George Carpenter on it. 1975–1988.

"Josh — look! It's George from the playground," I called.

"Amanda, we have to get Petey," he insisted.

But I couldn't pull myself away from the gravestones. I went from one to the next, moving the flashlight over the engraved letters.

To my growing horror, I found Jerry Franklin. And then Bill Gregory.

All the kids we had played softball with. They all had gravestones here.

My heart thudding, I moved down the crooked row, my sneakers sinking into the soft grass. I felt numb, numb with fear. I struggled to hold the light steady as I beamed it onto the last stone in the row.

RAY THURSTON. 1977–1988.

"Huh?"

I could hear Josh calling me, but I couldn't make out what he was saying.

The rest of the world seemed to fall away. I read the deeply etched inscription again:

RAY THURSTON. 1977–1988.

I stood there, staring at the letters and numbers. I stared at them till they didn't make sense anymore, until they were just a gray blur.

Suddenly, I realized that Ray had crept up beside the gravestone and was staring at me.

"Ray — " I managed to say, moving the light over the name on the stone. "Ray, this one is . . . *you!*"

His eyes flared, glowing like dying embers.

"Yes, it's me," he said softly, moving toward me. "I'm so sorry, Amanda."

13

I took a step back, my sneakers sinking into the soft ground. The air was heavy and still. No one made a sound. Nothing moved.

Dead.

I'm surrounded by death, I thought.

Then, frozen to the spot, unable to breathe, the darkness swirling around me, the gravestones spinning in their own black shadows, I thought: What is he going to do to me?

"Ray — " I managed to call out. My voice sounded faint and far away. "Ray, are you really dead?"

"I'm sorry. You weren't supposed to find out yet," he said, his voice floating low and heavy on the stifling night air.

"But — how? I mean . . . I don't understand. . . ." I looked past him to the darting white light of the flashlight. Josh was several rows away, almost to the street, still searching for Petey.

"Petey!" I whispered, dread choking my throat, my stomach tightening in horror.

"Dogs always know," Ray said in a low, flat tone. "Dogs always recognize the living dead. That's why they have to go first. They always know."

"You mean — Petey's . . . dead?" I choked out the words.

Ray nodded. "They kill the dogs first."

"No!" I screamed and took another step back, nearly losing my balance as I bumped into a low marble gravestone. I jumped away from it.

"You weren't supposed to see this," Ray said, his narrow face expressionless except for his dark eyes, which revealed real sadness. "You weren't supposed to know. Not for another few weeks, anyway. I'm the watcher. I was supposed to watch, to make sure you didn't see until it was time."

He took a step toward me, his eyes lighting up red, burning into mine.

"Were you watching me from the window?" I cried. "Was that you in my room?"

Again he nodded yes. "I used to live in your house," he said, taking another step closer, forcing me back against the cold marble stone. "I'm the watcher."

I forced myself to look away, to stop staring into his glowing eyes. I wanted to scream to Josh to run and get help. But he was too far away. And I was frozen there, frozen with fear.

"We need fresh blood," Ray said.

"What?" I cried. "What are you saying?"

"The town — it can't survive without fresh blood. None of us can. You'll understand soon, Amanda. You'll understand why we had to invite you to the house, to the . . . Dead House."

In the darting, zigzagging beam of light, I could see Josh moving closer, heading our way.

Run, Josh, I thought. Run away. Fast. Get someone. Get *anyone*.

I could think the words. Why couldn't I scream them?

Ray's eyes glowed brighter. He was standing right in front of me now, his features set, hard and cold.

"Ray?" Even through my jeans, the marble gravestone felt cold against the back of my legs.

"I messed up," he whispered. "I was the watcher. But I messed up."

"Ray — what are you going to do?"

His red eyes flickered. "I'm really sorry."

He started to raise himself off the ground, to float over me.

I could feel myself start to choke. I couldn't breathe. I couldn't move. I opened my mouth to call out to Josh, but no sound came out.

Josh? Where was he?

I looked down the rows of gravestones but couldn't see his light.

Ray floated up a little higher. He hovered over me, choking me somehow, blinding me, suffocating me.

I'm dead, I thought. Dead.

Now I'm dead, too.

14

And then, suddenly, light broke through the darkness.

The light shone in Ray's face, the bright white halogen light.

"What's going on?" Josh asked, in a high-pitched, nervous voice. "Amanda — what's happening?"

Ray cried out and dropped back to the ground. "Turn that off! Turn it off!" he screeched, his voice a shrill whisper, like wind through a broken windowpane.

But Josh held the bright beam of light on Ray. "What's going on? What are you doing?"

I could breathe again. As I stared into the light, I struggled to stop my heart from pounding so hard.

Ray moved his arms to shield himself from the light. But I could see what was happening to him. The light had already done its damage.

Ray's skin seemed to be melting. His whole face

sagged, then fell, dropping off his skull.

I stared into the circle of white light, unable to look away, as Ray's skin folded and drooped and melted away. As the bone underneath was revealed, his eyeballs rolled out of their sockets and fell silently to the ground.

Josh, frozen in horror, somehow held the bright light steady, and we both stared at the grinning skull, its dark craters staring back at us.

"Oh!" I shrieked as Ray took a step toward me.

But then I realized that Ray wasn't walking. He was falling.

I jumped aside as he crumpled to the ground. And gasped as his skull hit the top of the marble gravestone, and cracked open with a sickening *splat*.

"Come on!" Josh shouted. "Amanda — come *on*!" He grabbed my hand and tried to pull me away.

But I couldn't stop staring down at Ray, now a pile of bones inside a puddle of crumpled clothes.

"Amanda, come on!"

Then, before I even realized it, I was running, running beside Josh as fast as I could down the long row of graves toward the street. The light flashed against the blur of gravestones as we ran, slipping on the soft, dew-covered grass, gasping in the still, hot air.

"We've got to tell Mom and Dad. Got to get *away* from here!" I cried.

"They — they won't believe it!" Josh said, as we reached the street. We kept running, our sneakers thudding hard against the pavement. "I'm not sure I believe it myself!"

"They've *got* to believe us!" I told him. "If they don't, we'll *drag* them out of that house."

The white beam of light pointed the way as we ran through the dark, silent streets. There were no streetlights, no lights on in the windows of the houses we passed, no car headlights.

Such a dark world we had entered.

And now it was time to get out.

We ran the rest of the way home. I kept looking back to see if we were being followed. But I didn't see anyone. The neighborhood was still and empty.

I had a sharp pain in my side as we reached home. But I forced myself to keep running, up the gravel driveway with its thick blanket of dead leaves, and onto the front porch.

I pushed open the door and both Josh and I started to scream. "Mom! Dad! Where are you?"

Silence.

We ran into the living room. The lights were all off.

"Mom? Dad? Are you here?"

Please be here, I thought, my heart racing, the pain in my side still sharp. Please be here.

We searched the house. They weren't home.

"The potluck party," Josh suddenly remembered. "Can they still be at that party?"

We were standing in the living room, both of us breathing hard. The pain in my side had let up just a bit. I had turned on all the lights, but the room still felt gloomy and menacing.

I glanced at the clock on the mantel. Nearly two in the morning.

"They should be home by now," I said, my voice shaky and weak.

"Where did they go? Did they leave a number?" Josh was already on his way to the kitchen.

I followed him, turning on lights as we went. We went right to the memo pad on the counter where Mom and Dad always leave us notes.

Nothing. The pad was blank.

"We've *got* to find them!" Josh cried. He sounded very frightened. His wide eyes reflected his fear. "We have to get away from here."

What if something has happened to them?

That's what I started to say. But I caught myself just in time. I didn't want to scare Josh any more than he was already.

Besides, he'd probably thought of that, too.

"Should we call the police?" he asked, as we walked back to the living room and peered out the front window into the darkness.

"I don't know," I said, pressing my hot forehead against the cool glass. "I just don't know *what* to do. I want them to be home. I want them here so we can all leave."

"What's your hurry?" a girl's voice said from behind me.

Josh and I both cried out and spun around.

Karen Somerset was standing in the center of the room, her arms crossed over her chest.

"But — you're *dead!*" I blurted out.

She smiled, a sad smile, a bitter smile.

And then two more kids stepped in from the hallway. One of them clicked off the lights. "Too bright in here," he said. They moved next to Karen.

And another kid, Jerry Franklin — another dead kid — appeared by the fireplace. And I saw the girl with short black hair, the one I had seen on the stairs, move beside me by the curtains.

They were all smiling, their eyes glowing dully in the dim light, all moving in on Josh and me.

"What do you *want?*" I screamed in a voice I didn't even recognize. "What are you going to do?"

"We used to live in your house," Karen said softly.

"Huh?" I cried.

"We used to live in your house," George said.

"And now, guess what?" Jerry added. *"Now we're dead in your house!"*

The others started to laugh, crackling, dry laughs, as they all closed in on Josh and me.

15

"They're going to kill us!" Josh cried.

I watched them move forward in silence. Josh and I had backed up to the window. I looked around the dark room for an escape route.

But there was nowhere to run.

"Karen — you seemed so nice," I said. The words just tumbled out. I hadn't thought before I said them.

Her eyes glowed a little brighter. "I *was* nice," she said in a glum monotone, "until I moved here."

"We were all nice," George Carpenter said in the same low monotone. "But now we're dead."

"Let us go!" Josh cried, raising his hands in front of him as if to shield himself. "Please — let us go."

They laughed again, the dry, hoarse laughter. Dead laughter.

"Don't be scared, Amanda," Karen said. "Soon you'll be with us. That's why they invited you to this house."

"Huh? I don't understand," I cried, my voice shaking.

"This is the Dead House. This is where everyone lives when they first arrive in Dark Falls. When they're still alive."

This seemed to strike the others as funny. They all snickered and laughed.

"But our great-uncle — " Josh started.

Karen shook her head, her eyes glowing with amusement. "No. Sorry, Josh. No great-uncle. It was just a trick to bring you here. Once every year, someone new has to move here. Other years, it was us. We lived in this house — until we died. This year, it's your turn."

"We need new blood," Jerry Franklin said, his eyes glowing red in the dim light. "Once a year, you see, we need new blood."

Moving forward in silence, they hovered over Josh and me.

I took a deep breath. A last breath, perhaps. And shut my eyes.

And then I heard the knock on the door.

A loud knock, repeated several times.

I opened my eyes. The ghostly kids all vanished. The air smelled sour.

Josh and I stared at each other, dazed, as the loud knocking started again.

"It's Mom and Dad!" Josh cried.

We both ran to the door. Josh stumbled over

the coffee table in the dark, so I got to the door first.

"Mom! Dad!" I cried, pulling open the door. "Where have you been?"

I reached out my arms to hug them both — and stopped with my arms in the air. My mouth dropped open and I uttered a silent cry.

"Mr. Dawes!" Josh exclaimed, coming up beside me. "We thought — "

"Oh, Mr. Dawes, I'm so glad to see you!" I cried happily, pushing open the screen door for him.

"Kids — you're okay?" he asked, eyeing us both, his handsome face tight with worry. "Oh, thank God!" he cried. "I got here in time!"

"Mr. Dawes — " I started, feeling so relieved, I had tears in my eyes. "I — "

He grabbed my arm. "There's no time to talk," he said, looking behind him to the street. I could see his car in the driveway. The engine was running. Only the parking lights were on. "I've got to get you kids out of here while there's still time."

Josh and I started to follow him, then hesitated.

What if Mr. Dawes was one of them?

"Hurry," Mr. Dawes urged, holding open the screen door, gazing nervously out into the darkness. "I think we're in terrible danger."

"But — " I started, staring into his frightened eyes, trying to decide if we could trust him.

"I was at the party with your parents," Mr.

Dawes said. "All of a sudden, they formed a circle. Everyone. Around your parents and me. They — they started to close in on us."

Just like when the kids started to close in on Josh and me, I thought.

"We broke through them and ran," Mr. Dawes said, glancing to the driveway behind him. "Somehow the three of us got away. Hurry. We've all got to get away from here — *now!*"

"Josh, let's go," I urged. Then I turned to Mr. Dawes. "Where are Mom and Dad?"

"Come on. I'll show you. They're safe for now. But I don't know for how long."

We followed him out of the house and down the driveway to his car. The clouds had parted. A sliver of moon shone low in a pale, early morning sky.

"There's something wrong with this whole town," Mr. Dawes said, holding the front passenger door open for me as Josh climbed into the back.

I slumped gratefully into the seat, and he slammed the door shut. "I know," I said, as he slid behind the wheel. "Josh and I. We both — "

"We've got to get as far away as we can before they catch up with us," Mr. Dawes said, backing down the drive quickly, the tires sliding and squealing as he pulled onto the street.

"Yes," I agreed. "Thank goodness you came.

My house — it's filled with kids. Dead kids and — "

"So you've seen them," Mr. Dawes said softly, his eyes wide with fear. He pushed down harder on the gas pedal.

As I looked out into the purple darkness, a low, orange sun began to show over the green treetops. "Where are our parents?" I asked anxiously.

"There's a kind of outdoor theater next to the cemetery," Mr. Dawes said, staring straight ahead through the windshield, his eyes narrow, his expression tense. "It's built right into the ground, and it's hidden by a big tree. I left them there. I told them not to move. I think they'll be safe. I don't think anyonc'll think to look there."

"We've seen it," Josh said. A bright light suddenly flashed on in the backseat.

"What's that?" Mr. Dawes asked, looking into the rearview mirror.

"My flashlight," Josh answered, clicking it off. "I brought it just in case. But the sun will be up soon. I probably won't need it."

Mr. Dawes hit the brake and pulled the car to the side of the road. We were at the edge of the cemetery. I climbed quickly out of the car, eager to see my parents.

The sky was still dark, streaked with violet now. The sun was a dark orange balloon just barely poking over the trees. Across the street, beyond the jagged rows of gravestones, I could see the dark outline of the leaning tree that hid the mysterious amphitheater.

"Hurry," Mr. Dawes urged, closing his car door quietly. "I'm sure your parents are desperate to see you."

We headed across the street, half-walking, half-jogging, Josh swinging the flashlight in one hand.

Suddenly, at the edge of the cemetery grass, Josh stopped. "Petey!" he cried.

I followed his gaze, and saw our white terrier walking slowly along a slope of gravestones.

"Petey!" Josh yelled again, and began running to the dog.

My heart sank. I hadn't had a chance to tell Josh what Ray had revealed to me about Petey. "No — Josh!" I called.

Mr. Dawes looked very alarmed. "We don't have time. We have to hurry," he said to me. Then he began shouting for Josh to come back.

"I'll go get him," I said, and took off, running as fast as I could along the rows of graves, calling to my brother. "Josh! Josh, wait up! Don't! Don't go after him! Josh — Petey is *dead!*"

Josh had been gaining on the dog, which was ambling along, sniffing the ground, not looking up, not paying any attention to Josh. Then suddenly, Josh tripped over a low grave marker.

He cried out as he fell, and the flashlight flew out of his hand and clattered against a gravestone.

I quickly caught up with him. "Josh — are you okay?"

He was lying on his stomach, staring straight ahead.

"Josh — answer me. Are you okay?"

I grabbed him by the shoulders and tried to pull him up, but he kept staring straight ahead, his mouth open, his eyes wide.

"Josh?"

"Look," he said finally.

I breathed a sigh of relief, knowing that Josh wasn't knocked out or something.

"Look," he repeated, and pointed to the gravestone he had tripped over.

I turned and squinted at the grave. I read the inscription, silently mouthing the words as I read:

COMPTON DAWES. R.I.P. 1950–1980.

My head began to spin. I felt dizzy. I steadied myself, holding onto Josh.

COMPTON DAWES.

It wasn't his father or his grandfather. He had told us he was the only Compton in his family.

So Mr. Dawes was dead, too.

Dead. Dead. Dead.

Dead as everyone else.

He was one of them. One of the dead ones.

Josh and I stared at each other in the purple darkness. Surrounded. Surrounded by the dead.

Now what? I asked myself.

Now what?

16

"Get up, Josh," I said, my voice a choked whisper. "We've got to get away from here."

But we were too late.

A hand grabbed me firmly by the shoulder.

I spun around to see Mr. Dawes, his eyes narrowing as he read the inscription on his own gravestone.

"Mr. Dawes — you, too!" I cried, so disappointed, so confused, so . . . scared.

"Me, too," he said, almost sadly. "All of us." His eyes burned into mine. "This was a normal town once. And we were normal people. Most of us worked in the plastics factory on the outskirts of town. Then there was an accident. Something escaped from the factory. A yellow gas. It floated over the town. So fast we didn't see it . . . didn't realize. And then, it was too late, and Dark Falls wasn't a normal town anymore. We were all dead, Amanda. Dead and buried. But we couldn't rest.

We couldn't sleep. Dark Falls was a town of living dead."

"What — what are you going to do to us?" I managed to ask. My knees were trembling so hard, I could barely stand. A dead man was squeezing my shoulder. A dead man was staring hard into my eyes.

Standing this close, I could smell his sour breath. I turned my head, but the smell already choked my nostrils.

"Where are Mom and Dad?" Josh asked, climbing to his feet and standing rigidly across from us, glaring accusingly at Mr. Dawes.

"Safe and sound," Mr. Dawes said with a faint smile. "Come with me. It's time for you to join them."

I tried to pull away from him, but his hand was locked on my shoulder. "Let go!" I shouted.

His smile grew wider. "Amanda, it doesn't hurt to die," he said softly, almost soothingly. "Come with me."

"No!" Josh shouted. And with sudden quickness, he dived to the ground and picked up his flashlight.

"Yes!" I cried. "Shine it on him, Josh!" The light could save us. The light could defeat Mr. Dawes, as it had Ray. The light could destroy him. "Quick — shine it on him!" I pleaded.

Josh fumbled with the flashlight, then pointed

it toward Mr. Dawes's startled face, and clicked it on.

Nothing.

No light.

"It — it's broken," Josh said. "I guess when it hit the gravestone. . . ."

My heart pounding, I looked back at Mr. Dawes. The smile on his face was a smile of victory.

17

"Nice try," Mr. Dawes said to Josh. The smile faded quickly from his face.

Close up, he didn't look so young and handsome. His skin, I could see, was dry and peeling and hung loosely beneath his eyes.

"Let's go, kids," he said, giving me a shove. He glanced up at the brightening sky. The sun was raising itself over the treetops.

Josh hesitated.

"I *said* let's go," Mr. Dawes snapped impatiently. He loosened his grip on my shoulder and took a menacing step toward Josh.

Josh glanced down at the worthless flashlight. Then he pulled his arm back and heaved the flashlight at Mr. Dawes's head.

The flashlight hit its target with a sickening *crack*. It hit Mr. Dawes in the center of his forehead, splitting a large hole in the skin.

Mr. Dawes uttered a low cry. His eyes widened in surprise. Dazed, he reached a hand up to the hole where a few inches of gray skull poked through.

"Run, Josh!" I cried.

But there was no need to tell him that. He was already zigzagging through the rows of graves, his head ducked low. I followed him, running as fast as I could.

Glancing back, I saw Mr. Dawes stagger after us, still holding his ripped forehead. He took several steps, then abruptly stopped, staring up at the sky.

It's too bright for him, I realized. He has to stay in the shade.

Josh had ducked down behind a tall marble monument, old and slightly tilted, cracked down the middle. I slid down beside him, gasping for breath.

Leaning on the cool marble, we both peered around the sides of the monument. Mr. Dawes, a scowl on his face, was heading back toward the amphitheater, keeping in the shadows of the trees.

"He — he's not chasing us," Josh whispered, his chest heaving as he struggled to catch his breath and stifle his fear. "He's going back."

"The sun is too bright for him," I said, holding onto the side of the monument. "He must be going to get Mom and Dad."

"That stupid flashlight," Josh cried.

"Never mind that," I said, watching Mr. Dawes

116

until he disappeared behind the big leaning tree. "What are we going to do now? I don't know — "

"Shhh. Look!" Josh poked me hard on the shoulder, and pointed. "Who's that?"

I followed his stare and saw several dark figures hurrying through the rows of tombstones. They seemed to have appeared from out of nowhere.

Did they rise out of the graves?

Walking quickly, seeming to float over the green, sloping ground, they headed into the shadows. All were walking in silence, their eyes straight ahead. They didn't stop to greet one another. They strode purposefully toward the hidden amphitheater, as if they were being drawn there, as if they were puppets being pulled by hidden strings.

"Whoa. Look at them all!" Josh whispered, ducking his head back behind the marble monument.

The dark, moving forms made all the shadows ripple. It looked as if the trees, the gravestones, the entire cemetery had come to life, had started toward the hidden seats of the amphitheater.

"There goes Karen," I whispered, pointing. "And George. And all the rest of them."

The kids from our house were moving quickly in twos and threes, following the other shadows, as silent and businesslike as everyone else.

Everyone was here except Ray, I thought.

Because we killed Ray.

We killed someone who was already dead.

"Do you think Mom and Dad are really down in that weird theater?" Josh asked, interrupting my morbid thoughts, his eyes on the moving shadows.

"Come on," I said, taking Josh's hand and pulling him away from the monument. "We've got to find out."

We watched the last of the dark figures float past the enormous leaning tree. The shadows stopped moving. The cemetery was still and silent. A solitary crow floated high above in the clear blue, cloudless sky.

Slowly, Josh and I edged our way toward the amphitheater, ducking behind gravestones, keeping low to the ground.

It was a struggle to move. I felt as if I weighed five hundred pounds. The weight of my fear, I guess.

I was desperate to see if Mom and Dad were there.

But at the same time, I didn't want to see.

I didn't want to see them being held prisoner by Mr. Dawes and the others.

I didn't want to see them . . . killed.

The thought made me stop. I reached out an arm and halted Josh.

We were standing behind the leaning tree, hidden by its enormous clump of upraised roots. Beyond the tree, down in the theater below, I could hear the low murmur of voices.

"Are Mom and Dad there?" Josh whispered. He started to poke his head around the side of the bent tree trunk, but I cautiously pulled him back.

"Be careful," I whispered. "Don't let them see you. They're practically right beneath us."

"But I've *got* to know if Mom and Dad are really here," he whispered, his eyes frightened, pleading.

"Me, too," I agreed.

We both leaned over the massive trunk. The bark felt smooth under my hands as I gazed into the deep shadows cast by the tree.

And then I saw them.

Mom and Dad. They were tied up, back-to-back, standing in the center of the floor at the bottom of the amphitheater in front of everyone.

They looked so uncomfortable, so terrified. Their arms were tied tightly down at their sides. Dad's face was bright red. Mom's hair was all messed up, hanging wildly down over her forehead, her head bowed.

Squinting into the darkness cast by the tree, I saw Mr. Dawes standing beside them along with another, older man. And I saw that the rows of long benches built into the ground were filled with people. Not a single empty space.

Everyone in town must be here, I realized.

Everyone except Josh and me.

"They're going to kill Mom and Dad," Josh whispered, grabbing my arm, squeezing it in fear. "They're going to make Mom and Dad just like them."

"Then they'll come after us," I said, thinking out loud, staring through the shadows at my poor parents. Both of them had their heads bowed now as they stood before the silent crowd. Both of them were awaiting their fates.

"What are we going to do?" Josh whispered.

"Huh?" I was staring so hard at Mom and Dad, I guess I momentarily blanked out.

"What are we going to do?" Josh repeated urgently, still holding desperately to my arm. "We can't just stand here and — "

I suddenly knew what we were going to do.

It just came to me. I didn't even have to think hard.

"Maybe we can save them," I whispered, backing away from the tree. "Maybe we *can* do something."

Josh let go of my arm. He stared at me eagerly.

"We're going to push this tree over," I whispered with so much confidence that I surprised myself. "We're going to push the tree over so the sunlight will fill the amphitheater."

"Yes!" Josh cried immediately. "Look at this tree. It's practically down already. We can do it!"

I *knew* we could do it. I don't know where my confidence came from. But I *knew* we could do it.

And I knew we had to do it fast.

Peering over the top of the trunk again, struggling to see through the shadows, I could see that everyone in the theater had stood up. They were all starting to move forward, down toward Mom and Dad.

"Come on, Josh," I whispered. "We'll take a running jump, and push the tree over. Come on!"

Without another word, we both took several steps back.

We just had to give the trunk a good, hard push, and the tree would topple right over. The roots were already almost entirely up out of the ground, after all.

One hard push. That's all it would take. And the sunlight would pour into the theater. Beautiful, golden sunlight. Bright, bright sunlight.

The dead people would all crumble.

And Mom and Dad would be saved.

All four of us would be saved.

"Come on, Josh," I whispered. "Ready?"

He nodded, his face solemn, his eyes frightened.

"Okay. Let's *go!*" I cried.

We both ran forward, digging our sneakers into the ground, moving as fast as we could, our arms outstretched and ready.

In a second, we hit the tree trunk and pushed with all of our strength, shoving it with our hands and then moving our shoulders into it, pushing . . . pushing . . . pushing . . .

It didn't budge.

18

"Push!" I cried. "Push it again!"

Josh let out an exasperated, defeated sigh. "I can't, Amanda. I can't move it."

"Josh — " I glared at him.

He backed up to try again.

Below, I could hear startled voices, angry voices.

"Quick!" I yelled. *"Push!"*

We hurtled into the tree trunk with our shoulders, both of us grunting from the effort, our muscles straining, our faces bright red.

"Push! Keep pushing!"

The veins at my temples felt about to pop.

Was the tree moving?

No.

It gave a little, but bounced right back.

The voices from below were getting louder.

"We can't do it!" I cried, so disappointed, so frustrated, so terrified. "We can't move it!"

Defeated, I slumped over onto the tree trunk,

and started to bury my face in my hands.

I pulled back with a gasp when I heard the soft cracking sound. The cracking sound grew louder until it was a rumble, then a roar. It sounded as if the ground were ripping apart.

The old tree fell quickly. It didn't have far to fall. But it hit with a thundering crash that seemed to shake the ground.

I grabbed Josh and we both stood in amazement and disbelief as bright sunlight poured into the amphitheater.

The cries went up instantly. Horrified cries. Angry cries. Frantic cries.

The cries became howls. Howls of pain, of agony.

The people in the amphitheater, the living dead caught in the golden light, began scrambling over one another, screeching, pulling, climbing, pushing, trying to claw their way to shade.

But it was too late.

Their skin began to drop off their bones and, as I stared open-mouthed, they crumbled to powder and dissolved to the ground, their clothes disintegrating along with them.

The painful cries continued to ring out as the bodies fell apart, the skin melted away, the dry bones collapsed. I saw Karen Somerset staggering across the floor. I saw her hair fall to the ground in a heap, revealing the dark skull underneath. She cast a glance up at me, a longing look, a look of regret. And then her eyeballs rolled out of their sockets, and she opened her toothless mouth, and she cried, "Thank you, Amanda! Thank you!" and collapsed.

Josh and I covered our ears to shut out the ghastly cries. We both looked away, unable to keep watching the entire town fall in agony and crumble to powder, destroyed by the sun, the clear, warm sun.

When we looked back, they had all disappeared.

Mom and Dad were standing right where they had been, tied back-to-back, their expressions a mixture of horror and disbelief.

"Mom! Dad!" I cried.

I'll never forget their smiles as Josh and I ran forward to free them.

It didn't take our parents long to get us packed up and to arrange for the movers to take us back to our old neighborhood and our old house. "I guess it's lucky after all that we couldn't sell the old place," Dad said, as we eagerly piled into the car to leave.

Dad backed down the driveway and started to roar away.

"Stop!" I cried suddenly. I'm not sure why, but I had a sudden, powerful urge to take one last look at the old house.

As both of my parents called out to me in confusion, I pushed open the door and jogged back to the driveway. Standing in the middle of the yard, I stared up at the house, silent, empty, still covered in thick layers of blue-gray shadows.

I found myself gazing up at the old house as if I were hypnotized. I don't know how long I stood there.

The crunch of tires on the gravel driveway snapped me out of my spell. Startled, I turned to see a red station wagon parked in the driveway.

Two boys about Josh's age jumped out of the back. Their parents followed. Staring up at the house, they didn't seem to notice me.

"Here we are, kids," the mother said, smiling at them. "Our new house."

"It doesn't look new. It looks old," one of the boys said.

And then his brother's eyes widened as he noticed me. "Who are *you*?" he demanded.

The other members of his family turned to stare at me.

"Oh. I . . . uh . . ." His question caught me by surprise. I could hear my dad honking his horn impatiently down on the street. "I . . . uh . . . used to live in your house," I found myself answering.

And then I turned and ran full speed down to the street.

Wasn't that Mr. Dawes standing at the porch, clipboard in hand? I wondered, catching a glimpse of a dark figure as I ran to the car.

No, it couldn't be Mr. Dawes up there waiting for them, I decided.

It just couldn't be.

I didn't look back. I slammed the car door behind me, and we sped away.

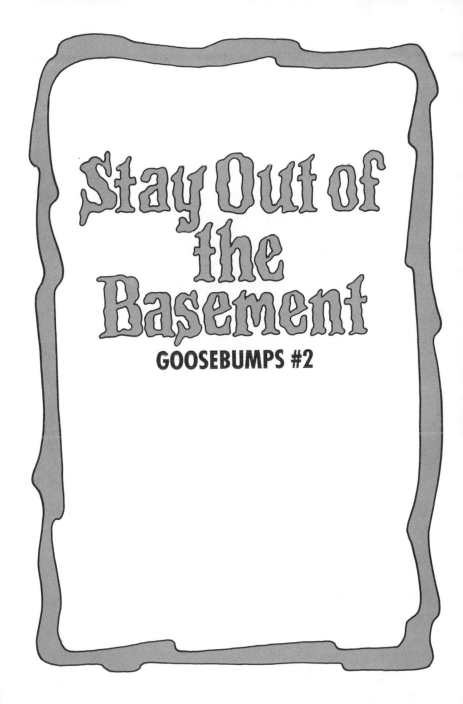

Stay Out of the Basement

the

Basement

GOOSEBUMPS #2

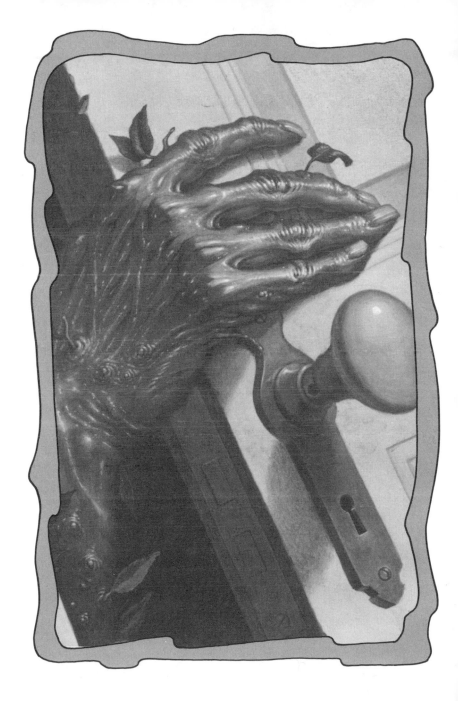

1

"Hey, Dad — catch!"

Casey tossed the Frisbee across the smooth, green lawn. Casey's dad made a face, squinting into the sun. The Frisbee hit the ground and skipped a few times before landing under the hedge at the back of the house.

"Not today. I'm busy," Dr. Brewer said, and abruptly turned and loped into the house. The screen door slammed behind him.

Casey brushed his straight blond hair back off his forehead. "What's *his* problem?" he called to Margaret, his sister, who had watched the whole scene from the side of the redwood garage.

"You know," Margaret said quietly. She wiped her hands on the legs of her jeans and held them both up, inviting a toss. "I'll play Frisbee with you for a little while," she said.

"Okay," Casey said without enthusiasm. He walked slowly over to retrieve the Frisbee from under the hedge.

Margaret moved closer. She felt sorry for Casey. He and their dad were really close, always playing ball or Frisbee or Nintendo together. But Dr. Brewer didn't seem to have time for that anymore.

Jumping up to catch the Frisbee, Margaret realized she felt sorry for herself, too. Dad hadn't been the same to her, either. In fact, he spent so much time down in the basement, he barely said a word to her.

He doesn't even call me Princess anymore, Margaret thought. It was a nickname she hated. But at least it was a nickname, a sign of closeness.

She tossed the red Frisbee back. A bad toss. Casey chased after it, but it sailed away from him. Margaret looked up to the golden hills beyond their backyard.

California, she thought.

It's so weird out here. Here it is, the middle of winter, and there isn't a cloud in the sky, and Casey and I are out in jeans and T-shirts as if it were the middle of summer.

She made a diving catch for a wild toss, rolling over on the manicured lawn and raising the Frisbee above her head triumphantly.

"Show off," Casey muttered, unimpressed.

"You're the hot dog in the family," Margaret called.

"Well, you're a dork."

"Hey, Casey — you want me to play with you or not?"

He shrugged.

Everyone was so edgy these days, Margaret realized.

It was easy to figure out why.

She made a high toss. The Frisbee sailed over Casey's head. *"You* chase it!" he cried angrily, putting his hands on his hips.

"No, *you!*" she cried.

"You!"

"Casey — you're eleven years old. Don't act like a two-year-old," she snapped.

"Well, you act like a *one*-year-old," was his reply as he grudgingly went after the Frisbee.

It was all Dad's fault, Margaret realized. Things had been so tense ever since he started working at home. Down in the basement with his plants and weird machines. He hardly ever came up for air.

And when he did, he wouldn't even catch a Frisbee.

Or spend two minutes with either of them.

Mom had noticed it, too, Margaret thought, running full-out and making another grandstand catch just before colliding with the side of the garage.

Having Dad home has made Mom really tense, too. She pretends everything is fine. But I can tell she's worried about him.

"Lucky catch, Fatso!" Casey called.

Margaret hated the name Fatso even more than she hated Princess. People in her family jokingly called her Fatso because she was so thin, like her father. She also was tall like him, but she had her mother's straight brown hair, brown eyes, and dark coloring.

"Don't call me that." She heaved the red disc at him. He caught it at his knees and flipped it back to her.

They tossed it back and forth without saying much for another ten or fifteen minutes. "I'm getting hot," Margaret said, shielding her eyes from the afternoon sun with her hand. "Let's go in."

Casey tossed the Frisbee against the garage wall. It dropped onto the grass. He came trotting over to her. "Dad always plays longer," he said peevishly. "And he throws better. You throw like a girl."

"Give me a break," Margaret groaned, giving him a playful shove as she jogged to the back door. "You throw like a chimpanzee."

"How come Dad got fired?" he asked.

She blinked. And stopped running. The question had caught her by surprise. "Huh?"

His pale, freckled face turned serious. "You

know. I mean, why?" he asked, obviously uncomfortable.

She and Casey had never discussed this in the four weeks since Dad had been home. Which was unusual since they were pretty close, being only a year apart.

"I mean, we came all the way out here so he could work at PolyTech, right?" Casey asked.

"Yeah. Well . . . he got fired," Margaret said, half-whispering in case her dad might be able to hear.

"But why? Did he blow up the lab or something?" Casey grinned. The idea of his dad blowing up a huge campus science lab appealed to him.

"No, he didn't blow anything up," Margaret said, tugging at a strand of dark hair. "Botanists work with plants, you know. They don't get much of a chance to blow things up."

They both laughed.

Casey followed her into the narrow strip of shade cast by the low ranch-style house.

"I'm not sure exactly what happened," Margaret continued, still half-whispering. "But I overheard Dad on the phone. I think he was talking to Mr. Martinez. His department head. Remember? The quiet little man who came to dinner that night the barbecue grill caught fire?"

Casey nodded. "Martinez fired Dad?"

"Probably," Margaret whispered. "From what

I overheard, it had something to do with the plants Dad was growing, some experiments that had gone wrong or something."

"But Dad's real smart," Casey insisted, as if Margaret were arguing with him. "If his experiments went wrong, he'd know how to fix them."

Margaret shrugged. "That's all I know," she said. "Come on, Casey. Let's go inside. I'm dying of thirst!" She stuck her tongue out and moaned, demonstrating her dire need of liquid.

"You're gross," Casey said. He pulled open the screen door, then dodged in front of her so he could get inside first.

"Who's gross?" Mrs. Brewer asked from the sink. She turned to greet the two of them. "Don't answer that."

Mom looks very tired today, Margaret thought, noticing the crisscross of fine lines at the corners of her mother's eyes and the first strands of gray in her mother's shoulder-length brown hair. "I hate this job," Mrs. Brewer said, turning back to the sink.

"What are you doing?" Casey asked, pulling open the refrigerator and removing a box of juice.

"I'm deveining shrimp."

"Yuck!" Margaret exclaimed.

"Thanks for the support," Mrs. Brewer said dryly. The phone rang. Wiping her shrimpy hands with a dish towel, she hurried across the room to pick up the phone.

Margaret got a box of juice from the fridge, popped the straw into the top, and followed Casey into the front hallway. The basement door, usually shut tight when Dr. Brewer was working down there, was slightly ajar.

Casey started to close it, then stopped. "Let's go down and see what Dad is doing," he suggested.

Margaret sucked the last drops of juice through the straw and squeezed the empty box flat in her hand. "Okay."

She knew they probably shouldn't disturb their father, but her curiosity got the better of her. He had been working down there for four weeks now. All kinds of interesting equipment, lights, and plants had been delivered. Most days he spent at least eight or nine hours down there, doing whatever it was he was doing. And he hadn't shown it to them once.

"Yeah. Let's go," Margaret said. It was *their* house, too, after all.

Besides, maybe their dad was just waiting for them to show some interest. Maybe he was hurt that they hadn't bothered to come downstairs in all this time.

She pulled the door open the rest of the way,

and they stepped onto the narrow stairway. "Hey, Dad — " Casey called excitedly. "Dad — can we see?"

They were halfway down when their father appeared at the foot of the stairs. He glared up at them angrily, his skin strangely green under the fluorescent light fixture. He was holding his right hand, drops of red blood falling onto his white lab coat.

"*Stay out of the basement!*" he bellowed, in a voice they'd never heard before.

Both kids shrank back, surprised to hear their father scream like that. He was usually so mild and soft-spoken.

"*Stay out of the basement,*" he repeated, holding his bleeding hand. "Don't *ever* come down here — I'm warning you."

2

"Okay. All packed," Mrs. Brewer said, dropping her suitcases with a thud in the front hallway. She poked her head into the living room where the TV was blaring. "Do you think you could stop the movie for one minute to say good-bye to your mother?"

Casey pushed a button on the remote control, and the screen went blank. He and Margaret obediently walked to the hallway to give their mother hugs.

Margaret's friend, Diane Manning, who lived just around the corner, followed them into the hallway. "How long are you going to be gone, Mrs. Brewer?" she asked, her eyes on the two bulging suitcases.

"I don't know," Mrs. Brewer replied fretfully. "My sister went into the hospital in Tucson this morning. I guess I'll have to stay until she's able to go home."

"Well, I'll be glad to baby-sit for Casey and

Margaret while you're away," Diane joked.

"Give me a break," Margaret said, rolling her eyes. "I'm older than you are, Diane."

"And I'm smarter than both of you," Casey added with typical modesty.

"I'm not worried about you kids," Mrs. Brewer said, glancing nervously at her watch. "I'm worried about your father."

"Don't worry," Margaret told her seriously. "We'll take good care of him."

"Just make sure that he eats something once in a while," Mrs. Brewer said. "He's so obsessed with his work, he doesn't remember to eat unless you tell him."

It's going to be really lonely around here without Mom, Margaret thought. Dad hardly ever comes up from the basement.

It had been two weeks since he yelled at Casey and her to stay out of the basement. They had been tiptoeing around ever since, afraid to get him angry again. But in the past two weeks, he had barely spoken to them, except for the occasional "good morning" and "good night."

"Don't worry about anything, Mom," she said, forcing a smile. "Just take good care of Aunt Eleanor."

"I'll call as soon as I get to Tucson," Mrs. Brewer said, nervously lowering her eyes to her watch again. She took three long strides to the basement door, then shouted down, "Michael — time to take me to the airport!"

After a long wait, Dr. Brewer called up a reply. Then Mrs. Brewer turned back to the kids. "Think he'll even notice I'm gone?" she asked in a loud whisper. She meant it to be a light remark, but her eyes revealed some sadness.

A few seconds later, they heard footsteps on the basement stairs, and their dad appeared. He pulled off his stained lab coat, revealing tan slacks and a bright yellow T-shirt, and tossed the lab coat onto the banister. Even though it was two weeks later, his right hand, the hand that had been bleeding, was still heavily bandaged.

"Ready?" he asked his wife.

Mrs. Brewer sighed. "I guess." She gave Margaret and Casey a helpless look, then moved quickly to give them each one last hug.

"Let's go, then," Dr. Brewer said impatiently. He picked up the two bags and groaned. "Wow. How long are you planning to stay? A year?" Then he headed out the front door with them, not waiting for an answer.

"Bye, Mrs. Brewer," Diane said, waving. "Have a good trip."

"How can she have a good trip?" Casey asked sharply. "Her sister's in the hospital."

"You know what I mean," Diane replied, tossing back her long red hair and rolling her eyes.

They watched the station wagon roll down the driveway, then returned to the living room. Casey picked up the remote control and started the movie.

Diane sprawled on the couch and picked up the bag of potato chips she'd been eating.

"Who picked this movie?" Diane asked, crinkling the foil bag noisily.

"I did," Casey said. "It's neat." He had pulled a couch cushion down to the living room carpet and was lying on it.

Margaret was sitting cross-legged on the floor, her back against the base of an armchair, still thinking about her mother and her aunt Eleanor. "It's neat if you like to see a lot of people blown up and their guts flying all over," she said, making a face for Diane's benefit.

"Yeah. It's neat," Casey said, not taking his eyes off the glowing TV screen.

"I've got so much homework. I don't know why I'm sitting here," Diane said, reaching her hand into the potato chip bag.

"Me, too," Margaret sighed. "I guess I'll do it after dinner. Do you have the math assignment? I think I left my math book at school."

"Sshhh!" Casey hissed, kicking a sneakered foot in Margaret's direction. "This is a good part."

"You've seen this tape before?" Diane shrieked.

"Twice," Casey admitted. He ducked, and the

sofa pillow Diane threw sailed over his head.

"It's a pretty afternoon," Margaret said, stretching her arms above her head. "Maybe we should go outside. You know. Ride bikes or something."

"You think you're still back in Michigan? It's *always* a pretty afternoon here," Diane said, chewing loudly. "I don't even notice it anymore."

"Maybe we should do the math assignment together," Margaret suggested hopefully. Diane was much better in math than she was.

Diane shrugged. "Yeah. Maybe." She crinkled up the bag and set it on the floor. "Your dad looked kind of nervous, you know?"

"Huh? What do you mean?"

"Just nervous," Diane said. "How's he doing?"

"Sshhh," Casey insisted, picking up the potato chip bag and tossing it at Diane.

"You know. Being laid off and all."

"I guess he's okay," Margaret said wistfully. "I don't know, really. He spends all his time down in the basement with his experiments."

"Experiments? Hey — let's go take a look." Tossing her hair back behind her shoulders, Diane jumped up from the chrome and white leather couch.

Diane was a science freak. Math and science. The two subjects Margaret hated.

She should have been in the Brewer family,

145

Margaret thought with a trace of bitterness. Maybe Dad would pay some attention to her since she's into the same things he is.

"Come on — " Diane urged, bending over to pull Margaret up from the floor. "He's a botanist, right? What's he doing down there?"

"It's complicated," Margaret said, shouting over the explosions and gunfire on the TV. "He tried to explain it to me once. But — " Margaret allowed Diane to pull her to her feet.

"Shut up!" Casey yelled, staring at the movie, the colors from the TV screen reflecting over his clothes.

"Is he building a Frankenstein monster or something?" Diane demanded. "Or some kind of RoboCop? Wouldn't that be cool?"

"Shut up!" Casey repeated shrilly as Arnold Schwarzenegger bounded across the screen.

"He's got all these machines and plants down there," Margaret said uncomfortably. "But he doesn't want us to go down there."

"Huh? It's like top secret?" Diane's emerald green eyes lit up with excitement. "Come on. We'll just take a peek."

"No, I don't think so," Margaret told her. She couldn't forget the angry look on her father's face two weeks before when she and Casey had tried to pay a visit. Or the way he had screamed at them never to come down to the basement.

"Come on. I dare you," Diane challenged. "Are you chicken?"

"I'm not afraid," Margaret insisted shrilly. Diane was always daring her to do things she didn't want to do. Why is it so important for Diane to think she's so much braver than everyone else? Margaret wondered.

"Chicken," Diane repeated. Tossing her mane of red hair behind her shoulder, she strode quickly toward the basement door.

"Diane — stop!" Margaret cried, following after her.

"Hey, wait!" Casey cried, clicking off the movie. "Are we going downstairs? Wait for me!" He climbed quickly to his feet and enthusiastically hurried to join them at the basement door.

"We can't — " Margaret started, but Diane clamped a hand over her mouth.

"We'll take a quick peek," Diane insisted. "We'll just look. We won't touch anything. And then we'll come right back upstairs."

"Okay. I'll go first," Casey said, grabbing for the doorknob.

"Why do you want to do this?" Margaret asked her friend. "Why are you so eager to go down there?"

Diane shrugged. "It beats doing our math," she replied, grinning.

Margaret sighed, defeated. "Okay, let's go. But

remember — just looking, no touching."

Casey pulled open the door and led the way onto the stairway. Stepping onto the landing, they were immediately engulfed in hot, steamy air. They could hear the buzz and hum of electronic machinery. And off to the right, they could see the glare of the bright white lights from Dr. Brewer's workroom.

This is kind of fun, Margaret thought as the three of them made their way down the linoleum-covered stairway.

It's an adventure.

There's no harm in taking a peek.

So why was her heart pounding? Why did she have this sudden tingle of fear?

"Yuck! It's so hot in here!"

As they stepped away from the stairs, the air became unbearably hot and thick.

Margaret gasped. The sudden change in temperature was suffocating.

"It's so moist," Diane said. "Good for your hair and skin."

"We studied the rain forest in school," Casey said. "Maybe Dad's building a rain forest."

"Maybe," Margaret said uncertainly.

Why did she feel so strange? Was it just because they were invading their father's domain? Doing something he had told them not to do?

She held back, gazing in both directions. The basement was divided into two large, rectangular rooms. To the left, an unfinished rec room stood in darkness. She could barely make out the outlines of the Ping-Pong table in the center of the room.

The workroom to the right was brightly lit, so

bright they had to blink and wait for their eyes to adjust. Beams of white light poured down from large halogen lamps on tracks in the ceiling.

"Wow! Look!" Casey cried, his eyes wide as he stepped excitedly toward the light.

Reaching up toward the lights were shiny, tall plants, dozens of them, thick-stalked and broad-leafed, planted close together in an enormous, low trough of dark soil.

"It's like a jungle!" Margaret exclaimed, following Casey into the white glare.

The plants, in fact, resembled jungle plants — leafy vines and tall, treelike plants with long, slender tendrils, fragile-looking ferns, plants with gnarled, cream-colored roots poking up like bony knees from the soil.

"It's like a swamp or something," Diane said. "Did your father really grow these things in just five or six weeks?"

"Yeah. I'm pretty sure," Margaret replied, staring at the enormous red tomatoes on a slender, yellow stalk.

"Ooh. Feel this one," Diane said.

Margaret glanced over to find her friend rubbing her hand over a large, flat leaf the shape of a teardrop. "Diane — we shouldn't touch — "

"I know, I know," Diane said, not letting go of the leaf. "But just rub your hand on it."

Margaret reluctantly obeyed. "It doesn't feel like a leaf," she said as Diane moved over to examine a large fern. "It's so smooth. Like glass."

The three of them stood under the bright, white lights, examining the plants for several minutes, touching the thick stalks, running their hands over the smooth, warm leaves, surprised by the enormous size of the fruits some of the plants had produced.

"It's too hot down here," Casey complained. He pulled his T-shirt off over his head and dropped it onto the floor.

"What a bod!" Diane teased him.

He stuck out his tongue at her. Then his pale blue eyes grew wide and he seemed to freeze in surprise. "Hey!"

"Casey — what's the matter?" Margaret asked, hurrying over to him.

"This one — " He pointed to a tall, treelike plant. "It's *breathing!*"

Diane laughed.

But Margaret heard it, too. She grabbed Casey's bare shoulder and listened. Yes. She could hear breathing sounds, and they seemed to be coming from the tall, leafy tree.

"What's your problem?" Diane asked, seeing the amazed expressions on Casey's and Margaret's faces.

"Casey's right," Margaret said softly, listening to the steady, rhythmic sound. "You can hear it breathing."

Diane rolled her eyes. "Maybe it has a cold. Maybe its vine is stuffed up." She laughed at her own joke, but her two companions didn't join in. "I don't hear it." She moved closer.

All three of them listened.

Silence.

"It — stopped," Margaret said.

"Stop it, you two," Diane scolded. "You're not going to scare me."

"No. Really," Margaret protested.

"Hey — look at this!" Casey had already moved on to something else. He was standing in front of a tall glass case that stood on the other side of the plants. It looked a little like a phone booth, with a shelf inside about shoulder-high, and dozens of wires attached to the back and sides.

Margaret's eyes followed the wires to a similar glass booth a few feet away. Some kind of electrical generator stood between the two booths and appeared to be connected to both of them.

"What could that be?" Diane asked, hurrying over to Casey.

"Don't touch it," Margaret warned, giving the breathing plant one final glance, then joining the others.

But Casey reached out to the glass door on the

front of the booth. "I just want to see if this opens," he said.

He grabbed the glass — and his eyes went wide with shock.

His entire body began to shake and vibrate. His head jerked wildly from side to side. His eyes rolled up in his head.

"Oh, help!" he managed to cry, his body vibrating and shaking harder and faster. "Help me! I — can't stop!"

4

"Help me!"

Casey's whole body shook as if an electrical current were charging through him. His head jerked on his shoulders, and his eyes looked wild and dazed.

"Please!"

Margaret and Diane stared in open-mouthed horror. Margaret was the first to move. She lunged at Casey, and reached out to try to pull him away from the glass.

"Margaret — don't!" Diane screamed. "Don't touch him!"

"But we have to do something!" Margaret cried.

It took both girls a while to realize that Casey had stopped shaking. And was laughing.

"Casey?" Margaret asked, staring at him, her terrified expression fading to astonishment.

He was leaning against the glass, his body still now, his mouth wrapped in a broad, mischievous grin.

"Gotcha!" he declared. And then began to laugh even harder, pointing at them and repeating the phrase through his triumphant laughter. "Gotcha! Gotcha!"

"That wasn't funny!" Margaret screamed.

"You were faking it?! I don't believe it!" Diane cried, her face as pale as the white lights above them, her lower lip trembling.

Both girls leapt onto Casey and pushed him to the floor. Margaret sat on top of him while Diane held his shoulders down.

"Gotcha! Gotcha!" he continued, stopping only when Margaret tickled his stomach so hard he couldn't talk.

"You rat!" Diane cried. "You little rat!"

The free-for-all was brought to a sudden halt by a low moan from across the room. All three kids raised their heads and stared in the direction of the sound.

The large basement was silent now except for their heavy breathing.

"What was that?" Diane whispered.

They listened.

Another low moan, a mournful sound, muffled, like air through a saxophone.

The tendrils of a treelike plant suddenly drooped, like snakes lowering themselves to the ground.

Another low, sad moan.

155

"It's — the plants!" Casey said, his expression frightened now. He pushed his sister off him and climbed to his feet, brushing back his disheveled blond hair as he stood up.

"Plants don't cry and moan," Diane said, her eyes on the vast trough of plants that filled the room.

"These do," Margaret said.

Tendrils moved, like human arms shifting their position. They could hear breathing again, slow, steady breathing. Then a sigh, like air escaping.

"Let's get out of here," Casey said, edging toward the stairs.

"It's definitely creepy down here," Diane said, following him, her eyes remaining on the shifting, moaning plants.

"I'm sure Dad could explain it," Margaret said. Her words were calm, but her voice trembled, and she was backing out of the room, following Diane and Casey.

"Your dad is weird," Diane said, reaching the doorway.

"No, he isn't," Casey quickly insisted. "He's doing important work here."

A tall treelike plant sighed and appeared to bend toward them, raising its tendrils as if beckoning to them, calling them back.

"Let's just get out of here!" Margaret exclaimed.

All three of them were out of breath by the time they ran up the stairs. Casey closed the door tightly, making sure it clicked shut.

"Weird," Diane repeated, playing nervously with a strand of her long red hair. "Definitely weird." It was her word of the day. But Margaret had to admit it was appropriate.

"Well, Dad warned us not to go down there," Margaret said, struggling to catch her breath. "I guess he knew it would look scary to us, and we wouldn't understand."

"I'm getting out of here," Diane said, only half-kidding. She stepped out of the screen door and turned back toward them. "Want to go over the math later?"

"Yeah. Sure," Margaret said, still thinking about the moaning, shifting plants. Some of them had seemed to be reaching out to them, crying out to them. But of course that was impossible.

"Later," Diane said, and headed at a trot down the drive.

Just as she disappeared, their father's dark blue station wagon turned the corner and started up the drive. "Back from the airport," Margaret said. She turned from the door back to Casey a few yards behind her in the hallway. "Is the basement door closed?"

"Yeah," Casey replied, looking again to make sure. "No way Dad will know we — "

157

He stopped. His mouth dropped open, but no sound came out.

His face went pale.

"My T-shirt!" Casey exclaimed, slapping his bare chest. "I left it in the basement!"

5

"I've got to get it," Casey said. "Otherwise Dad'll know — "

"It's too late," Margaret interrupted, her eyes on the driveway. "He's already pulled up the drive."

"It'll only take a second," Casey insisted, his hand on the basement doorknob. "I'll run down and run right up."

"No!" Margaret stood tensely in the center of the narrow hallway, halfway between the front door and the basement door, her eyes toward the front. "He's parked. He's getting out of the car."

"But he'll know! He'll know!" Casey cried, his voice high and whiny.

"So?"

"Remember how mad he got last time?" Casey asked.

"Of course I remember," Margaret replied. "But he's not going to kill us, Casey, just because we took a peek at his plants. He's — "

Margaret stopped. She moved closer to the screen door. "Hey, wait."

"What's going on?" Casey asked.

"Hurry!" Margaret turned and gestured with both hands. "Go! Get downstairs — fast! Mr. Henry from next door. He stopped Dad. They're talking about something in the drive."

With a loud cry, Casey flung open the basement door and disappeared. Margaret heard him clumping rapidly down the stairs. Then she heard his footsteps fade as he hurried into their father's workroom.

Hurry, Casey, she thought, standing guard at the front door, watching her father shielding his eyes from the sun with one hand as he talked with Mr. Henry.

Hurry.

You know Dad never talks for long with the neighbors.

Mr. Henry seemed to be doing all the talking. Probably asking Dad some kind of favor, Margaret thought. Mr. Henry wasn't handy at all, not like Dr. Brewer. And so he was always asking Margaret's dad to come over and help repair or install things.

Her father was nodding now, a tight smile on his face.

Hurry, Casey.

Get back up here. Where are you?

Still shielding his eyes, Dr. Brewer gave Mr. Henry a quick wave. Then both men spun around and began walking quickly toward their houses.

Hurry, Casey.

Casey — he's coming! Hurry! Margaret urged silently.

It doesn't take this long to pick your T-shirt up from the floor and run up the stairs.

It *shouldn't* take this long.

Her dad was on the front walk now. He spotted her in the doorway and waved.

Margaret returned the wave and looked back through the hallway to the basement door. "Casey — where are you?" she called aloud.

No reply.

No sound from the basement.

No sound at all.

Dr. Brewer had paused outside to inspect the rosebushes at the head of the front walk.

"Casey?" Margaret called.

Still no reply.

"Casey — hurry!"

Silence.

Her father was crouching down, doing something to the soil beneath the rosebushes.

With a feeling of dread weighing down her entire body, Margaret realized she had no choice.

She had to go downstairs and see what was keeping Casey.

6

Casey ran down the steps, leaning on the metal banister so that he could jump down two steps at a time. He landed hard on the cement basement floor and darted into the bright white light of the plant room.

Stopping at the entranceway, he waited for his eyes to adjust to the brighter-than-day light. He took a deep breath, inhaling the steamy air, and held it. It was so hot down here, so sticky. His back began to itch. The back of his neck tingled.

The jungle of plants stood as if at attention under the bright white lights.

He saw his T-shirt, lying crumpled on the floor a few feet from a tall, leafy tree. The tree seemed to lean toward the T-shirt, its long tendrils hanging down, loosely coiled on the soil around its trunk.

Casey took a timid step into the room.

Why am I so afraid? he wondered.

It's just a room filled with strange plants.

Why do I have the feeling that they're watching me? Waiting for me?

He scolded himself for being so afraid and took a few more steps toward the crumpled T-shirt on the floor.

Hey — wait.

The breathing.

There it was again.

Steady breathing. Not too loud. Not too soft, either.

Who could be breathing? What could be breathing?

Was the big tree breathing?

Casey stared at the shirt on the floor. So near. What was keeping him from grabbing it and running back upstairs? What was holding him back?

He took a step forward. Then another.

Was the breathing growing louder?

He jumped, startled by a sudden, low moan from the big supply closet against the wall.

It sounded so human, as if someone were in there, moaning in pain.

"Casey — where are you?"

Margaret's voice sounded so far away, even though she was just at the head of the stairs.

"Okay so far," he called back to her. But his voice came out in a whisper. She probably couldn't hear him.

He took another step. Another.

The shirt was about three yards away.

A quick dash. A quick dive, and he'd have it.

Another low moan from the supply closet. A plant seemed to sigh. A tall fern suddenly dipped low, shifting its leaves.

"Casey?" He could hear his sister from upstairs, sounding very worried. "Casey — hurry!"

I'm trying, he thought. I'm trying to hurry.

What was holding him back?

Another low moan, this time from the other side of the room.

He took two more steps, then crouched low, his arms straight out in front of him.

The shirt was almost within reach.

He heard a groaning sound, then more breathing.

He raised his eyes to the tall tree. The long, ropy tendrils had tensed. Stiffened. Or had he imagined it?

No.

They had been drooping loosely. Now they were taut. Ready.

Ready to grab him?

"Casey — hurry!" Margaret called, sounding even farther away.

He didn't answer. He was concentrating on the shirt. Just a few feet away. Just a few feet. Just a foot.

The plant groaned again.

"Casey? Casey?"

The leaves quivered all the way up the trunk. Just a foot away. Almost in reach.

"Casey? Are you okay? *Answer* me!"

He grabbed the shirt.

Two snakelike tendrils swung out at him.

"Huh?" he cried out, paralyzed with fear. "What's happening?"

The tendrils wrapped themselves around his waist.

"Let go!" he cried, holding the T-shirt tightly in one hand, grabbing at the tendrils with the other.

The tendrils hung on, and gently tightened around him.

Margaret? Casey tried calling, but no sound came out of his mouth. Margaret?

He jerked violently, then pulled straight ahead.

The tendrils held on.

They didn't squeeze him. They weren't trying to strangle him. Or pull him back.

But they didn't let go.

They felt warm and wet against his bare skin. Like animal arms. Not like a plant.

Help! He again tried to shout. He pulled once more, leaning forward, using all his strength.

No good.

He ducked low, hit the floor, tried to roll away.

The tendrils hung on.

The plant uttered a loud sigh.

"Let go!" Casey cried, finally finding his voice.

And then suddenly Margaret was standing beside him. He hadn't heard her come down the stairs. He hadn't seen her enter the room.

"Casey!" she cried. "What's — "

Her mouth dropped open and her eyes grew wide.

"It — won't let go!" he told her.

"No!" she screamed. And grabbed one of the tendrils with both hands. And tugged with all her strength.

The tendril resisted for only a moment, then went slack.

Casey uttered a joyful cry and spun away from the remaining tendril. Margaret dropped the tendril and grabbed Casey's hand and began running toward the stairs.

"Oh!"

They both stopped short at the bottom of the stairway.

Standing at the top was their father, glaring down at them, his hands balled into tight fists at his sides, his face rigid with anger.

7

"Dad — the plants!" Margaret cried.

He stared down at them, his eyes cold and angry, unblinking. He was silent.

"It grabbed Casey!" Margaret told him.

"I just went down to get my shirt," Casey said, his voice trembling.

They stared up at him expectantly, waiting for him to move, to unball his fists, to relax his hard expression, to speak. But he glared down at them for the longest time.

Finally, he said, "You're okay?"

"Yeah," they said in unison, both of them nodding.

Margaret realized she was still holding Casey's hand. She let go of it and reached for the banister.

"I'm very disappointed in you both," Dr. Brewer said in a low, flat voice, cool but not angry.

"Sorry," Margaret said. "We knew we shouldn't — "

"We didn't touch anything. Really!" Casey exclaimed.

"Very disappointed," their father repeated.

"Sorry, Dad."

Dr. Brewer motioned for them to come upstairs, then he stepped into the hallway.

"I thought he was going to yell at us," Casey whispered to Margaret as he followed her up the steps.

"That's not Dad's style," Margaret whispered back.

"He sure yelled at us the *last* time we started into the basement," Casey replied.

They followed their father into the kitchen. He motioned for them to sit down at the white Formica table, then dropped into a chair across from them.

His eyes went from one to the other, as if studying them, as if seeing them for the first time. His expression was totally flat, almost robotlike, revealing no emotion at all.

"Dad, what's with those plants?" Casey asked.

"What do you mean?" Dr. Brewer asked.

"They're — so weird," Casey said.

"I'll explain them to you some day," he said flatly, still staring at the two of them.

"It looks very interesting," Margaret said, struggling to say the right thing.

Was their dad *trying* to make them feel uncomfortable? she wondered. If so, he was doing a good job of it.

This wasn't like him. Not at all. He was always a very direct person, Margaret thought. If he was angry, he said he was angry. If he was upset, he'd tell them he was upset.

So why was he acting so strange, so silent, so . . . cold?

"I asked you not to go in the basement," he said quietly, crossing his legs and leaning back so that the kitchen chair tilted back on two legs. "I thought I made it clear."

Margaret and Casey glanced at each other. Finally, Margaret said, "We won't do it again."

"But can't you take us down there and tell us what you're doing?" Casey asked. He still hadn't put the T-shirt on. He was holding it in a ball between his hands on the kitchen table.

"Yeah. We'd really like to understand it," Margaret added enthusiastically.

"Some day," their father said. He returned the chair to all four legs and then stood up. "We'll do it soon, okay?" He raised his arms above his head and stretched. "I've got to get back to work." He disappeared into the front hallway.

Casey raised his eyes to Margaret and shrugged. Their father reappeared carrying the lab coat he had tossed over the front banister.

"Mom got off okay?" Margaret asked.

He nodded. "I guess." He pulled on the lab coat over his head.

"I hope Aunt Eleanor is okay," Margaret said.

Dr. Brewer's reply was muffled as he adjusted the lab coat and straightened the collar. "Later," he said. He disappeared into the hallway. They heard him shut the basement door behind him.

"I guess he's not going to ground us or anything for going down there," Margaret said, leaning against the table and resting her chin in her hands.

"I guess," Casey said. "He sure is acting . . . weird."

"Maybe he's upset because Mom is gone," Margaret said. She sat up and gave Casey a push. "Come on. Get up. I've got work to do."

"I can't believe that plant grabbed me," Casey said thoughtfully, not budging.

"You don't have to push," Casey griped, but he climbed to his feet and stepped out of Margaret's way. "I'm going to have bad dreams tonight," he said glumly.

"Just don't think about the basement," Margaret advised. That's really lame advice, she told herself. But what else could she say?

She went up to her room, thinking about how she missed her mother already. Then the scene in the basement with Casey trying to pull himself free of the enormous, twining plant tendrils played once again through her mind.

With a shudder, she grabbed her textbook and threw herself onto her stomach on the bed, prepared to read.

But the words on the page blurred as the moaning, breathing plants kept creeping back into her thoughts.

At least we're not being punished for going down there, she thought.

At least Dad didn't yell and frighten us this time.

And at least Dad has promised to take us downstairs with him soon and explain to us what he's working on down there.

That thought made Margaret feel a lot better.

She felt better until the next morning when she awoke early and went downstairs to make some breakfast. To her surprise, her father was already at work, the basement door was shut tight, and a lock had been installed on the door.

The next Saturday afternoon, Margaret was up in her room, lying on top of the bed, talking to her mom on the phone. "I'm really sorry about Aunt Eleanor," she said, twisting the white phone cord around her wrist.

"The surgery didn't go as well as expected," her mother said, sounding very tired. "The doctors say she may have to have more surgery. But they have to build up her strength first."

"I guess this means you won't be coming home real soon," Margaret said sadly.

Mrs. Brewer laughed. "Don't tell me you actually miss me!"

"Well . . . yes," Margaret admitted. She raised her eyes to the bedroom window. Two sparrows had landed outside on the window ledge and were chattering excitedly, distracting Margaret, making it hard to hear her mother over the crackling line from Tucson.

"How's your father doing?" Mrs. Brewer asked. "I spoke to him last night, but he only grunted."

"He doesn't even grunt to us!" Margaret complained. She held her hand over her ear to drown out the chattering birds. "He hardly says a word."

"He's working really hard," Mrs. Brewer replied. In the background, Margaret could hear some kind of loudspeaker announcement. Her mother was calling from a pay phone at the hospital.

"He never comes out of the basement," Margaret complained, a little more bitterly than she had intended.

"Your father's experiments are very important to him," her mother said.

"More important than *we* are?" Margaret cried. She hated the whiny tone in her voice. She wished she hadn't started complaining about her dad over the phone. Her mother had enough to worry about at the hospital. Margaret knew she shouldn't make her feel even worse.

"Your dad has a lot to prove," Mrs. Brewer said. "To himself, and to others. I think he's working so hard because he wants to prove to Mr. Martinez and the others at the university that they were wrong to fire him. He wants to show them that they made a big mistake."

"But we used to see him more *before* he was home all the time!" Margaret complained.

She could hear her mother sigh impatiently. "Margaret, I'm trying to explain to you. You're old enough to understand."

"I'm sorry," Margaret said quickly. She decided to change the subject. "He's wearing a baseball cap all of a sudden."

"Who? Casey?"

"No, Mom," Margaret replied. "Dad. He's wearing a Dodgers cap. He never takes it off."

"Really?" Mrs. Brewer sounded very surprised.

Margaret laughed. "We told him he looks really dorky in it, but he refuses to take it off."

Mrs. Brewer laughed, too. "Uh-oh. I'm being

174

called," she said. "Got to run. Take care, dear. I'll try to call back later."

A click, and she was gone.

Margaret stared up at the ceiling, watching shadows from trees in the front yard move back and forth. The sparrows had flown away, leaving silence behind.

Poor Mom, Margaret thought.

She's so worried about her sister, and I had to go and complain about Dad.

Why did I do that?

She sat up, listening to the silence. Casey was over at a friend's. Her dad was no doubt working in the basement, the door carefully locked behind him.

Maybe I'll give Diane a call, Margaret thought. She reached for the phone, then realized she was hungry. Lunch first, she decided. Then Diane.

She brushed her dark hair quickly, shaking her head at the mirror over her dressing table, then hurried downstairs.

To her surprise, her dad was in the kitchen. He was huddled over the sink, his back to her.

She started to call out to him, but stopped. What was he doing?

Curious, she pressed against the wall, gazing at him through the doorway to the kitchen.

Dr. Brewer appeared to be eating something. With one hand, he was holding a bag on the counter beside the sink. As Margaret watched in surprise, he dipped his hand into the bag, pulled out a big handful of something, and shoved it into his mouth.

Margaret watched him chew hungrily, noisily, then pull out another handful from the bag and eat it greedily.

What on earth is he eating? she wondered. He never eats with Casey and me. He always says he isn't hungry. But he sure is hungry now! He acts as if he's starving!

She watched from the doorway as Dr. Brewer continued to grab handful after handful from the bag, gulping down his solitary meal. After a while, he crinkled up the bag and tossed it into the trash can under the sink. Then he wiped his hands off on the sides of his white lab coat.

Margaret quickly backed away from the door, tiptoed through the hall and ducked into the living room. She held her breath as her father came into the hall, clearing his throat loudly.

The basement door closed behind him. She heard him carefully lock it.

When she was sure that he had gone downstairs, Margaret walked eagerly into the kitchen. She had to know what her father had been eating so greedily, so hungrily.

She pulled open the sink cabinet, reached into

the trash, and pulled out the crinkled-up bag.

Then she gasped aloud as her eyes ran over the label.

Her father, she saw, had been devouring *plant food.*

Margaret swallowed hard. Her mouth felt dry as cotton. She suddenly realized she was squeezing the side of the counter so tightly, her hand ached.

Forcing herself to loosen her grip, she stared down at the half-empty plant food bag, which she had dropped onto the floor.

She felt sick. She couldn't get the disgusting picture out of her mind. How could her dad eat *mud*?

He didn't just eat it, she realized. He shoveled it into his mouth and gulped it down.

As if he *liked* it.

As if he *needed* it.

Eating the plant food had to be part of his experiments, Margaret told herself. But what *kind* of experiments? What was he trying to prove with those strange plants he was growing?

The stuff inside the bag smelled sour, like fertilizer. Margaret took a deep breath and held it. She suddenly felt sick to her stomach. Staring at the bag, she couldn't help but imagine what the disgusting muck inside must taste like.

Ohh.

She nearly gagged.

How could her own father shove this horrid stuff into his mouth?

Still holding her breath, she grabbed the nearly empty bag, wadded it up, and tossed it back into the trash. She started to turn away from the counter when a hand grabbed her shoulder.

Margaret uttered a silent cry and spun around. "Casey!"

"I'm home," he said, grinning at her. "What's for lunch?"

Later, after making him a peanut butter sandwich, she told Casey what she had seen.

Casey laughed.

"It isn't funny," she said crossly. "Our own dad was eating dirt."

Casey laughed again. For some reason, it struck him funny.

Margaret punched him hard on the shoulder, so hard that he dropped his sandwich. "Sorry," she said quickly, "but I don't see what you're laughing at. It's sick! There's something wrong with Dad. Something really wrong."

"Maybe he just had a craving for plant food," Casey cracked, still not taking her seriously. "You know. Like you get a craving for those honey-roasted peanuts."

"That's different," Margaret snapped. "Eating dirt is disgusting. Why won't you admit it?"

But before Casey could reply, Margaret continued, letting all of her unhappiness out at once. "Don't you see? Dad has changed. A lot. Even since Mom has been gone. He spends even more time in the basement — "

"That's because Mom isn't around," Casey interrupted.

"And he's so quiet all the time and so cold to us," Margaret continued, ignoring him. "He hardly says a word to us. He used to kid around all the time and ask us about our homework. He never says a human word. He never calls me Princess or Fatso the way he used to. He never — "

"You hate those names, Fatso," Casey said, giggling with a mouthful of peanut butter.

"I know," Margaret said impatiently. "That's just an example."

"So what are you trying to say?" Casey asked. "That Dad is out of his tree? That he's gone totally bananas?"

"I — I don't know," Margaret answered in frustration. "Watching him gulp down that disgusting plant food, I — I had this horrible thought that he's turning *into* a plant!"

Casey jumped up, causing his chair to scrape

back across the floor. He began staggering around the kitchen, zombielike, his eyes closed, his arms stretched out stiffly in front of him. "I am The Incredible Plant Man!" he declared, trying to make his voice sound bold and deep.

"Not funny," Margaret insisted, crossing her arms over her chest, refusing to be amused.

"Plant Man versus Weed Woman!" Casey declared, staggering toward Margaret.

"Not funny," she repeated.

He bumped into the counter, banging his knee. "Ow!"

"Serves you right," Margaret said.

"Plant Man kills!" he cried, and rushed at her. He ran right into her, using his head as a battering ram against her shoulder.

"Casey — will you stop it!" she screamed. "Give me a break!"

"Okay, okay." He backed off. "If you'll do me one favor."

"What favor?" Margaret asked, rolling her eyes.

"Make me another sandwich."

Monday afternoon after school, Margaret, Casey, and Diane were tossing a Frisbee back and forth in Diane's backyard. It was a warm, breezy day, the sky dotted with small, puffy white clouds.

Diane tossed the disc high. It sailed over

Casey's head into the row of fragrant lemon trees that stretched from behind the clapboard garage. Casey went running after it and tripped over an in-ground sprinkler that poked up just an inch above the lawn.

Both girls laughed.

Casey, on the run, flung the Frisbee toward Margaret. She reached for it, but the breeze sent it sailing from her hand.

"What's it like to have a mad scientist for a dad?" Diane asked suddenly.

"What?" Margaret wasn't sure she heard right.

"Don't just stand there. Throw it!" Casey urged from beside the garage.

Margaret tossed the Frisbee high in the air in her brother's general direction. He liked to run and make diving catches.

"Just because he's doing strange experiments doesn't mean he's a mad scientist," Margaret said sharply.

"Strange is right," Diane said, her expression turning serious. "I had a nightmare last night about those gross plants in your basement. They were crying and reaching for me."

"Sorry," Margaret said sincerely. "I've had nightmares, too."

"Look out!" Casey cried. He tossed a low one that Diane caught around her ankles.

Mad scientist, Margaret thought. Mad scientist. Mad scientist.

The words kept repeating in her mind.

Mad scientists were only in the movies — right?

"My dad was talking about your dad the other night," Diane said, flipping the disc to Casey.

"You didn't tell him about — going down in the basement? Did you?" Margaret asked anxiously.

"No," Diane replied, shaking her head.

"Hey, are these lemons ripe?" Casey asked, pointing at one of the low trees.

"Why don't you suck one to find out?" Margaret snapped, annoyed that he kept interrupting.

"Why don't *you*?" he predictably shot back.

"My dad said that your dad was fired from PolyTech because his experiments got out of control, and he wouldn't stop them," Diane confided. She ran along the smooth, closely cropped grass, chasing down the Frisbee.

"What do you mean?" Margaret asked.

"The university told him he had to stop whatever it was he was doing, and he refused. He said he couldn't stop. At least that's what my dad heard from a guy who came into the salesroom."

Margaret hadn't heard this story. It made her feel bad, but she thought it was probably true.

"Something really bad happened in your dad's

lab," Diane continued. "Someone got really hurt or killed or something."

"That's not true," Margaret insisted. "We would've heard if that happened."

"Yeah. Probably," Diane admitted. "But my dad said your dad was fired because he refused to stop his experiments."

"Well, that doesn't make him a mad scientist," Margaret said defensively. She suddenly felt she had to stick up for her father. She wasn't sure why.

"I'm just telling you what I heard," Diane said, brusquely tossing back her red hair. "You don't have to bite my head off."

They played for a few more minutes. Diane changed the subject and talked about some kids they knew who were eleven but were going steady. Then they talked about school for a while.

"Time to go," Margaret called to Casey. He picked the Frisbee up from the lawn and came running over. "Call you later," Margaret told Diane, giving her a little wave. Then she and Casey began to jog home, cutting through familiar backyards.

"We need a lemon tree," Casey said as they slowed to a walk. "They're cool."

"Oh, yeah," Margaret replied sarcastically. "That's just what we need at our house. Another plant!"

As they stepped through the hedges into their backyard, they were both surprised to see their dad. He was standing at the rose trellis examining clusters of pink roses.

"Hey, Dad!" Casey called. "Catch!" He tossed the Frisbee to his father.

Dr. Brewer turned around a little too slowly. The Frisbee glanced off his head, knocking the Dodgers cap off. His mouth opened wide in surprise. He raised his hands to cover his head.

But it was too late.

Margaret and Casey both shrieked in surprise as they saw his head.

At first, Margaret thought her father's hair had turned green.

But then she clearly saw that it wasn't hair on his scalp.

His hair was gone. It had all fallen out.

In place of hair, Dr. Brewer had bright green leaves sprouting from his head.

"Kids — it's okay!" Dr. Brewer called. He bent down quickly, picked up the baseball cap, and replaced it on his head.

A crow flew low overhead, cawing loudly. Margaret raised her eyes to follow the bird, but the sight of the hideous leaves sprouting from her father's head wouldn't go away.

Her whole head began to itch as she imagined what it must feel like to have leaves uncurling from your scalp.

"It's okay. Really," Dr. Brewer repeated, hurrying over to them.

"But, Dad — your head," Casey stammered. He suddenly looked very pale.

Margaret felt sick. She kept swallowing hard, trying to ride out the waves of nausea.

"Come here, you two," their father said softly, putting an arm around each of their shoulders. "Let's sit down in the shade over there and have a talk. I spoke to your mom on the phone this morning. She told me you're upset about my work."

"Your head — it's all green!" Casey repeated.

"I know," Dr. Brewer said, smiling. "That's why I put on the cap. I didn't want you two to worry."

He led them to the shade of the tall hedges that ran along the garage, and they sat down on the grass. "I guess you two think your dad has gotten pretty weird, huh?"

He stared into Margaret's eyes. Feeling uncomfortable, she looked away.

Cawing frantically, the crow flew over again, heading in the other direction.

"Margaret, you haven't said a word," her father said, squeezing her hand tenderly between his. "What's wrong? What do you want to say to me?"

Margaret sighed and still avoided her father's glance. "Come on. Tell us. Why do you have leaves growing out of your head?" she asked bluntly.

"It's a side effect," he told her, continuing to hold her hand. "It's only temporary. It'll go away soon and my hair will grow back."

"But how did it happen?" Casey asked, staring at his father's Dodgers cap. A few green leaves poked out from under the brim.

"Maybe you two would feel better if I explained what I'm trying to do down in the basement," Dr. Brewer said, shifting his weight and leaning back on his hands. "I've been so wrapped up in my experiments, I haven't had much time to talk to you."

"You haven't had *any* time," Margaret corrected him.

"I'm sorry," he said, lowering his eyes. "I really am. But this work I'm doing is so exciting and so difficult."

"Did you discover a new kind of plant?" Casey asked, crossing his legs beneath him.

"No, I'm trying to *build* a new kind of plant," Dr. Brewer explained.

"Huh?" Casey exclaimed.

"Have you ever talked about DNA in school?" their father asked. They shook their heads. "Well, it's pretty complicated," he continued. Dr. Brewer thought for a moment. "Let me try and put it in simple terms," he said, fiddling with the bandage around his hand. "Let's say we took a person who had a very high IQ. You know. Real brain power."

"Like me," Casey interrupted.

"Casey, shut up," Margaret said edgily.

"A real brain. Like Casey," Dr. Brewer said agreeably. "And let's say we were able to isolate the molecule or gene or tiny part of a gene that enabled the person to have such high intelligence. And then let's say we were able to transmit it into other brains. And then this brain power could be passed along from generation to generation. And lots of people would have a high IQ. Do you understand?" He looked first at Casey, then at Margaret.

"Yeah. Kind of," Margaret said. "You take a good quality from one person and put it into other people. And then they have the good quality, too, and they pass it on to their children, and on and on."

"Very good," Dr. Brewer said, smiling for the first time in weeks. "That's what a lot of botanists do with plants. They try to take the fruit-bearing building block from one plant and put it into another. Create a new plant that will bear five times as much fruit, or five times as much grain, or vegetables."

"And that's what you're doing?" Casey asked.

"Not exactly," their father said, lowering his voice. "I'm doing something a little more unusual. I really don't want to go into detail now. But I'll tell you that what I'm trying to do is build a kind of plant that has never existed and *could* never exist. I'm trying to build a plant that's *part animal*."

Casey and Margaret stared at their father in surprise. Margaret was the first to speak. "You mean you're taking cells from an animal and putting them into a plant?"

He nodded. "I really don't want to say more. You two understand why this must be kept secret." He turned his eyes on Margaret, then Casey, studying their reactions.

"How do you do it?" Margaret asked, thinking hard about everything he had just told them. "How do you get these cells from the animals to the plant?"

"I'm trying to do it by breaking them down electronically," he answered. "I have two glass booths connected by a powerful electron generator. You may have seen them when you were snooping around down there." He made a sour face.

"Yeah. They look like phone booths," Casey said.

"One booth is a sender, and one is a receiver," he explained. "I'm trying to send the right DNA, the right building blocks, from one booth to the other. It's very delicate work."

"And have you done it?" Margaret asked.

"I've come very close," Dr. Brewer said, a pleased smile crossing his face. The smile lasted only a few seconds. Then, his expression thoughtful, he abruptly climbed to his feet. "Got to get back to work," he said quietly. "See you two later." He started walking across the lawn, taking long strides.

"But, Dad," Margaret called after him. She and Casey climbed to their feet, too. "Your head. The leaves. You didn't explain it," she said as she and her brother hurried to catch up to him.

Dr. Brewer shrugged. "Nothing to explain," he said curtly. "Just a side effect." He adjusted his Dodgers cap. "Don't worry about it. It's only temporary. Just a side effect."

Then he hurried into the house.

Casey seemed really pleased by their dad's explanation of what was going on in the basement. "Dad's doing really important work," he said, with unusual seriousness.

But, as Margaret made her way into the house, she found herself troubled by what her dad had said. And even more troubled by what he *hadn't* said.

Margaret closed the door to her room and lay down on the bed to think about things. Her father hadn't really explained the leaves growing on his head. "Just a side effect" didn't explain much at all.

A side effect from what? What actually caused it? What made his hair fall out? When will his hair grow back?

It was obvious that he hadn't wanted to discuss it with them. He had certainly hurried back to his basement after telling them it was just a side effect.

A side effect.

It made Margaret feel sick every time she thought about it.

What must it feel like? Green leaves pushing up from your pores, uncurling against your head.

Yuck. Thinking about it made her itch all over. She knew she'd have hideous dreams tonight.

She grabbed her pillow and hugged it over her stomach, wrapping her arms tightly around it.

There were lots of other questions Casey and I should have asked, she decided. Like, why were the plants moaning down there? Why did some of them sound like they were breathing? Why did that plant grab Casey? What animal was Dad using?

Lots of questions.

Not to mention the one Margaret wanted to ask most of all: Why were you gulping down that disgusting plant food?

But she couldn't ask that one. She couldn't let her dad know she'd been spying on him.

She and Casey hadn't really asked any of the questions they'd wanted answered. They were just so pleased that their father had decided to sit down and talk with them, even for a few minutes.

His explanation was really interesting, as far as it went, Margaret decided. And it was good to know that he was close to doing something truly amazing, something that would make him really famous.

But what about the rest of it?

A frightening thought entered her mind: Could he have been lying to them?

No, she quickly decided. No. Dad wouldn't lie to us.

There are just some questions he hasn't answered yet.

She was still thinking about all of these questions late that night — after dinner, after talking to Diane on the phone for an hour, after homework, after watching a little TV, after going to bed. And she was still puzzling over them.

When she heard her father's soft footsteps coming up the carpeted stairs, she sat up in bed. A soft breeze fluttered the curtains across the room. She listened to her father's footsteps pass her room, heard him go into the bathroom, heard the water begin to run into the sink.

I've got to ask him, she decided.

Glancing at the clock, she saw that it was two-thirty in the morning.

But she realized she was wide awake.

I've got to ask him about the plant food.

Otherwise, it will drive me crazy. I'll think about it and think about it and think about it. Every time I see him, I'll picture him standing over the sink, shoving handful after handful into his mouth.

There's got to be a simple explanation, she told herself, climbing out of bed. There's got to be a *logical* explanation.

And I have to know it.

She padded softly down the hall, a sliver of light escaping through the bathroom door, which was slightly ajar. Water still ran into the sink.

She heard him cough, then heard him adjust the water.

I have to know the answer, she thought.

I'll just ask him point-blank.

She stepped into the narrow triangle of light and peered into the bathroom.

He was standing at the sink, leaning over it, his chest bare, his shirt tossed behind him on the floor. He had put the baseball cap on the closed toilet lid, and the leaves covering his head shone brightly under the bathroom light.

Margaret held her breath.

The leaves were so geeen, so thick.

He didn't notice her. He was concentrating on the bandage on his hand. Using a small scissors, he cut the bandage, then pulled it off.

The hand was still bleeding, Margaret saw.

Or was it?

What *was* that dripping from the cut on her father's hand?

Still holding her breath, she watched him wash it off carefully under the hot water. Then he examined it, his eyes narrowed in concentration.

After washing, the cut continued to bleed.

Margaret stared hard, trying to better focus her eyes.

It couldn't be blood — could it?

It couldn't be blood dripping into the sink.

It was bright green!

She gasped and started to run back to her room. The floor creaked under her footsteps.

"Who's there?" Dr. Brewer cried. "Margaret? Casey?"

He poked his head into the hallway as Margaret disappeared back into her room.

He saw me, she realized, leaping into bed.

He saw me — and now he's coming after me.

10

Margaret pulled the covers up to her chin. She realized she was trembling, her whole body shaking and chilled.

She held her breath and listened.

She could still hear water splashing into the bathroom sink.

But no footsteps.

He isn't coming after me, she told herself, letting out a long, silent sigh.

How could I have thought that? How could I have been so terrified — of my own father?

Terrified.

It was the first time the word had crossed her mind.

But sitting there in bed, trembling so violently, holding onto the covers so hard, listening for his approaching footsteps, Margaret realized that she was terrified.

Of her own father.

If only Mom were home, she thought.

Without thinking, she reached for the phone. She had the idea in her head to call her mother, wake her up, tell her to come home as fast as she could. Tell her something terrible was happening to Dad. That he was changing. That he was acting so weird. . . .

She glanced at the clock. Two-forty-three.

No. She couldn't do that. Her poor mother was having such a terrible time in Tucson trying to care for her sister. Margaret couldn't frighten her like that.

Besides, what could she say? How could she explain to her mother how she had become terrified of her own father?

Mrs. Brewer would just tell her to calm down. That her father still loved her. That he would never harm her. That he was just caught up in his work.

Caught up. . . .

He had leaves growing out of his head, he was eating dirt, and his blood was green.

Caught up. . . .

She heard the water in the sink shut off. She heard the bathroom light being clicked off. Then she heard her father pad slowly to his room at the end of the hall.

Margaret relaxed a little, slid down in the bed, loosened her grip on the blankets. She closed her eyes and tried to clear her mind.

She tried counting sheep.

That never worked. She tried counting to one thousand. At 375, she sat up. Her head throbbed. Her mouth was as dry as cotton.

She decided to go downstairs and get a drink of cold water from the refrigerator.

I'm going to be a wreck tomorrow, she thought, making her way silently through the hall and down the stairs.

It *is* tomorrow.

What am I going to do? I've got to get to sleep.

The kitchen floor creaked beneath her bare feet. The refrigerator motor clicked on noisily, startling her.

Be cool, she told herself. You've got to be cool.

She had opened the refrigerator and was reaching for the water bottle when a hand grabbed her shoulder.

"Aii!" She cried out and dropped the open bottle onto the floor. Ice-cold water puddled around her feet. She leapt back, but her feet were soaked.

"Casey — you scared me!" she exclaimed. "What are you doing up?"

"What are *you* doing up?" he replied, half asleep, his blond hair matted against his forehead.

"I couldn't sleep. Help me mop up this water."

"I didn't spill it," he said, backing away. "You mop it up."

"You *made* me spill it!" Margaret declared

shrilly. She grabbed a roll of paper towels off the counter and handed him a wad of them. "Come on. Hurry."

They both got down on their knees and, by the light from the refrigerator, began mopping up the cold water.

"I just keep thinking about things," Casey said, tossing a soaking wad of paper towel onto the counter. "That's why I can't sleep."

"Me, too," Margaret said, frowning.

She started to say something else, but a sound from the hallway stopped her. It was a plaintive cry, a moan filled with sadness.

Margaret gasped and stopped dabbing at the water. "What was that?"

Casey's eyes filled with fear.

They heard it again, such a sad sound, like a plea, a mournful plea.

"It — it's coming from the basement," Margaret said.

"Do you think it's a plant?" Casey asked very quietly. "Do you think it's one of Dad's plants?"

Margaret didn't answer. She crouched on her knees, not moving, just listening.

Another moan, softer this time but just as mournful.

"I don't think Dad told us the truth," she told Casey, staring into his eyes. He looked pale and frightened in the dim refrigerator light. "I don't think a tomato plant would make a sound like that."

Margaret climbed to her feet, collected the wet clumps of paper towel, and deposited them in the trash can under the sink. Then she closed the refrigerator door, covering the room in darkness.

Her hand on Casey's shoulder, she guided him out of the kitchen and through the hall. They stopped at the basement door, and listened.

Silence now.

Casey tried the door. It was locked.

Another low moan, sounding very nearby now.

"It's so human," Casey whispered.

Margaret shuddered. What was going on down in the basement? What was *really* going on?

She led the way up the stairs and waited at her doorway until Casey was safely in his room. He gave her a wave, yawning silently, and closed the door behind him.

A few seconds later, Margaret was back in her bed, the covers pulled up to her chin despite the warmth of the night. Her mouth was still achingly dry, she realized. She had never managed to get a drink.

Somehow she drifted into a restless sleep.

Her alarm went off at seven-thirty. She sat up and thought about school. Then she remembered there was no school for the next two days because of some kind of teachers' conference.

She turned off the clock radio, slumped back onto her pillow, and tried to go back to sleep. But she was awake now, thoughts of the night before pouring back into her mind, flooding her with the fear she had felt just a few hours earlier.

She stood up and stretched, and decided to go talk to her father, to confront him first thing, to ask all the questions she wanted to ask.

If I don't, he'll disappear down to the basement, and I'll sit around thinking these frightening thoughts all day, she told herself.

I don't want to be terrified of my own father.

I don't.

She pulled a light cotton robe over her pajamas, found her slippers in the cluttered closet, and stepped out into the hallway. It was hot and stuffy in the hall, almost suffocating. Pale, morning light filtered down from the skylight overhead.

She stopped in front of Casey's room, wondering if she should wake him so that he could ask their father questions, too.

No, she decided. The poor guy was up half the night. I'll let him sleep.

Taking a deep breath, she walked the rest of the hall and stopped at her parents' bedroom. The door was open.

"Dad?"

No reply.

"Dad? Are you up?"

She stepped into the room. "Dad?"

He didn't seem to be there.

The air in here was heavy and smelled strangely sour. The curtains were drawn. The bedclothes were rumpled and tossed down at the foot of the bed. Margaret took a few more steps toward the bed.

"Dad?"

No. She had missed him. He was probably already locked in his basement workroom, she realized unhappily.

He must have gotten up very early and —

What was that in the bed?

Margaret clicked on a dresser lamp and stepped up beside the bed.

"Oh, no!" she cried, raising her hands to her face in horror.

The bedsheet was covered with a thick layer of dirt. Clumps of dirt.

Margaret stared down at it, not breathing, not moving.

The dirt was black and appeared to be moist.

And the dirt was moving.

Moving?

It can't be, Margaret thought. That's impossible.

She leaned down to take a closer look at the layer of dirt.

No. The dirt wasn't moving.

The dirt was filled with dozens of moving insects. And long, brown earthworms. All crawling through the wet, black clumps that lined her father's bed.

11

Casey didn't come downstairs until ten-thirty. Before his arrival, Margaret had made herself breakfast, managed to pull on jeans and a T-shirt, had talked to Diane on the phone for half an hour, and had spent the rest of the time pacing back and forth in the living room, trying to decide what to do.

Desperate to talk to her dad, she had banged a few times on the basement door, timidly at first and then loudly. But he either couldn't hear her or chose not to. He didn't respond.

When Casey finally emerged, she poured him a tall glass of orange juice and led him out to the backyard to talk. It was a hazy day, the sky mostly yellow, the air already stifling hot even though the sun was still hovering low over the hills.

Walking toward the block of green shade cast by the hedges, she told her brother about their dad's green blood and about the insect-filled dirt in his bed.

Casey stood open-mouthed, holding the glass of orange juice in front of him, untouched. He stared at Margaret, and didn't say anything for a very long time.

Finally, he set the orange juice down on the lawn and said, "What should we do?" in a voice just above a whisper.

Margaret shrugged. "I wish Mom would call."

"Would you tell her everything?" Casey asked, shoving his hands deep into the pockets of his baggy shorts.

"I guess," Margaret said. "I don't know if she'd believe it, but —"

"It's so scary," Casey said. "I mean, he's our dad. We've known him our whole lives. I mean —"

"I know," Margaret said. "But he's not the same. He's —"

"Maybe he can explain it all," Casey said thoughtfully. "Maybe there's a good reason for everything. You know. Like the leaves on his head."

"We asked him about that," Margaret reminded her brother. "He just said it was a side effect. Not much of an explanation."

Casey nodded, but didn't reply.

"I told some of it to Diane," Margaret admitted.

Casey looked up at her in surprise.

"Well, I had to tell *somebody*," she snapped

edgily. "Diane thought I should call the police."

"Huh?" Casey shook his head. "Dad hasn't done anything wrong — has he? What would the police do?"

"I know," Margaret replied. "That's what I told Diane. But she said there's got to be some kind of law against being a mad scientist."

"Dad isn't a mad scientist," Casey said angrily. "That's stupid. He's just — He's just —"

Just what? Margaret thought. What *is* he?

A few hours later, they were still in the backyard, trying to figure out what to do, when the kitchen door opened and their father called them to come in.

Margaret looked at Casey in surprise. "I don't believe it. He came upstairs."

"Maybe we can talk to him," Casey said.

They both raced into the kitchen. Dr. Brewer, his Dodgers cap in place, flashed them a smile as he set two soup bowls down on the table. "Hi," he said brightly. "Lunchtime."

"Huh? You made lunch?" Casey exclaimed, unable to conceal his astonishment.

"Dad, we've got to talk," Margaret said seriously.

"Afraid I don't have much time," he said, avoiding her stare. "Sit down. Try this new dish. I want to see if you like it."

Margaret and Casey obediently took their places at the table. "What *is* this stuff?" Casey cried.

The two bowls were filled with a green, pulpy substance. "It looks like green mashed potatoes," Casey said, making a face.

"It's something different," Dr. Brewer said mysteriously, standing over them at the head of the table. "Go ahead. Taste it. I'll bet you'll be surprised."

"Dad — you've never made lunch for us before," Margaret said, trying to keep the suspicion out of her voice.

"I just wanted you to try this," he said, his smile fading. "You're my guinea pigs."

"We have some things we want to ask you," Margaret said, lifting her spoon, but not eating the green mess.

"Your mother called this morning," their father said.

"When?" Margaret asked eagerly.

"Just a short while ago. I guess you were outside and didn't hear the phone ring."

"What did she say?" Casey asked, staring down at the bowl in front of him.

"Aunt Eleanor's doing better. She's been moved out of intensive care. Your mom may be able to come home soon."

"Great!" Margaret and Casey cried in unison.

"Eat," Dr. Brewer instructed, pointing to the bowls.

"Uh . . . aren't you going to have some?" Casey asked, rolling his spoon around in his fingers.

"No," their father replied quickly. "I already ate." He leaned with both hands against the tabletop. Margaret saw that his cut hand was freshly bandaged.

"Dad, last night —" she started.

But he cut her off. "Eat, will you? Try it."

"But what *is* it?" Casey demanded, whining. "It doesn't smell too good."

"I think you'll like the taste," Dr. Brewer insisted impatiently. "It should taste very sweet."

He stared at them, urging them to eat the green stuff.

Staring into the bowl at the mysterious substance, Margaret was suddenly frozen with fear. He's too eager for us to eat this, she thought, glancing up at her brother.

He's too desperate.

He's never made lunch before. Why did he make this?

And why won't he tell us what it is?

What's going on here? she wondered. And Casey's expression revealed that he was wondering the same thing.

Is Dad trying to do something to us? Is this

green stuff going to change us, or hurt us . . . or make us grow leaves, too?

What crazy thoughts, Margaret realized.

But she also realized that she was terrified of whatever this stuff was he was trying to feed them.

"What's the matter with you two?" their father cried impatiently. He raised his hand in an eating gesture. "Pick up your spoons. Come on. What are you waiting for?"

Margaret and Casey raised their spoons and dropped them into the soft, green substance. But they didn't raise the spoons to their mouths.

They couldn't.

"Eat! Eat!" Dr. Brewer screamed, pounding the table with his good hand. "What are you waiting for? Eat your lunch. Go ahead. Eat it!"

He's giving us no choice, Margaret thought.

Her hand was trembling as she reluctantly raised the spoon to her mouth.

12

"Go ahead. You'll like it," Dr. Brewer insisted, leaning over the table.

Casey watched as Margaret raised the spoon to her lips.

The doorbell rang.

"Who could that be?" Dr. Brewer asked, very annoyed at the interruption. "I'll be right back, kids." He lumbered out to the front hall.

"Saved by the bell," Margaret said, dropping the spoon back into the bowl with a sickening plop.

"This stuff is disgusting," Casey whispered. "It's some kind of plant food or something. Yuck!"

"Quick —" Margaret said, jumping up and grabbing the two bowls. "Help me."

They rushed to the sink, pulled out the wastebasket, and scooped the contents of both bowls into the garbage. Then they carried both bowls back to the table and set them down beside the spoons.

"Let's go see who's at the door," Casey said.

They crept into the hall in time to see a man carrying a black briefcase step into the front entranceway and greet their father with a short handshake. The man had a tanned bald head and was wearing large, blue-lensed sunglasses. He had a brown mustache and was wearing a navy blue suit with a red-and-white striped tie.

"Mr. Martinez!" their father exclaimed. "What a . . . surprise."

"That's Dad's old boss from PolyTech," Margaret whispered to Casey.

"I *know*," Casey replied peevishly.

"I said weeks ago I'd come check up on how your work is coming along," Martinez said, sniffing the air for some reason. "Wellington gave me a lift. My car is in the garage — for a change."

"Well, I'm not really ready," Dr. Brewer stammered, looking very uncomfortable even from Margaret's vantage point behind him. "I wasn't expecting anyone. I mean . . . I don't think this is a good time."

"No problem. I'll just have a quick look," Martinez said, putting a hand on Dr. Brewer's shoulder as if to calm him. "I've always been so interested in your work. You know that. And you know that it wasn't *my* idea to let you go. The board forced me. They gave me no choice. But

I'm not giving up on you. I promise you that. Come on. Let's see what kind of progress you're making."

"Well . . ." Dr. Brewer couldn't hide his displeasure at Mr. Martinez's surprise appearance. He scowled and tried to block the path to the basement steps.

At least, it seemed that way to Margaret, who watched silently beside her brother.

Mr. Martinez stepped past Dr. Brewer and pulled open the basement door. "Hi, guys." Mr. Martinez gave the two kids a wave, hoisting his briefcase as if it weighed two tons.

Their father looked surprised to see them there. "Did you kids finish your lunch?"

"Yeah, it was pretty good," Casey lied.

The answer seemed to please Dr. Brewer. Adjusting the brim of his Dodgers cap, he followed Mr. Martinez into the basement, carefully closing and locking the door behind him.

"Maybe he'll give Dad his job back," Casey said, walking back into the kitchen. He pulled open the refrigerator to look for something for lunch.

"Don't be stupid," Margaret said, reaching over him to pull out a container of egg salad. "If Dad really is growing plants that are part animal, he'll be famous. He won't need a job."

"Yeah, I guess," Casey said thoughtfully. "Is that all there is? Just egg salad?"

"I'll make you a sandwich," Margaret offered.

"I'm not really hungry," Casey replied. "That green stuff made me sick. Why do you think he wanted us to eat it?"

"I don't know," Margaret said. She put a hand on Casey's slender shoulder. "I'm really scared, Casey. I wish Mom were home."

"Me, too," he said quietly.

Margaret put the egg salad back into the refrigerator. She closed the door, then leaned her hot forehead against it. "Casey —"

"What?"

"Do you think Dad is telling us the truth?"

"About what?"

"About *anything*?"

"I don't know," Casey said, shaking his head. Then his expression suddenly changed. "There's one way to find out," he said, his eyes lighting up.

"Huh? What do you mean?" Margaret pushed herself away from the refrigerator.

"The first chance we get, the first time Dad is away," Casey whispered, "let's go back down in the basement and see for ourselves what Dad is doing."

13

They got their chance the next afternoon when their father emerged from the basement, red metal toolchest in hand. "I promised Mr. Henry next door I'd help him install a new sink in his bathroom," he explained, adjusting his Dodgers cap with his free hand.

"When are you coming back?" Casey asked, glancing at Margaret.

Not very subtle, Casey, Margaret thought, rolling her eyes.

"It shouldn't take more than a couple of hours," Dr. Brewer said. He disappeared out the kitchen door.

They watched him cut through the hedges in the backyard and head to Mr. Henry's back door. "It's now or never," Margaret said, glancing doubtfully at Casey. "Think we can do this?" She tried the door. Locked, as usual.

"No problem," Casey said, a mischievous grin spreading across his face. "Go get a paper clip.

I'll show you what my friend Kevin taught me last week."

Margaret obediently found a paper clip on her desk and brought it to him. Casey straightened the clip out, then poked it into the lock. In a few seconds, he hummed a triumphant fanfare and pulled the door open.

"Now you're an expert lock picker, huh? Your friend Kevin is a good guy to know," Margaret said, shaking her head.

Casey grinned and motioned for Margaret to go first.

"Okay. Let's not think about it. Let's just do it," Margaret said, summoning her courage and stepping onto the landing.

A few seconds later, they were in the basement.

Knowing a little of what to expect down here didn't make it any less frightening. They were hit immediately by a blast of steamy, hot air. The air, Margaret realized, was so wet, so thick, that droplets immediately clung to her skin.

Squinting against the sudden bright light, they stopped in the doorway to the plant room. The plants seemed taller, thicker, more plentiful than the first time they had ventured down here.

Long, sinewy tendrils drooped from thick yellow stalks. Broad green and yellow leaves bobbed and trembled, shimmering under the white light. Leaves slapped against each other, making a soft, wet sound. A fat tomato plopped to the ground.

Everything seemed to shimmer. The plants all seemed to quiver expectantly. They weren't standing still. They seemed to be reaching up, reaching out, quaking with energy as they grew.

Long brown tendrils snaked along the dirt, wrapping themselves around other plants, around each other. A bushy fern had grown to the ceiling, curved, and started its way back down again.

"Wow!" Casey cried, impressed with this trembling, glistening jungle. "Are all these plants really brand-new?"

"I guess so," Margaret said softly. "They look prehistoric!"

They heard breathing sounds, loud sighing, a low moan coming from the direction of the supply closet against the wall.

A tendril suddenly swung out from a long stalk. Margaret pulled Casey back. "Look out. Don't get too close," she warned.

"I know," he said sharply, moving away from her. "Don't grab me like that. You scared me."

The tendril slid harmlessly to the dirt.

"Sorry," she said, squeezing his shoulder affectionately. "It's just . . . well, you remember last time."

"I'll be careful," he said.

Margaret shuddered.

She heard breathing. Steady, quiet breathing.

These plants are definitely not normal, she thought. She took a step back, letting her eyes roam over the amazing jungle of slithering, sighing plants.

She was still staring at them when she heard Casey's terrified scream.

"Help! It's got me! It's *got* me!"

14

Margaret uttered a shriek of terror and spun away from the plants to find her brother.

"Help!" Casey cried.

Gripped with fear, Margaret took a few steps toward Casey, then saw the small, gray creature scampering across the floor.

She started to laugh.

"Casey, it's a squirrel!"

"What?" His voice was several octaves higher than normal. "It — it grabbed my ankle and — "

"Look," Margaret said, pointing. "It's a squirrel. Look how scared it is. It must have run right into you."

"Oh." Casey sighed. The color began to return to his ash-gray face. "I thought it was a . . . plant."

"Right. A furry gray plant," Margaret said, shaking her head. Her heart was still thudding in her chest. "You sure gave me a scare, Casey."

The squirrel stopped several yards away,

turned, stood up on its hind legs, and stared back at them, quivering all over.

"How did a squirrel get down here?" Casey demanded, his voice still shaky.

Margaret shrugged. "Squirrels are always getting in," she said. "And remember that chipmunk we couldn't get rid of?" Then she glanced over to the small ground-level window at the top of the opposite wall. "That window — it's open," she told Casey. "The squirrel must have climbed in over there."

"Shoo!" Casey yelled at the squirrel. He started to chase it. The squirrel's tail shot right up in the air, and then it took off, running through the tangled plants. "Get out! Get out!" Casey screamed.

The terrified squirrel, with Casey in close pursuit, circled the plants twice. Then it headed to the far wall, leapt onto a carton, then onto a higher carton, then bounded out the open window.

Casey stopped running and stared up at the window.

"Good work," Margaret said. "Now, let's get out of here. We don't know what anything is. We have no idea what to look for. So we can't tell if Dad is telling the truth or not."

She started toward the stairs, but stopped when she heard the bumping sound. "Casey — did you hear that?" She searched for her brother, but he was hidden by the thick leaves of the plants. "Casey?"

"Yeah. I heard it," he answered, still out of her view. "It's coming from the supply closet."

The loud thumping made Margaret shudder. It sounded to her exactly like someone banging on the closet wall.

"Casey, let's check it out," she said.

No reply.

The banging got louder.

"Casey?"

Why wasn't he answering her?

"Casey — where *are* you? You're frightening me," Margaret called, moving closer to the shimmering plants. Another tomato plopped to the ground, so near her foot, it made her jump.

Despite the intense heat, she suddenly felt cold all over.

"Casey?"

"Margaret — come here. I've found something," he finally said. He sounded uncertain, worried.

She hurried around the plants and saw him standing in front of the worktable beside the supply closet. The banging from the closet had stopped.

"Casey, what's the matter? You scared me," Margaret scolded. She stopped and leaned against the wooden worktable.

"Look," her brother said, holding up a dark, folded-up bundle. "I found this. On the floor. Shoved under this worktable."

"Huh? What is it?" Margaret asked.

Casey unfolded it. It was a suit jacket. A blue suit jacket. A red-striped necktie was folded inside it.

"It's Mr. Martinez's," Casey said, squeezing the collar of the wrinkled jacket between his hands. "It's his jacket and tie."

Margaret's mouth dropped open into a wide O of surprise. "You mean he left it here?"

"If he left it, why was it bundled up and shoved back under the table?" Casey asked.

Margaret stared at the jacket. She ran her hand over the silky striped tie.

"Did you see Mr. Martinez leave the house yesterday afternoon?" Casey asked.

"No," Margaret answered. "But he *must* have left. I mean, his car was gone."

"He didn't drive, remember? He told Dad he got a lift."

Margaret raised her eyes from the wrinkled jacket to her brother's worried face. "Casey — what are you saying? That Mr. Martinez didn't leave? That he was eaten by a plant or something? That's ridiculous!"

"Then why were his coat and tie hidden like that?" Casey demanded.

Margaret didn't have a chance to respond.

They both gasped as they heard loud footsteps on the stairs.

Someone was hurrying down to the basement.

"Hide!" Margaret whispered.

"Where?" Casey asked, his eyes wide with panic.

15

Margaret leapt up onto the carton, then pulled herself through the small, open window. A tight squeeze, but she struggled out onto the grass. Then she turned around to help Casey.

That squirrel turned out to be a friend, she thought, tugging her brother's arms as he scrambled out of the basement. It showed us the only escape route.

The afternoon air felt quite cool compared to the steamy basement. Breathing hard, they both squatted down to peer into the window. "Who is it?" Casey whispered.

Margaret didn't have to answer. They both saw their father step into the white light, his eyes searching the plant room.

"Why did Dad come back?" Casey asked.

"Sshhh!" Margaret held a finger to her lips. Then she climbed to her feet and pulled Casey toward the back door. "Come on. Hurry."

The back door was unlocked. They stepped into

the kitchen just as their father emerged from the basement, a concerned expression on his face. "Hey — *there* you are!" he exclaimed.

"Hi, Dad," Margaret said, trying to sound casual. "Why'd you come back?"

"Had to get more tools," he answered, studying their faces. He eyed them suspiciously. "Where *were* you two?"

"Out in the backyard," Margaret said quickly. "We came in when we heard the back door slam."

Dr. Brewer scowled and shook his head. "You never used to lie to me before," he said. "I know you went down into the basement again. You left the door wide open."

"We just wanted to look," Casey said quickly, glancing at Margaret, his expression fearful.

"We found Mr. Martinez's jacket and tie," Margaret said. "What happened to him, Dad?"

"Huh?" The question seemed to catch Dr. Brewer by surprise.

"Why did he leave his jacket and tie down there?" Margaret asked.

"I'm raising two snoops," her father griped. "Martinez got hot, okay? I have to keep the basement at a very high, tropical temperature with lots of humidity. Martinez became uncomfortable. He removed his jacket and tie and put them down on the worktable. Then he forgot them when he left."

Dr. Brewer chuckled. "I think he was in a state of shock from everything I showed him down there. It's no wonder he forgot his things. But I called Martinez this morning. I'm going to drive over and return his stuff when I finish at Mr. Henry's."

Margaret saw a smile break out on Casey's face. She felt relieved, too. It was good to know that Mr. Martinez was okay.

How awful to suspect my own father of doing something terrible to someone, she thought.

But she couldn't help herself. The fear returned every time she saw him.

"I'd better get going," Dr. Brewer said. Carrying the tools he had picked up, he started toward the back door. But he stopped at the end of the hall and turned around. "Don't go back in the basement, okay? It really could be dangerous. You could be very sorry."

Margaret listened to the screen door slam behind him.

Was that a warning — or a threat? she wondered.

16

Margaret spent Saturday morning biking up in the golden hills with Diane. The sun burned through the morning smog, and the skies turned blue. A strong breeze kept them from getting too hot. The narrow road was lined with red and yellow wildflowers, and Margaret felt as if she were traveling somewhere far, far away.

They had lunch at Diane's house — tomato soup and avocado salad — then wandered back to Margaret's house, trying to figure out how to spend the rest of a beautiful afternoon.

Dr. Brewer was just backing the station wagon down the drive as Margaret and Diane rode up on their bikes. He rolled down the window, a broad smile on his face. "Good news!" he shouted. "Your mom is on her way home. I'm going to the airport to get her!"

"Oh, that's great!" Margaret exclaimed, so happy she could almost cry. Margaret and Diane waved and pedaled up the driveway.

I'm so happy, Margaret thought. It'll be so good to have her back. Someone I can talk to. Someone who can explain . . . about Dad.

They looked through some old copies of *Sassy* and *People* in Margaret's room, listening to some tapes that Margaret had recently bought. At a little past three, Diane suddenly remembered that she had a make-up piano lesson that she was late for. She rushed out of the house in a panic, jumped on her bike, yelled, "Say hi to your mom for me!" and disappeared down the drive.

Margaret stood behind the house looking out at the rolling hills, wondering what to do next to make the time pass before her mother got home. The strong, swirling breeze felt cool against her face. She decided to get a book and go sit down with it under the shady sassafras tree in the middle of the yard.

She turned and pulled open the kitchen door, and Casey came running up. "Where are our kites?" he asked, out of breath.

"Kites? I don't know. Why?" Margaret asked. "Hey — " She grabbed his shoulder to get his attention. "Mom's coming home. She should be here in an hour or so."

"Great!" he cried. "Just enough time to fly some kites. It's so windy. Come on. Want to fly 'em with me?"

"Sure," Margaret said. It would help pass the

time. She thought hard, trying to remember where they put the kites. "Are they in the garage?"

"No," Casey told her. "I know. They're in the basement. On those shelves. The string, too." He pushed past her into the house. "I'll jimmy the lock and go down and get them."

"Hey, Casey — be careful down there," she called after him. He disappeared into the hallway. Margaret had second thoughts. She didn't want Casey down there by himself in the plant room. "Wait up," she called. "I'll come with you."

They made their way down the stairs quickly, into the hot, steamy air, into the bright lights.

The plants seemed to bend toward them, to reach out to them as they walked by. Margaret tried to ignore them. Walking right behind Casey, she kept her eyes on the tall metal shelves straight ahead.

The shelves were deep and filled with old, unwanted toys, games, and sports equipment, a plastic tent, some old sleeping bags. Casey got there first and started rummaging around on the lower shelves. "I know they're here somewhere," he said.

"Yeah. I remember storing them here," Margaret said, running her eyes over the top shelves.

Casey, down on his knees, started pulling boxes

off the bottom shelf. Suddenly, he stopped. "Whoa — Margaret."

"Huh?" She took a step back. "What is it?"

"Look at this," Casey said softly. He pulled something out from behind the shelves, then stood up with it bundled in his hands.

Margaret saw that he was holding a pair of black shoes. And a pair of blue trousers.

Blue suit trousers?

His face suddenly pale, his features drawn, Casey let the shoes drop to the floor. He unfurled the trousers and held them up in front of him.

"Hey — look in the back pocket," Margaret said, pointing.

Casey reached into the back pocket and pulled out a black leather wallet.

"I don't believe this," Margaret said.

Casey's hands trembled as he opened the wallet and searched inside. He pulled out a green American Express card and read the name on it.

"It belongs to Mr. Martinez," he said, swallowing hard. He raised his eyes to Margaret's. "This is Mr. Martinez's stuff."

17

"Dad lied," Casey said, staring in horror at the wallet in his hands. "Mr. Martinez might leave without his jacket. But he wouldn't leave without his pants and shoes."

"But — what *happened* to him?" Margaret asked, feeling sick.

Casey slammed the wallet shut. He shook his head sadly, but didn't reply.

In the center of the room, a plant seemed to groan, the sound startling the two kids.

"Dad lied," Casey repeated, staring down at the pants and shoes on the floor. "Dad lied to us."

"What are we going to *do*?" Margaret cried, panic and desperation in her voice. "We've got to tell someone what's happening here. But who?"

The plant groaned again. Tendrils snaked along the dirt. Leaves clapped against each other softly, wetly.

And then the banging began again in the supply closet next to the shelves.

Margaret stared at Casey. "That thumping. What is it?"

They both listened to the insistent banging sounds. A low moan issued from the closet, followed by a higher-pitched one, both mournful, both very human-sounding.

"I think someone's *in* there!" Margaret exclaimed.

"Maybe it's Mr. Martinez," Casey suggested, still gripping the wallet tightly in his hand.

Thud thud thud.

"Do you think we should open the closet?" Casey asked timidly.

A plant groaned as if answering.

"Yes. I think we should," Margaret replied, suddenly cold all over. "If it's Mr. Martinez in there, we've got to let him out."

Casey set the wallet down on the shelf. Then they moved quickly to the supply closet.

Across from them, the plants seemed to shift and move as the two kids did. They heard breathing sounds, another groan, scurrying noises. Leaves bristled on their stalks. Tendrils drooped and slid.

"Hey — look!" Casey cried.

"I see," Margaret said. The closet door wasn't just locked. A two-by-four had been nailed over it.

Thud thud. Thud thud thud.

"There's someone in there — I *know* it!" Margaret cried.

"I'll get the hammer," Casey said. Keeping close to the wall and as far away from the plants as he could, he edged his way toward the worktable.

A few seconds later, he returned with a claw hammer.

Thud thud.

Working together, they pried the two-by-four off the door. It clattered noisily to the floor.

The banging from inside the supply closet grew louder, more insistent.

"Now what do we do about the lock?" Margaret asked, staring at it.

Casey scratched his head. They both had perspiration dripping down their faces. The steamy, hot air made it hard to catch their breaths.

"I don't know how to unlock it," Casey said, stumped.

"What if we tried to pry the door off the way we pulled off the two-by-four?" Margaret asked.

Thud thud thud.

Casey shrugged. "I don't know. Let's try."

Working the claw of the hammer into the narrow crack, they tried prying the door on the side of the lock. When it wouldn't budge, they moved to the hinged side of the door and tried there.

"It's not moving," Casey said, mopping his forehead with his arm.

"Keep trying," Margaret said. "Here. Let's both push it."

Digging the claw in just above the lower hinge, they both pushed the handle of the hammer with all their strength.

"It — it moved a little," Margaret said, breathing hard.

They kept at it. The wet wood began to crack. They both pushed against the hammer, wedging the claw into the crack.

Finally, with a loud ripping sound, they managed to pull the door off.

"Huh?" Casey dropped the hammer.

They both squinted into the dark closet.

And screamed in horror when they saw what was inside.

18

"Look!" Margaret cried, her heart thudding. She suddenly felt dizzy. She gripped the side of the closet to steady herself.

"I — don't believe this," Casey said quietly, his voice trembling as he stared into the long, narrow supply closet.

They both gaped at the weird plants that filled the closet.

Were they plants?

Under the dim ceiling bulb, they bent and writhed, groaning, breathing, sighing. Branches shook, leaves shimmered and moved, tall plants leaned forward as if reaching out to Margaret and Casey.

"Look at that one!" Casey cried, taking a step back, stumbling into Margaret. "It has an arm!"

"Ohh." Margaret followed Casey's stare. Casey was right. The tall, leafy plant appeared to have a green, human arm descending from its stalk.

Margaret's eyes darted around the closet. To her horror, she realized that several plants seemed to have human features — green arms, a yellow hand with three fingers poking from it, two stumpy legs where the stem should be.

She and her brother both cried out when they saw the plant with the face. Inside a cluster of broad leaves there appeared to grow a round, green tomato. But the tomato had a human-shaped nose and an open mouth, from which it repeatedly uttered the most mournful sighs and groans.

Another plant, a short plant with clusters of broad, oval leaves, had two green, nearly human faces partly hidden by the leaves, both wailing through open mouths.

"Let's get out of here!" Casey cried, grabbing Margaret's hand in fear and tugging her away from the closet. "This is — gross!"

The plants moaned and sighed. Green, finger-less hands reached out to Margaret and Casey. A yellow, sick-looking plant near the wall made choking sounds. A tall flowering plant staggered toward them, thin, tendril-like arms outstretched.

"Wait!" Margaret cried, pulling her hand out of Casey's. She spotted something on the closet floor behind the moaning, shifting plants. "Casey — what's that?" she asked, pointing.

She struggled to focus her eyes in the dim light of the closet. On the floor behind the plants, near the shelves on the back wall, were two human feet.

Margaret stepped cautiously into the closet. The feet, she saw, were attached to legs.

"Margaret — let's go!" Casey pleaded.

"No. Look. There's someone back there," Margaret said, staring hard.

"Huh?"

"A person. Not a plant," Margaret said. She took another step. A soft green arm brushed against her side.

"Margaret, what are you doing?" Casey asked, his voice high and frightened.

"I have to see who it is," Margaret said.

She took a deep breath and held it. Then, ignoring the moans, the sighs, the green arms reaching out to her, the hideous green-tomato faces, she plunged through the plants to the back of the closet.

"Dad!" she cried.

Her father was lying on the floor, his hands and feet tied tightly with plant tendrils, his mouth gagged by a wide strip of elastic tape.

"Margaret —" Casey was beside her. He lowered his eyes to the floor. "Oh, no!"

Their father stared up at them, pleading with

his eyes. "Mmmmm!" he cried, struggling to talk through the gag.

Margaret dived to the floor and started to untie him.

"No — stop!" Casey cried, and pulled her back by the shoulders.

"Casey, let go of me. What's wrong with you?" Margaret cried angrily. "It's Dad. He —"

"It can't be Dad!" Casey said, still holding her by the shoulders. "Dad is at the airport — remember?"

Behind them, the plants seemed to be moaning in unison, a terrifying chorus. A tall plant fell over and rolled toward the open closet door.

"Mmmmmmm!" their father continued to plead, struggling at the tendrils that imprisoned him.

"I've got to untie him," Margaret told her brother. "Let go of me."

"No," Casey insisted. "Margaret — look at his head."

Margaret turned her eyes to her father's head. He was bareheaded. No Dodgers cap. He had tufts of green leaves growing where his hair should be.

"We've already seen that," Margaret snapped. "It's a side effect, remember?" She reached down to pull at her father's ropes.

"No — don't!" Casey insisted.

"Okay, okay," Margaret said. "I'll just pull the tape off his mouth. I won't untie him."

She reached down and tugged at the elastic tape until she managed to get it off.

"Kids — I'm so glad to see you," Dr. Brewer said. "Quick! Untie me."

"How did you get in here?" Casey demanded, standing above him, hands on his hips, staring down at him suspiciously. "We saw you leave for the airport."

"That wasn't me," Dr. Brewer said. "I've been locked in here for days."

"Huh?" Casey cried.

"But we saw you —" Margaret started.

"It wasn't me. It's a plant," Dr. Brewer said. "It's a plant copy of me."

"Dad —" Casey said.

"Please. There's no time to explain," their father said urgently, raising his leaf-covered head to look toward the closet doorway. "Just untie me. Quick!"

"The father we've been living with? He's a plant?" Margaret cried, swallowing hard.

"Yes. Please — untie me!"

Margaret reached for the tendrils.

"No!" Casey insisted. "How do we know you're telling the truth?"

"I'll explain everything. I promise," he pleaded.

"Hurry. Our lives are at stake. Mr. Martinez is in here, too."

Startled, Margaret turned her eyes to the far wall. Sure enough, Mr. Martinez also lay on the floor, bound and gagged.

"Let me out — please!" her father cried.

Behind them, plants moaned and cried.

Margaret couldn't stand it anymore. "I'm untying him," she told Casey, and bent down to start grappling with the tendrils.

Her father sighed gratefully. Casey bent down and reluctantly began working at the tendrils, too.

Finally, they had loosened them enough so their father could slip out. He climbed to his feet slowly, stretching his arms, moving his legs, bending his knees. "Man, that feels good," he said, giving Margaret and Casey a grim smile.

"Dad — should we untie Mr. Martinez?" Margaret asked.

But, without warning, Dr. Brewer pushed past the two kids and made his way out of the closet.

"Dad — whoa! Where are you going?" Margaret called.

"You said you'd explain everything!" Casey insisted. He and his sister ran through the moaning plants, following their father.

"I will. I will." Breathing hard, Dr. Brewer strode quickly to the woodpile against the far wall.

Margaret and Casey both gasped as he picked up an axe.

He spun around to face them, holding the thick axe handle with both hands. His face frozen with determination, he started toward them.

"Dad — what are you *doing*?" Margaret cried.

19

Swinging the axe onto his shoulder, Dr. Brewer advanced on Margaret and Casey. He groaned from the effort of raising the heavy tool, his face reddening, his eyes wide, excited.

"Dad, please!" Margaret cried, gripping Casey's shoulder, backing up toward the jungle of plants in the center of the room.

"What are you *doing*?" she repeated.

"He's not our real father!" Casey cried. "I *told* you we shouldn't untie him!"

"He *is* our real father!' Margaret insisted. I *know* he is!" She turned her eyes to her father, looking for an answer.

But he stared back at them, his face filled with confusion — and menace, the axe in his hands gleaming under the bright ceiling lights.

"Dad — answer us!" Margaret demanded. "Answer us!"

Before Dr. Brewer could reply, they heard

loud, rapid footsteps clumping down the basement steps.

All four of them turned to the doorway of the plant room — to see an alarmed-looking Dr. Brewer enter. He grabbed the bill of his Dodgers cap as he strode angrily toward the two kids.

"What are you two doing down here?" he cried. "You promised me. Here's your mother. Don't you want to —?"

Mrs. Brewer appeared at his side. She started to call out a greeting, but stopped, freezing in horror when she saw the confusing scene.

"No!" she screamed, seeing the other Dr. Brewer, the capless Dr. Brewer, holding an axe in front of him with both hands. "No!" Her face filled with horror. She turned to the Dr. Brewer that had just brought her home.

He glared accusingly at Margaret and Casey. "What have you *done*? You let him escape?"

"He's our dad," Margaret said, in a tiny little voice she barely recognized.

"*I'm* your dad!" the Dr. Brewer at the doorway bellowed. "Not him! He's not your dad. He's not even human! He's a plant!"

Margaret and Casey both gasped and drew back in terror.

"*You're* the plant!" the bareheaded Dr. Brewer accused, raising the axe.

"He's dangerous!" the other Dr. Brewer exclaimed. "How could you have let him out?"

Caught in the middle, Margaret and Casey stared from one father to the other.

Who was their *real* father?

20

"That's not your father!" Dr. Brewer with the Dodgers cap cried again, moving into the room. "He's a copy. A plant copy. One of my experiments that went wrong. I locked him in the supply closet because he's dangerous."

"*You're* the copy!" the other Dr. Brewer accused, and raised the axe again.

Margaret and Casey stood motionless, exchanging terrified glances.

"Kids — what have you done?" Mrs. Brewer cried, her hands pressed against her cheeks, her eyes wide with disbelief.

"What *have* we done?" Margaret asked her brother in a low voice.

Staring wide-eyed from one man to the other, Casey seemed too frightened to reply.

"I — I don't know what to do," Casey managed to whisper.

What *can* we do? Margaret wondered silently, realizing that her entire body was trembling.

"He has to be destroyed!" the axe-wielding Dr. Brewer shouted, staring at his look-alike across the room.

Beside them, plants quivered and shook, sighing loudly. Tendrils slithered across the dirt. Leaves shimmered and whispered.

"Put down the axe. You're not fooling anyone," the other Dr. Brewer said.

"You have to be destroyed!" Dr. Brewer with no cap repeated, his eyes wild, his face scarlet, moving closer, the axe gleaming as if electrified under the white light.

Dad would *never* act like this, Margaret realized. Casey and I were idiots. We let him out of the closet. And now he's going to kill our real dad. And mom.

And then . . . us!

What can I do? she wondered, trying to think clearly even though her mind was whirring wildly out of control.

What can I do?

Uttering a desperate cry of protest, Margaret leapt forward and grabbed the axe from the imposter's hands.

He gaped in surprise as she steadied her grip on the handle. It was heavier than she'd imagined. "Get back!" she screamed. "Get back — now!"

"Margaret — wait!" her mother cried, still too frightened to move from the doorway.

The capless Dr. Brewer reached for the axe. "Give it back to me! You don't know what you're doing!" he pleaded, and made a wild grab for it.

Margaret pulled back and swung the axe. "Stay back. *Everyone*, stay back."

"Thank goodness!" Dr. Brewer with the Dodgers cap exclaimed. "We've got to get him back in the closet. He's very dangerous." He stepped up to Margaret. "Give *me* the axe."

Margaret hesitated.

"Give *me* the axe," he insisted.

Margaret turned to her mother. "What should I do?"

Mrs. Brewer shrugged helplessly. "I — I don't know."

"Princess — don't do it," the capless Dr. Brewer said softly, staring into Margaret's eyes.

He called me Princess, Margaret realized.

The other one never had.

Does this mean that the Dad in the closet is my real dad?

"Margaret — give me the axe." The one in the cap made a grab for it.

Margaret backed away and swung the axe again.

"Get back! Both of you — stay back!" she warned.

"I'm warning you," Dr. Brewer in the cap

246

said. "He's dangerous. Listen to me, Margaret."

"Get back!" she repeated, desperately trying to decide what to do.

Which one is my real dad?

Which one? Which one? Which one?

Her eyes darting back and forth from one to the other, she saw that each of them had a bandage around his right hand. And it gave her an idea.

"Casey, there's a knife on the wall over there," she said, still holding the axe poised. "Get it for me — fast!"

Casey obediently hurried to the wall. It took him a short while to find the knife among all the tools hanging there. He reached up on tiptoes to pull it down, then hurried back to Margaret with it.

Margaret lowered the axe and took the long-bladed knife from him.

"Margaret — give me the axe," the man in the Dodgers cap insisted impatiently.

"Margaret, what are you doing?" the man from the supply closet asked, suddenly looking frightened.

"I — I have an idea," Margaret said hesitantly.

She took a deep breath.

Then she stepped over to the man from the supply closet and pushed the knife blade into his arm.

21

"Ow!" he cried out as the blade cut through the skin.

Margaret pulled the knife back, having made a tiny puncture hole.

Red blood trickled from the hole.

"He's our real dad," she told Casey, sighing with relief. "Here, Dad." She handed him the axe.

"Margaret — you're wrong!" the man in the baseball cap cried in alarm. "He's tricked you! He's *tricked* you!"

The capless Dr. Brewer moved quickly. He picked up the axe, took three steps forward, pulled the axe back, and swung with all his might.

The Dr. Brewer in the cap opened his mouth wide and uttered a hushed cry of alarm. The cry was choked off as the axe cut easily through his body, slicing him in two.

A thick green liquid oozed from the wound. And as the man fell, his mouth locking open in disbelief and horror, Margaret could see that his body was actually a stem. He had no bones, no human organs.

The body thudded to the floor. Green liquid puddled around it.

"Princess — we're okay!" Dr. Brewer cried, flinging the axe aside. "You guessed right!"

"It wasn't a guess," Margaret said, sinking into his arms. "I remembered the green blood. I saw it. Late at night. One of you was in the bathroom, bleeding green blood. I knew my real dad would have red blood."

"We're okay!" Mrs. Brewer cried, rushing into her husband's arms. "We're okay. We're all okay!"

All four of them rushed together in an emotional family hug.

"One more thing we have to do," their father said, his arms around the two kids. "Let's get Mr. Martinez out of the closet."

By dinnertime, things had almost returned to normal.

They had finally managed to welcome their mother home, and tried to explain to her all that had happened in her absence.

Mr. Martinez had been rescued from the supply closet, not too much the worse for wear. He and Dr. Brewer had had a long discussion about what had happened and about Dr. Brewer's work.

He expressed total bewilderment as to what Dr.

Brewer had accomplished, but he knew enough to realize that it was historic. "Perhaps you need the structured environment the lab on campus offers. I'll talk to the board members about getting you back on staff," Martinez said. It was his way of inviting their father back to work.

After Mr. Martinez was driven home, Dr. Brewer disappeared into the basement for about an hour. He returned grim-faced and exhausted. "I destroyed most of the plants," he explained, sinking into an armchair. "I had to. They were suffering. Later, I'll destroy the rest."

"Every single plant?" Mrs. Brewer asked.

"Well . . . there are a few normal ones that I can plant out back in the garden," he replied. He shook his head sadly. "Only a few."

At dinner, he finally had the strength to explain to Margaret, Casey, and Mrs. Brewer what had happened down in the basement.

"I was working on a super plant," he said, "trying to electronically make a new plant using DNA elements from other plants. Then I accidentally cut my hand on a slide. I didn't realize it, but some of my blood got mixed in with the plant molecules I was using. When I turned on the machine, my molecules got mixed in with plant molecules — and I ended up with something that was part human, part plant."

"That's gross!" Casey exclaimed, dropping a forkful of mashed potatoes.

"Well, I'm a scientist," Dr. Brewer replied, "so I didn't think it was gross. I thought it was pretty exciting. I mean, here I was, inventing an entirely new kind of creature."

"Those plants with faces — " Margaret started.

Her father nodded. "Yes. Those were things I made by inserting human materials into plant materials. I kept putting them in the supply closet. I got carried away. I didn't know how far I could go, how human I could make the plants. I could see that my creations were unhappy, suffering. But I couldn't stop. It was too exciting."

He took a long drink of water from his glass.

"You didn't tell me any of this," Mrs. Brewer said, shaking her head.

"I couldn't," he said. "I couldn't tell anyone. I — I was too involved. Then one day, I went too far. I created a plant that was an exact copy of me in almost every way. He looked like me. He sounded like me. And he had my brain, my mind."

"But he still acted like a plant in some ways," Margaret said. "He ate plant food and — "

"He wasn't perfect," Dr. Brewer said, leaning forward over the dinner table, talking in a low, serious voice. "He had flaws. But he was strong enough and smart enough to overpower me, to

251

lock me in the closet, to take my place — and to continue my experiments. And when Martinez arrived unexpectedly, he locked Martinez in the closet, too, so that his secret would be safe."

"Was the head full of leaves one of the flaws?" Casey asked.

Dr. Brewer nodded. "Yes, he was almost a perfect clone of me, almost a perfect human, but not quite."

"But, Dad," Margaret said, pointing, "you have leaves on your head, too."

He reached up and pulled one off. "I know," he said, making a disgusted face. "That's really gross, huh?"

Everyone agreed.

"Well, when I cut my hand, some of the plant materials mixed with my blood, got into my system," he explained. "And then I turned on the machine. The machine created a strong chemical reaction between the plant materials and my blood. Then, my hair fell out overnight. And the leaves immediately started to sprout. Don't worry, guys. The leaves are falling out already. I think my hair will grow back."

Margaret and Casey cheered.

"I guess things will return to normal around here," Mrs. Brewer said, smiling at her husband.

"Better than normal," he said, smiling back. "If Martinez convinces the board to give me my job back, I'll clear out the basement and turn it into the best game room you ever saw!"

Margaret and Casey cheered again.

"We're all alive and safe," Dr. Brewer said, hugging both kids at once. "Thanks to you two."

It was the happiest dinner Margaret could remember. After they had cleaned up, they all went out for ice cream. It was nearly ten o'clock when they returned.

Dr. Brewer headed for the basement.

"Hey — where are you going?" his wife called suspiciously.

"I'm just going down to deal with the rest of the plants," Dr. Brewer assured her. "I want to make sure that everything is gone, that this horrible chapter in our lives is over."

By the end of the week, most of the plants had been destroyed. A giant pile of leaves, roots, and stalks were burned in a bonfire that lasted for hours. A few tiny plants had been transplanted outside. All of the equipment had been dismantled and trucked to the university.

On Saturday, all four Brewers went to select a pool table for the new basement rec room. On Sunday, Margaret found herself standing in back by the garden, staring up at the golden hills.

It's so peaceful now, she thought happily.

So peaceful here. And so beautiful.

The smile faded from her face when she heard the whisper at her feet. "Margaret."

She looked down to see a small yellow flower nudging her ankle.

"Margaret," the flower whispered, "help me. Please — help me. I'm your father. Really! I'm your real father."

Say Cheese and Die!

GOOSEBUMPS #4

1

"There's nothing to do in Pitts Landing," Michael Warner said, his hands shoved into the pockets of his faded denim cutoffs.

"Yeah. Pitts Landing is the pits," Greg Banks said.

Doug Arthur and Shari Walker muttered their agreement.

Pitts Landing is the Pits. That was the town slogan, according to Greg and his three friends. Actually, Pitts Landing wasn't much different from a lot of small towns with quiet streets of shady lawns and comfortable, old houses.

But here it was, a balmy fall afternoon, and the four friends were hanging around Greg's driveway, kicking at the gravel, wondering what to do for fun and excitement.

"Let's go to Grover's and see if the new comic books have come in," Doug suggested.

"We don't have any money, Bird," Greg told him.

Everyone called Doug "Bird" because he looked

259

a lot like a bird. A better nickname might have been "Stork." He had long, skinny legs and took long, storklike steps. Under his thick tuft of brown hair, which he seldom brushed, he had small, birdlike brown eyes and a long nose that curved like a beak. Doug didn't really like being called Bird, but he was used to it.

"We can still *look* at the comics," Bird insisted.

"Until Grover starts yelling at you," Shari said. She puffed out her cheeks and did a pretty good imitation of the gruff store owner: *"Are you paying or staying?"*

"He thinks he's cool," Greg said, laughing at her imitation. "He's such a jerk."

"I think the new *X-Force* is coming in this week," Bird said.

"You should join the X-Force," Greg said, giving his pal a playful shove. "You could be Bird Man. You'd be great!"

"We should *all* join the X-Force," Michael said. "If we were super-heroes, maybe we'd have something to do."

"No, we wouldn't," Shari quickly replied. "There's no crime to fight in Pitts Landing."

"We could fight crabgrass," Bird suggested. He was the joker in the group.

The others laughed. The four of them had been friends for a long time. Greg and Shari lived next door to each other, and their parents were best friends. Bird and Michael lived on the next block.

"How about a baseball game?" Michael suggested. "We could go down to the playground."

"No way," Shari said. "You can't play with only four people." She pushed back a strand of her crimped, black hair that had fallen over her face. Shari was wearing an oversized yellow sweatshirt over bright green leggings.

"Maybe we'll find some other kids there," Michael said, picking up a handful of gravel from the drive and letting it sift through his chubby fingers. Michael had short red hair, blue eyes, and a face full of freckles. He wasn't exactly fat, but no one would ever call him skinny.

"Come on, let's play baseball," Bird urged. "I need the practice. My Little League starts in a couple of days."

"Little League? In the fall?" Shari asked.

"It's a new fall league. The first game is Tuesday after school," Bird explained.

"Hey — we'll come watch you," Greg said.

"We'll come watch you strike out," Shari added. Her hobby was teasing Bird.

"What position are you playing?" Greg asked.

"Backstop," Michael cracked.

No one laughed. Michael's jokes always fell flat.

Bird shrugged. "Probably the outfield. How come *you're* not playing, Greg?"

With his big shoulders and muscular arms and legs, Greg was the natural athlete of the group. He was blond and good-looking, with flashing gray-green eyes and a wide, friendly smile.

"My brother Terry was supposed to go sign me up, but he forgot," Greg said, making a disgusted face.

"Where *is* Terry?" Shari asked. She had a tiny crush on Greg's older brother.

"He got a job Saturdays and after school. At the Dairy Freeze," Greg told her.

"Let's go to the Dairy Freeze!" Michael exclaimed enthusiastically.

"We don't have any money — remember?" Bird said glumly.

"Terry'll give us free cones," Michael said, turning a hopeful gaze on Greg.

"Yeah. Free cones. But no ice cream in them," Greg told him. "You know what a straight-arrow my brother is."

"This is boring," Shari complained, watching a robin hop across the sidewalk. "It's boring standing around talking about how bored we are."

"We could *sit down* and talk about how bored we are," Bird suggested, twisting his mouth into the goofy half-smile he always wore when he was making a dumb joke.

"Let's take a walk or a jog or something," Shari insisted. She made her way across the lawn and began walking, balancing her white high-tops on the edge of the curb, waving her arms like a highwire performer.

The boys followed, imitating her in an impromptu game of Follow the Leader, all of them balancing on the curb edge as they walked.

A curious cocker spaniel came bursting out of the neighbors' hedge, yapping excitedly. Shari stopped to pet him. The dog, its stub of a tail wagging furiously, licked her hand a few times. Then the dog lost interest and disappeared back into the hedge.

The four friends continued down the block, playfully trying to knock each other off the curb as they walked. They crossed the street and continued on past the school. A couple of guys were shooting baskets, and some little kids played kickball on the practice baseball diamond, but no one they knew.

The road curved away from the school. They followed it past familiar houses. Then, just beyond a small wooded area, they stopped and looked up a sloping lawn, the grass uncut for weeks, tall weeds poking out everywhere, the shrubs ragged and overgrown.

At the top of the lawn, nearly hidden in the shadows of enormous, old oak trees, sprawled a large, ramshackle house. The house, anyone could see, had once been grand. It was gray shingle, three stories tall, with a wraparound screened porch, a sloping red roof, and tall chimneys on either end. But the broken windows on the second floor, the cracked, weather-stained shingles, the bare spots on the roof, and the shutters hanging loosely beside the dust-smeared windows were evidence of the house's neglect.

Everyone in Pitts Landing knew it as the Coffman house. Coffman was the name painted on the mailbox that tilted on its broken pole over the front walk.

But the house had been deserted for years — ever since Greg and his friends could remember.

And people liked to tell weird stories about the house: ghost stories and wild tales about murders and ghastly things that happened there. Most likely, none of them were true.

"Hey — I know what we can do for excitement," Michael said, staring up at the house bathed in shadows.

"Huh? What are you talking about?" Greg asked warily.

"Let's go into the Coffman house," Michael said, starting to make his way across the weed-choked lawn.

"Whoa. Are you crazy?" Greg called, hurrying to catch up to him.

"Let's go in," Michael said, his blue eyes catching the light of the late afternoon sun filtering down through the tall oak trees. "We wanted an adventure. Something a little exciting, right? Come on — let's check it out."

Greg hesitated and stared up at the house. A cold chill ran down his back.

Before he could reply, a dark form leapt up from the shadows of the tall weeds and attacked him!

2

Greg toppled backwards onto the ground. "Aah!" he screamed. Then he realized the others were laughing.

"It's that dumb cocker spaniel!" Shari cried. "He followed us!"

"Go home, dog. Go home!" Bird shooed the dog away.

The dog trotted to the curb, turned around, and stared back at them, its stubby tail wagging furiously.

Feeling embarrassed that he'd become so frightened, Greg slowly pulled himself to his feet, expecting his friends to give him grief. But they were staring up at the Coffman house thoughtfully.

"Yeah, Michael's right," Bird said, slapping Michael hard on the back, so hard Michael winced and turned to slug Bird. "Let's see what it's like in there."

"No way," Greg said, hanging back. "I mean,

the place is kind of creepy, don't you think?"

"So?" Shari challenged him, joining Michael and Bird, who repeated her question: "So?"

"So . . . I don't know," Greg replied. He didn't like being the sensible one of the group. Everyone always made fun of the sensible one. He'd rather be the wild and crazy one. But, somehow, he always ended up sensible.

"I don't think we should go in there," he said, staring up at the neglected old house.

"Are you chicken?" Bird asked.

"Chicken!" Michael joined in.

Bird began to cluck loudly, tucking his hands into his armpits and flapping his arms. With his beady eyes and beaky nose, he looked just like a chicken.

Greg didn't want to laugh, but he couldn't help it.

Bird *always* made him laugh.

The clucking and flapping seemed to end the discussion. They were standing at the foot of the broken concrete steps that led up to the screened porch.

"Look. The window next to the front door is broken," Shari said. "We can just reach in and open the door."

"This is cool," Michael said enthusiastically.

"Are we really doing this?" Greg, being the sensible one, had to ask. "I mean — what about Spidey?"

Spidey was a weird-looking man of fifty or sixty they'd all seen lurking about town. He dressed entirely in black and crept along on long, slender legs. He looked just like a black spider, so the kids all called him Spidey.

Most likely he was a homeless guy. No one really knew anything about him — where he'd come from, where he lived. But a lot of kids had seen him hanging around the Coffman house.

"Maybe Spidey doesn't like visitors," Greg warned.

But Shari was already reaching in through the broken windowpane to unlock the front door. And after little effort, she turned the brass knob and the heavy wooden door swung open.

One by one, they stepped into the front entryway, Greg reluctantly bringing up the rear. It was dark inside the house. Only narrow beams of sunlight managed to trickle down through the heavy trees in front, creating pale circles of light on the worn brown carpet at their feet.

The floorboards squeaked as Greg and his friends made their way past the living room, which was bare except for a couple of overturned grocery store cartons against one wall.

Spidey's furniture? Greg wondered.

The living room carpet, as threadbare as the one in the entryway, had a dark oval stain in the center of it. Greg and Bird, stopping in the doorway, both noticed it at the same time.

"Think it's blood?" Bird asked, his tiny eyes lighting up with excitement.

Greg felt a chill on the back of his neck. "Probably ketchup," he replied. Bird laughed and slapped him hard on the back.

Shari and Michael were exploring the kitchen. They were staring at the dust-covered kitchen counter as Greg stepped up behind them. He saw immediately what had captured their attention. Two fat, gray mice were standing on the countertop, staring back at them.

"They're cute," Shari said. "They look just like cartoon mice."

The sound of her voice made the two rodents scamper along the counter, around the sink, and out of sight.

"They're gross," Michael said, making a disgusted face. "I think they were rats — not mice."

"Rats have long tails. Mice don't," Greg told him.

"They were definitely rats," Bird muttered, pushing past them and into the hallway. He disappeared toward the front of the house.

Shari reached up and pulled open a cabinet over the counter. Empty. "I guess Spidey never uses the kitchen," she said.

"Well, I didn't *think* he was a gourmet chef," Greg joked.

He followed her into the long, narrow dining room, as bare and dusty as the other rooms. A low chandelier still hung from the ceiling, so brown with caked dust, it was impossible to tell that it was glass.

"Looks like a haunted house," Greg said softly.

"Boo," Shari replied.

"There's not much to see in here," Greg complained, following her back to the dark hallway. "Unless you get a thrill from dustballs."

Suddenly, a loud *crack* made him jump.

Shari laughed and squeezed his shoulder.

"What was *that*?" he cried, unable to stifle his fear.

"Old houses *do* things like that," she said. "They make noises for no reason at all."

"I think we should leave," Greg insisted, embarrassed again that he'd acted so frightened. "I mean, it's boring in here."

"It's kind of exciting being somewhere we're not supposed to be," Shari said, peeking into a dark, empty room — probably a den or study at one time.

"I guess," Greg replied uncertainly.

They bumped into Michael. "Where's Bird?" Greg asked.

"I think he went down in the basement," Michael replied.

"Huh? The basement?"

Michael pointed to an open door at the right of the hallway. "The stairs are there."

The three of them made their way to the top of

the stairs. They peered down into the darkness. "Bird?"

From somewhere deep in the basement, his voice floated up to them in a horrified scream: "Help! It's got me! Somebody — please help! It's *got* me!"

3

"It's got me! It's got me!"

At the sound of Bird's terrified cries, Greg pushed past Shari and Michael, who stood frozen in open-mouthed horror. Practically flying down the steep stairway, Greg called out to his friend. "I'm coming, Bird! What *is it?*"

His heart pounding, Greg stopped at the bottom of the stairs, every muscle tight with fear. His eyes searched frantically through the smoky light pouring in from the basement windows up near the ceiling.

"Bird?"

There he was, sitting comfortably, calmly, on an overturned metal trash can, his legs crossed, a broad smile on his birdlike face. "Gotcha," he said softly, and burst out laughing.

"What *is* it? What *happened?*" came the frightened voices of Shari and Michael. They clamored down the stairs, coming to a stop beside Greg.

It took them only a few seconds to scope out the situation.

"Another dumb joke?" Michael asked, his voice still trembling with fear.

"Bird — you were goofing on us again?" Shari asked, shaking her head.

Enjoying his moment, Bird nodded, with his peculiar half-grin. "You guys are too easy," he scoffed.

"But, Doug — " Shari started. She only called him Doug when she was upset with him. "Haven't you ever heard of the boy who cried wolf? What if something bad happens sometime, and you really need help, and we think you're just goofing?"

"What could happen?" Bird replied smugly. He stood up and gestured around the basement. "Look — it's brighter down here than upstairs."

He was right. Sunlight from the back yard cascaded down through four long windows at ground level, near the ceiling of the basement.

"I still think we should get out of here," Greg insisted, his eyes moving quickly around the large, cluttered room.

Behind Bird's overturned trash can stood an improvised table made out of a sheet of plywood resting on four paint cans. A nearly flat mattress, dirty and stained, rested against the wall, a faded wool blanket folded at the foot.

"Spidey must *live* down here!" Michael exclaimed.

Bird kicked his way through a pile of empty food boxes that had been tossed all over the floor — TV dinners, mostly. "Hey, a Hungry Man dinner!" he exclaimed. "Where does Spidey heat these up?"

"Maybe he eats them frozen," Shari suggested. "You know. Like Popsicles."

She made her way toward a towering oak wardrobe and pulled open the doors. "Wow! This is *excellent*!" she declared. "Look!" She pulled out a ratty-looking fur coat and wrapped it around her shoulders. "Excellent!" she repeated, twirling in the old coat.

From across the room, Greg could see that the wardrobe was stuffed with old clothing. Michael and Bird hurried to join Shari and began pulling out strange-looking pairs of bell-bottom pants, yellowed dress shirts with pleats down the front, tie-dyed neckties that were about a foot wide, and bright-colored scarves and bandannas.

"Hey, guys — " Greg warned. "Don't you think maybe those belong to somebody?"

Bird spun around, a fuzzy red boa wrapped around his neck and shoulders. "Yeah. These are Spidey's dress-up clothes," he cracked.

"Check out this *baad* hat," Shari said, turning around to show off the bright purple, wide-brimmed hat she had pulled on.

"Neat," Michael said, examining a long blue cape. "This stuff must be at least twenty-five years old. It's awesome. How could someone just leave it here?"

"Maybe they're coming back for it," Greg suggested.

As his friends explored the contents of the wardrobe, Greg wandered to the other end of the large basement. A furnace occupied the far wall, its ducts covered in thick cobwebs. Partially hidden by the furnace ducts, Greg could see stairs, probably leading to an outside exit.

Wooden shelves lined the adjoining wall, cluttered with old paint cans, rags, newspapers, and rusty tools.

Whoever lived here must have been a real handyman, Greg thought, examining a wooden worktable in front of the shelves. A metal vise was clamped to the edge of the worktable. Greg turned the handle, expecting the jaws of the vise to open.

But to his surprise, as he turned the vise handle, a door just above the worktable popped open. Greg pulled the door all the way open, revealing a hidden cabinet shelf.

Resting on the shelf was a camera.

4

For a long moment, Greg just stared at the camera.

Something told him the camera was hidden away for a reason.

Something told him he shouldn't touch it. He should close the secret door and walk away.

But he couldn't resist it.

He reached onto the hidden shelf and took the camera in his hands.

It pulled out easily. Then, to Greg's surprise, the door instantly snapped shut with a loud *bang*.

Weird, he thought, turning the camera in his hands.

What a strange place to leave a camera. Why would someone put it here? If it were valuable enough to hide in a secret cabinet, why didn't they take it with them?

Greg eagerly examined the camera. It was large and surprisingly heavy, with a long lens. Perhaps a telephoto lens, he thought.

Greg was very interested in cameras. He had an inexpensive automatic camera, which took okay snapshots. But he was saving his allowance in hopes of buying a really good camera with a lot of lenses.

He loved looking at camera magazines, studying the different models, picking out the ones he wanted to buy.

Sometimes he daydreamed about traveling around the world, going to amazing places, mountaintops and hidden jungle rivers. He'd take photos of everything he saw and become a famous photographer.

His camera at home was just too crummy. That's why all his pictures came out too dark or too light, and everyone in them had glowing red dots in their eyes.

Greg wondered if this camera was any good.

Raising the viewfinder to his eye, he sighted around the room. He came to a stop on Michael, who was wearing two bright yellow feather boas and a white Stetson hat and had climbed to the top of the steps to pose.

"Wait! Hold it!" Greg cried, moving closer, raising the camera to his eye. "Let me take your picture, Michael."

"Where'd you find that?" Bird asked.

"Does that thing have film in it?" Michael demanded.

"I don't know," Greg said. "Let's see."

Leaning against the railing, Michael struck what he considered a sophisticated pose.

Greg pointed the camera up and focused carefully. It took a short while for his finger to locate the shutter button. "Okay, ready? Say cheese."

"Cheddar," Michael said, grinning down at Greg as he held his pose against the railing.

"Very funny. Michael's a riot," Bird said sarcastically.

Greg centered Michael in the viewfinder frame, then pressed the shutter button.

The camera clicked and flashed.

Then it made an electronic whirring sound. A slot pulled open on the bottom, and a cardboard square slid out.

"Hey — it's one of those automatic-developing cameras," Greg exclaimed. He pulled the square of cardboard out and examined it. "Look — the picture is starting to develop."

"Let me see," Michael called down, leaning on the railing.

But before he could start down the stairs, everyone heard a loud crunching sound.

They all looked up to the source of the sound — and saw the railing break away and Michael go sailing over the edge.

"Noooooo!" Michael screamed as he toppled to the floor, arms outstretched, the feather boas flying behind him like animal tails.

He turned in the air, then hit the concrete hard

on his back, his eyes frozen wide in astonishment and fright.

He bounced once.

Then cried out again: "My ankle! Owwww! My ankle!" He grabbed at the injured ankle, then quickly let go with a loud gasp. It hurt too much to touch it.

"*Ohhh* — my ankle!"

Still holding the camera and the photo, Greg rushed to Michael. Shari and Bird did the same.

"We'll go get help," Shari told Michael, who was still on his back, groaning in pain.

But then they heard the ceiling creak.

Footsteps. Above them.

Someone was in the house.

Someone was approaching the basement stairs.

They were going to be caught.

5

The footsteps overhead grew louder.

The four friends exchanged frightened glances.
"We've got to get *out* of here," Shari whispered.

The ceiling creaked.

"You can't leave me here!" Michael protested.
He pulled himself to a sitting position.

"Quick — stand up," Bird instructed.

Michael struggled to his feet. "I can't stand on
this foot." His face revealed his panic.

"We'll help you," Shari said, turning her eyes
to Bird. "I'll take one arm. You take the other."

Bird obediently moved forward and pulled Michael's arm around his shoulder.

"Okay, let's move!" Shari whispered, support-
ing Michael from the other side.

"But how do we get out?" Bird asked breathlessly.

The footsteps grew louder. The ceiling creaked
under their weight.

"We can't go up the stairs," Michael whispered, leaning on Shari and Bird.

"There's another stairway behind the furnace," Greg told them, pointing.

"It leads out?" Michael asked, wincing from his ankle pain.

"Probably."

Greg led the way. "Just pray the door isn't padlocked or something."

"We're praying. We're praying!" Bird declared.

"We're outta here!" Shari said, groaning under the weight of Michael's arm.

Leaning heavily against Shari and Bird, Michael hobbled after Greg, and they made their way to the stairs behind the furnace. The stairs, they saw, led to wooden double doors up on ground level.

"I don't see a padlock," Greg said warily. "Please, doors — be open!"

"Hey — who's down there?" an angry man's voice called from behind them.

"It's — it's Spidey!" Michael stammered.

"Hurry!" Shari urged, giving Greg a frightened push. "Come *on!*"

Greg set the camera down on the top step. Then he reached up and grabbed the handles of the double doors.

"Who's down there?"

Spidey sounded closer, angrier.

"The doors could be locked from the outside," Greg whispered, hesitating.

"Just *push* them, man!" Bird pleaded.

Greg took a deep breath and pushed with all his strength.

The doors didn't budge.

"We're trapped," he told them.

6

"Now what?" Michael whined.

"Try again," Bird urged Greg. "Maybe they're just stuck." He slid out from under Michael's arm. "Here. I'll help you."

Greg moved over to give Bird room to step up beside him. "Ready?" he asked. "One, two, three — *push!*"

Both boys pushed against the heavy wooden doors with all their might.

And the doors swung open.

"Okay! *Now* we're outta here!" Shari declared happily.

Picking up the camera, Greg led the way out. The back yard, he saw, was as weed-choked and overgrown as the front. An enormous limb had fallen off an old oak tree, probably during a storm, and was lying half in the tree, half on the ground.

Somehow, Bird and Shari managed to drag Michael up the steps and onto the grass. "Can you walk? Try it," Bird said.

Still leaning against the two of them, Michael reluctantly pushed his foot down on the ground. He lifted it. Then pushed it again. "Hey, it feels a little better," he said, surprised.

"Then let's go," Bird said.

They ran to the overgrown hedge that edged along the side of the yard, Michael on his own now, stepping gingerly on the bad ankle, doing his best to keep up. Then, staying in the shadow of the hedge, they made their way around the house to the front.

"All *right*!" Bird cried happily as they reached the street. "We made it!"

Gasping for breath, Greg stopped at the curb and turned back toward the house. "Look!" he cried, pointing up to the living room window.

A dark figure stood in the window, hands pressed against the glass.

"It's Spidey," Shari said.

"He's just — staring at us," Michael cried.

"Weird," Greg said. "Let's go."

They didn't stop till they got to Michael's house, a sprawling redwood ranch-style house behind a shady front lawn.

"How's the ankle?" Greg asked.

"It's loosened up a lot. It doesn't even hurt that much," Michael said.

"Man, you could've been *killed!*" Bird declared, wiping sweat off his forehead with the sleeve of his T-shirt.

"Thanks for reminding me," Michael said dryly.

"Lucky thing you've got all that extra padding," Bird teased.

"Shut up," Michael muttered.

"Well, you guys wanted adventure," Shari said, leaning back against the trunk of a tree.

"That guy Spidey is definitely weird," Bird said, shaking his head.

"You see the way he was staring at us?" Michael asked. "All dressed in black and everything? He looked like some kind of zombie or something."

"He saw us," Greg said softly, suddenly feeling a chill of dread. "He saw us very clearly. We'd better stay away from there."

"What for?" Michael demanded. "It isn't his house. He's just sleeping there. We could call the police on him."

"But if he's really crazy or something, there's no telling what he might do," Greg replied thoughtfully.

"Aw, he's not going to do anything," Shari said quietly. "Spidey doesn't want trouble. He just wants to be left alone."

"Yeah," Michael agreed quickly. "He didn't want us messing with his stuff. That's why he yelled like that and came after us."

Michael was leaning over, rubbing his ankle.

"Hey, where's my picture?" he demanded, straightening up and turning to Greg.

"Huh?"

"You know. The picture you snapped. With the camera."

"Oh. Right." Greg suddenly realized he still had the camera gripped tightly in his hand. He set it down carefully on the grass and reached into his back pocket. "I put it in here when we started to run," he explained.

"Well? Did it come out?" Michael demanded.

The three of them huddled around Greg to get a view of the snapshot.

"Whoa — hold on a minute!" Greg cried, staring hard at the small, square photo. "Something's wrong. What's going *on* here?"

7

The four friends gaped at the photograph in Greg's hand, their mouths dropping open in surprise.

The camera had caught Michael in midair as he fell through the broken railing to the floor.

"That's impossible!" Shari cried.

"You snapped the picture *before* I fell!" Michael declared, grabbing the photo out of Greg's hand so that he could study it close up. "I remember it."

"You remembered wrong," Bird said, moving to get another look at it over Michael's shoulder. "You were falling, man. What a great action shot." He picked up the camera. "This is a good camera you stole, Greg."

"I didn't steal it" — Greg started — "I mean, I didn't realize — "

"I wasn't falling!" Michael insisted, tilting the picture in his hand, studying it from every angle. "I was posing, remember? I had a big, goofy smile on my face, and I was posing."

"I remember the goofy smile," Bird said, handing the camera back to Greg. "Do you have any *other* expression?"

"You're not funny, Bird," Michael muttered. He pocketed the picture.

"Weird," Greg said. He glanced at his watch. "Hey — I've got to get going."

He said good-bye to the others and headed for home. The afternoon sun was lowering behind a cluster of palm trees, casting long, shifting shadows over the sidewalk.

He had promised his mother he'd straighten up his room and help with the vacuuming before dinner. And now he was late.

What was that strange car in the drive? he wondered, jogging across the neighbor's lawn toward his house.

It was a navy-blue Taurus station wagon. Brand new.

Dad picked up our new car! he realized.

Wow! Greg stopped to admire it. It still had the sticker glued to the door window. He pulled open the driver's door, leaned in, and smelled the vinyl upholstery.

Mmmmmm. That new-car smell.

He inhaled deeply again. It smelled so good. So fresh and new.

He closed the door hard, appreciating the solid *clunk* it made as it closed.

What a great new car, he thought excitedly.

He raised the camera to his eye and took a few steps back off the drive.

I've *got* to take a picture of this, he thought. To remember what the car was like when it was totally new.

He backed up until he had framed the entire profile of the station wagon in the viewfinder. Then he pressed the shutter button.

As before, the camera clicked loudly, the flash flashed, and with an electronic *whirr*, a square undeveloped photo of gray and yellow slid out of the bottom.

Carrying the camera and the snapshot, Greg ran into the house through the front door. "I'm home!" he called. "Down in a minute!" And hurried up the carpeted stairs to his room.

"Greg? Is that you? Your father is home," his mother called from downstairs.

"I know. Be right down. Sorry I'm late!" Greg shouted back.

I'd better hide the camera, he decided. If Mom or Dad see it, they'll want to know whose it is and where I got it. And I won't be able to answer those questions.

"Greg — did you see the new car? Are you coming down?" his mother called impatiently from the foot of the stairs.

"I'm coming!" he yelled.

His eyes searched frantically for a good hiding place.

Under his bed?

No. His mom might vacuum under there and discover it.

Then Greg remembered the secret compartment in his headboard. He had discovered the compartment years ago when his parents had bought him a new bedroom set. Quickly, he shoved the camera in.

Peering into the mirror above his dresser, he gave his blond hair a quick brush, rubbed a black soot smudge off his cheek with one hand, then started for the door.

He stopped at the doorway.

The snapshot of the car. Where had he put it?

It took a few seconds to remember that he had tossed it onto his bed. Curious about how it came out, he turned back to retrieve it.

"Oh, no!"

He uttered a low cry as he gazed at the snapshot.

8

What's going on here? Greg wondered.

He brought the photo up close to his face.

This isn't right, he thought. How can this *be*?

The blue Taurus station wagon in the photo was a mess. It looked as if it had been in a terrible accident. The windshield was shattered. Metal was twisted and bent. The door on the driver's side was caved in.

The car appeared *totaled*!

"This is impossible!" Greg uttered aloud.

"Greg, where *are* you?" his mother called. "We're all hungry, and you're keeping us waiting."

"Sorry," he answered, unable to take his eyes off the snapshot. "Coming."

He shoved the photo into his top dresser drawer and made his way downstairs. The image of the totaled car burned in his mind.

Just to make sure, he crossed the living room

and peeked out of the front window to the driveway.

There stood the station wagon, sparkling in the glow of the setting sun. Shiny and perfect.

He turned and walked into the dining room where his brother and his parents were already seated. "The new wagon is awesome, Dad," Greg said, trying to shake the snapshot's image from his thoughts.

But he kept seeing the twisted metal, the caved-in driver's door, the shattered windshield.

"After dinner," Greg's dad announced happily, "I'm taking you all for a drive in the new car!"

9

"Mmmm. This is great chicken, Mom," Greg's brother Terry said, chewing as he talked.

"Thanks for the compliment," Mrs. Banks said dryly, "but it's veal — not chicken."

Greg and his dad burst out laughing. Terry's face grew bright red. "Well," he said, still chewing, "it's such excellent veal, it tastes as good as chicken!"

"I don't know why I bother to cook," Mrs. Banks sighed.

Mr. Banks changed the subject. "How are things at the Dairy Freeze?" he asked.

"We ran out of vanilla this afternoon," Terry said, forking a small potato and shoving it whole into his mouth. He chewed it briefly, then gulped it down. "People were annoyed about that."

"I don't think I can go for the ride," Greg said, staring down at his dinner, which he'd hardly touched. "I mean — "

"Why not?" his father asked.

"Well . . ." Greg searched his mind for a good reason. He needed to make one up, but his mind was a blank.

He couldn't tell them the truth.

That he had taken a snapshot of Michael, and it showed Michael falling. Then a few seconds later, Michael had fallen.

And now he had taken a picture of the new car. And the car was wrecked in the photo.

Greg didn't really know what it meant. But he was suddenly filled with this powerful feeling, of dread, of fear, of . . . he didn't know what.

A kind of troubled feeling he'd never had before.

But he couldn't tell them any of that. It was too weird. Too *crazy*.

"I . . . made plans to go over to Michael's," he lied, staring down at his plate.

"Well, call him and tell him you'll see him tomorrow," Mr. Banks said, slicing his veal. "That's no problem."

"Well, I'm kind of not feeling very well, either," Greg said.

"What's wrong?" Mrs. Banks asked with instant concern. "Do you have a temperature? I thought you looked a little flushed when you came in."

"No," Greg replied uncomfortably. "No temperature. I just feel kind of tired, not very hungry."

"Can I have your chicken — I mean, veal?" Terry asked eagerly. He reached his fork across the table and nabbed the cutlet off Greg's plate.

"Well, a nice ride might make you feel better," Greg's dad said, eyeing Greg suspiciously. "You know, some fresh air. You can stretch out in the back if you want."

"But, dad — " Greg stopped. He had used up all the excuses he could think of. They would *never* believe him if he said he needed to stay home and do homework on a Saturday night!

"You're coming with us, and that's final," Mr. Banks said, still studying Greg closely. "You've been dying for this new wagon to arrive. I really don't understand your problem."

Neither do I, Greg admitted to himself.

I don't understand it at all. Why am I so afraid of riding in the new car? Just because there's something wrong with that stupid camera?

I'm being silly, Greg thought, trying to shake away the feeling of dread that had taken away his appetite.

"Okay, Dad. Great," he said, forcing a smile. "I'll come."

"Are there any more potatoes?" Terry asked.

10

"It's so easy to drive," Mr. Banks said, accelerating onto the entry ramp to the freeway. "It handles like a small car, not like a station wagon."

"Plenty of room back here, Dad," Terry said, scooting low in the back seat beside Greg, raising his knees to the back of the front seat.

"Hey, look — there's a drink holder that pulls out from the dash!" Greg's mother exclaimed. "That's neat."

"Awesome, Mom," Terry said sarcastically.

"Well, we never had a drink holder before," Mrs. Banks replied. She turned back to the two boys. "Are your seat belts buckled? Do they work properly?"

"Yeah. They're okay," Terry replied.

"They checked them at the showroom, before I took the car," Mr. Banks said, signaling to move into the left lane.

A truck roared by, spitting a cloud of exhaust behind it. Greg stared out the front window. His door window was still covered by the new car sticker.

Mr. Banks pulled off the freeway, onto a nearly empty four-lane highway that curved toward the west. The setting sun was a red ball low on the horizon in a charcoal-gray sky.

"Put the pedal to the metal, Dad," Terry urged, sitting up and leaning forward. "Let's see what this car can do."

Mr. Banks obediently pressed his foot on the accelerator. "The cruising speed seems to be about sixty," he said.

"Slow down," Mrs. Banks scolded. "You know the speed limit is fifty-five."

"I'm just testing it," Greg's dad said defensively. "You know. Making sure the transmission doesn't slip or anything."

Greg stared at the glowing speedometer. They were doing seventy now.

"Slow down. I mean it," Mrs. Banks insisted. "You're acting like a crazy teenager."

"That's me!" Mr. Banks replied, laughing. "This is *awesome*!" he said, imitating Terry, ignoring his wife's pleas to slow down.

They roared past a couple of small cars in the right lane. Headlights of cars moving towards them were a bright white blur in the darkening night.

"Hey, Greg, you've been awfully quiet," his mother said. "You feeling okay?"

"Yeah. I'm okay," Greg said softly.

He wished his dad would slow down. He was doing seventy-five now.

"What do you think, Greg?" Mr. Banks asked, steering with his left hand as his right hand searched the dashboard. "Where's the light switch? I should turn on my headlights."

"The car's great," Greg replied, trying to sound enthusiastic. But he couldn't shake away the fear, couldn't get the photo of the mangled car out of his mind.

"Where's that stupid light switch? It's got to be here somewhere," Mr. Banks said.

As he glanced down at the unfamiliar dashboard, the station wagon swerved to the left.

"*Dad — look out for that truck!*" Greg screamed.

11

Horns blared.

A powerful blast of air swept over the station wagon, like a giant ocean wave pushing it to the side.

Mr. Banks swerved the station wagon to the right.

The truck rumbled past.

"Sorry," Greg's dad said, eyes straight ahead, slowing the car to sixty, fifty-five, fifty . . .

"I *told* you to slow down," Mrs. Banks scolded, shaking her head. "We could've been killed!"

"I was trying to find the lights," he explained. "Oh. Here they are. On the steering wheel." He clicked on the headlights.

"You boys okay?" Mrs. Banks asked, turning to check them out.

"Yeah. Fine," Terry said, sounding a little shaken. The truck would have hit his side of the car.

"I'm okay," Greg said. "Can we go back now?"

"Don't you want to keep going?" Mr. Banks asked, unable to hide his disappointment. "I thought we'd keep going to Santa Clara. Stop and get some ice cream or something."

"Greg's right," Mrs. Banks said softly to her husband. "Enough for tonight, dear. Let's turn around."

"The truck didn't come *that* close," Mr. Banks argued. But he obediently turned off the highway and they headed for home.

Later, safe and sound up in his room, Greg took the photograph out of his dresser and examined it. There was the new station wagon, the driver's side caved in, the windshield shattered.

"Weird," he said aloud, and placed the photo in the secret compartment in his headboard where he had stashed the camera. "Definitely weird."

He pulled the camera out of its hiding place and turned it around in his hands.

I'll try it one more time, he decided.

He walked to his dresser and aimed at the mirror above it.

I'll take a picture of myself in the mirror, he thought.

He raised the camera, then changed his mind. That won't work, he realized. The flash will reflect back and spoil the photo.

Gripping the camera in one hand, he made his way across the hall to Terry's room. His brother was at his desk, typing away on his computer keyboard, his face bathed in the blue light of the monitor screen.

"Terry, can I take your picture?" Greg asked meekly, holding up the camera.

Terry typed some more, then looked up from the screen. "Hey — where'd you get the camera?"

"Uh . . . Shari loaned it to me," Greg told him, thinking quickly. Greg didn't like to lie. But he didn't feel like explaining to Terry how he and his friends had sneaked into the Coffman house and he had made off with the camera.

"So can I take your picture?" Greg asked.

"I'll probably break your camera," Terry joked.

"I think it's already broken," Greg told him. "That's why I want to test it on you."

"Go ahead," Terry said. He stuck out his tongue and crossed his eyes.

Greg snapped the shutter. An undeveloped photo slid out of the slot in front.

"Thanks. See you." Greg headed to the door.

"Hey — don't I get to see it?" Terry called after him.

"If it comes out," Greg said, and hurried across the hall to his room.

He sat down on the edge of the bed. Holding the photo in his lap, he stared at it intently as it developed. The yellows filled in first. Then the reds appeared, followed by shades of blue.

"Whoa," Greg muttered as his brother's face

came into view. "There's something definitely wrong here."

In the photo, Terry's eyes weren't crossed, and his tongue wasn't sticking out. His expression was grim, frightened. He looked very upset.

As the background came into focus, Greg had another surprise. Terry wasn't in his room. He was outdoors. There were trees in the background. And a house.

Greg stared at the house. It looked so familiar.

Was that the house across the street from the playground?

He took one more look at Terry's frightened expression. Then he tucked the photo and the camera into his secret headboard compartment and carefully closed it.

The camera must be broken, he decided, getting changed for bed.

It was the best explanation he could come up with.

Lying in bed, staring up at the shifting shadows on the ceiling, he decided not to think about it anymore.

A broken camera wasn't worth worrying about.

Tuesday afternoon after school, Greg hurried to meet Shari at the playground to watch Bird's Little League game.

It was a warm fall afternoon, the sun high in a

cloudless sky. The outfield grass had been freshly mowed and filled the air with its sharp, sweet smell.

Greg crossed the grass and squinted into the bright sunlight, searching for Shari. Both teams were warming up on the sides of the diamond, yelling and laughing, the sound of balls popping into gloves competing with their loud voices.

A few parents and several kids had come to watch. Some were standing around, some sitting in the low bleachers along the first base line.

Greg spotted Shari behind the backstop and waved to her. "Did you bring the camera?" she asked eagerly, running over to greet him.

He held it up.

"Excellent," she exclaimed, grinning. She reached for it.

"I think it's broken," Greg said, holding on to the camera. "The photos just don't come out right. It's hard to explain."

"Maybe it's not the photos. Maybe it's the photographer," Shari teased.

"Maybe I'll take a photo of you getting a knuckle sandwich," Greg threatened. He raised the camera to his eye and pointed it at her.

"Snap that, and I'll take a picture of you *eating* the camera," Shari threatened playfully. She reached up quickly and pulled the camera from his hand.

"What do you want it for, anyway?" Greg asked, making a halfhearted attempt to grab it back.

Shari held it away from his outstretched hand. "I want to take Bird's picture when he comes to bat. He looks just like an ostrich at the plate."

"I heard that." Bird appeared beside them, pretending to be insulted.

He looked ridiculous in his starched white uniform. The shirt was too big, and the pants were too short. The cap was the only thing that fit. It was blue, with a silver dolphin over the bill and the words: PITTS LANDING DOLPHINS.

"What kind of name is 'Dolphins' for a baseball team?" Greg asked, grabbing the bill and turning the cap backwards on Bird's head.

"All the other caps were taken," Bird answered. "We had a choice between the Zephyrs and the Dolphins. None of us knew what Zephyrs were, so we picked Dolphins."

Shari eyed him up and down. "Maybe you guys should play in your street clothes."

"Thanks for the encouragement," Bird replied. He spotted the camera and took it from her. "Hey, you brought the camera. Does it have film?"

"Yeah. I think so," Greg told him. "Let me see." He reached for the camera, but Bird swung it out of his grasp.

"Hey — are you going to share this thing, Greg?" he asked.

"Huh? What do you mean?" Greg reached again for the camera, and again Bird swung it away from him.

"I mean, we all risked our lives down in that basement getting it, right?" Bird said. "We should all share it."

"Well . . ." Greg hadn't thought about it. "I guess you're right, Bird. But I'm the one who found it. So — "

Shari grabbed the camera out of Bird's hand. "I told Greg to bring it so we could take your picture when you're up."

"As an example of good form?" Bird asked.

"As a *bad* example," Shari said.

"You guys are just jealous," Bird replied, frowning, "because I'm a natural athlete, and you can't cross the street without falling on your face." He turned the cap back around to face the front.

"Hey, Bird — get back here!" one of the coaches called from the playing field.

"I've got to go," Bird said, giving them a quick wave and starting to trot back to his teammates.

"No. Wait. Let me take a fast picture now," Greg said.

Bird stopped, turned around, and struck a pose.

"No. I'll take it," Shari insisted.

She started to raise the camera to her eye, pointing it toward Bird. And as she raised it, Greg grabbed for it.

"Let *me* take it!"

And the camera went off. Clicked and then flashed.

An undeveloped photo slid out.

"Hey, why'd you do that?" Shari asked angrily.

"Sorry," Greg said. "I didn't mean to — "

She pulled the photo out and held it in her hand. Greg and Bird came close to watch it develop.

"What the heck is *that*?" Bird cried, staring hard at the small square as the colors brightened and took shape.

"Oh, wow!" Greg cried.

The photo showed Bird sprawled unconscious on his back on the ground, his mouth twisted open, his neck bent at a frightening angle, his eyes shut tight.

12

"Hey — what's with this stupid camera?" Bird asked, grabbing the snapshot out of Shari's hand. He tilted it from side to side, squinting at it. "It's out of focus or something."

"Weird," Greg said, shaking his head.

"Hey, Bird — get over here!" the Dolphins' coach called.

"Coming!" Bird handed the picture back to Shari and jogged over to his teammates.

Whistles blew. The two teams stopped their practicing and trotted to the benches along the third base line.

"How did this *happen?*" Shari asked Greg, shielding her eyes from the sun with one hand, holding the photo close to her face with the other. "It really looks like Bird is lying on the ground, knocked out or something. But he was standing right in front of us."

"I don't get it. I really don't," Greg replied thoughtfully. "The camera keeps doing that."

Carrying the camera at his side, swinging it by its slender strap, he followed her to a shady spot beside the bleachers.

"Look how his neck is bent," Shari continued. "It's so *awful*."

"There's something definitely wrong with the camera," Greg said. He started to tell her about the snapshot he took of the new station wagon, and the snapshot of his brother Terry. But she interrupted him before he could get the words out.

" — And that picture of Michael. It showed him falling down the stairs before he even fell. It's just so strange."

"I know," Greg agreed.

"Let me see that thing," Shari said and pulled the camera from his hand. "Is there any film left?"

"I can't tell," Greg admitted. "I couldn't find a film counter or anything."

Shari examined the camera closely, rolling it over in her hands. "It doesn't say anywhere. How can you tell if it's loaded or not?"

Greg shrugged.

The baseball game got under way. The Dolphins were the visiting team. The other team, the Cardinals, jogged out to take their positions on the field.

A kid in the bleachers dropped his soda can. It hit the ground and spilled, and the kid started to cry. An old station wagon filled with teenagers cruised by, its radio blaring, its horn honking.

"Where do you put the film in?" Shari asked impatiently.

Greg stepped closer to help her examine it. "Here, I think," he said, pointing. "Doesn't the back come off?"

Shari fiddled with it. "No, I don't think so. Most of these automatic-developing cameras load in the front."

She pulled at the back, but the camera wouldn't open. She tried pulling off the bottom. No better luck. Turning the camera, she tried pulling off the lens. It wouldn't budge.

Greg took the camera from her. "There's no slot or opening in the front."

"Well, what kind of camera is it, anyway?" Shari demanded.

"Uh . . . let's see." Greg studied the front, examined the top of the lens, then turned the camera over and studied the back.

He stared up at her with a surprised look on his face. "There's no brand name. Nothing."

"How can a camera not have a name?" Shari shouted in exasperation. She snatched the camera away from him and examined it closely, squinting her eyes against the bright afternoon sunshine.

Finally, she handed the camera back to him, defeated. "You're right, Greg. No name. No words of any kind. Nothing. What a stupid camera," she added angrily.

"Whoa. Hold on," Greg told her. "It's not my camera, remember? I didn't buy it. I took it from the Coffman house."

"Well, let's at least figure out how to open it up and look inside," Shari said.

The first Dolphin batter popped up to the second baseman. The second batter struck out on three straight swings. The dozen or so spectators shouted encouragement to their team.

The little kid who had dropped his soda continued to cry. Three kids rode by on bikes, waving to friends on the teams, but not stopping to watch.

"I've tried and tried, but I can't figure out how to open it," Greg admitted.

"Give me it," Shari said and grabbed the camera away from him. "There has to be a button or something. There has to be some way of opening it. This is ridiculous."

When she couldn't find a button or lever of any kind, she tried pulling the back off once again, prying it with her fingernails. Then she tried turning the lens, but it wouldn't turn.

"I'm not giving up," she said, gritting her teeth. "I'm not. This camera has to open. It *has* to!"

"Give up. You're going to wreck it," Greg warned, reaching for it.

"Wreck it? How could I wreck it?" Shari demanded. "It has no moving parts. Nothing!"

"This is impossible," Greg said.

Making a disgusted face, she handed the camera to him. "Okay, I give up. Check it out yourself, Greg."

He took the camera, started to raise it to his face, then stopped.

Uttering a low cry of surprise, his mouth dropped open and his eyes gaped straight ahead. Startled, Shari turned to follow his shocked gaze.

"Oh *no!*"

There on the ground a few yards outside the first base line, lay Bird. He was sprawled on his back, his neck bent at an odd and unnatural angle, his eyes shut tight.

13

"Bird!" Shari cried.

Greg's breath caught in his throat. He felt as if he were choking. "Oh!" he finally managed to cry out in a shrill, raspy voice.

Bird didn't move.

Shari and Greg, running side by side at full speed, reached him together.

"Bird?" Shari knelt down beside him. "Bird?"

Bird opened one eye. "Gotcha," he said quietly. The weird half-smile formed on his face, and he exploded in high-pitched laughter.

It took Shari and Greg a while to react. They both stood open-mouthed, gaping at their laughing friend.

Then, his heart beginning to slow to normal, Greg reached down, grabbed Bird with both hands, and pulled him roughly to his feet.

"I'll hold him while you hit him," Greg offered, holding Bird from behind.

"Hey, wait — " Bird protested, struggling to squirm out of Greg's grasp.

"Good plan," Shari said, grinning.

"Ow! Hey — let go! Come on! Let go!" Bird protested, trying unsuccessfully to wrestle free. "Come on! What's your problem? It was a joke, guys."

"Very funny," Shari said, giving Bird a playful punch on the shoulder. "You're a riot, Bird."

Bird finally freed himself with a hard tug and danced away from both of them. "I just wanted to show you how bogus it is to get all worked up about that dumb camera."

"But, Bird — " Greg started.

"It's just broken, that's all," Bird said, brushing blades of recently cut grass off his uniform pants. "You think because it showed Michael falling down those stairs, there's something strange with it. But that's dumb. Real dumb."

"I know it," Greg replied sharply. "But how do you explain it?"

"I told you, man. It's wrecked. Broken. That's it."

"Bird — get over here!" a voice called, and Bird's fielder's glove came flying at his head. He caught it, waved with a grin to Shari and Greg, and jogged to the outfield along with the other members of the Dolphins.

Carrying the camera tightly in one hand, Greg

led the way to the bleachers. He and Shari sat down on the end of the bottom bench.

Some of the spectators had lost interest in the game already and had left. A few kids had taken a baseball off the field and were having their own game of catch behind the bleachers. Across the playground, four or five kids were getting a game of kickball started.

"Bird is such a dork," Greg said, his eyes on the game.

"He scared me to death," Shari exclaimed. "I really thought he was hurt."

"What a clown," Greg muttered.

They watched the game in silence for a while. It wasn't terribly interesting. The Dolphins were losing 12–3 going into the third inning. None of the players were very good.

Greg laughed as a Cardinal batter, a kid from their class named Joe Garden, slugged a ball that sailed out to the field and right over Bird's head.

"That's the third ball that flew over his head!" Greg cried.

"Guess he lost it in the sun!" Shari exclaimed, joining in the laughter.

They both watched Bird's long legs storking after the ball. By the time he managed to catch up with it and heave it towards the diamond, Joe Garden had already rounded the bases and scored.

There were loud *boos* from the bleachers.

The next Cardinal batter stepped to the plate. A few more kids climbed down from the bleachers, having seen enough.

"It's so hot here in the sun," Shari said, shielding her eyes with one hand. "And I've got lots of homework. Want to leave?"

"I just want to see the next inning," Greg said, watching the batter swing and miss. "Bird is coming up next inning. I want to stay and *boo* him."

"What are friends for?" Shari said sarcastically.

It took a long while for the Dolphins to get the third out. The Cardinals batted around their entire order.

Greg's T-shirt was drenched with sweat by the time Bird came to the plate in the top of the fourth.

Despite the loud *booing* from Shari and Greg, Bird managed to punch the ball past the shortstop for a single.

"Lucky hit!" Greg yelled, cupping his hands into a megaphone.

Bird pretended not to hear him. He tossed away his batter's helmet, adjusted his cap, and took a short lead off first base.

The next batter swung at the first pitch and fouled it off.

"Let's go," Shari urged, pulling Greg's arm. "It's too hot. I'm dying of thirst."

"Let's just see if Bird — "

Greg didn't finish his sentence.

314

The batter hit the next ball hard. It made a loud *thunk* as it left the bat.

A dozen people — players and spectators — cried out as the ball flew across the diamond, a sharp line drive, and slammed into the side of Bird's head with another *thunk*.

Greg watched in horror as the ball bounced off Bird and dribbled away onto the infield grass. Bird's eyes went wide with disbelief, confusion.

He stood frozen in place on the base path for a long moment.

Then both of his hands shot up above his head, and he uttered a shrill cry, long and loud, like the high-pitched whinny of a horse.

His eyes rolled up in his head. He sank to his knees. Uttered another cry, softer this time. Then collapsed, sprawling onto his back, his neck at an unnatural angle, his eyes closed.

He didn't move.

14

In seconds, the two coaches and both teams were running out to the fallen player, huddling over him, forming a tight, hushed circle around him.

Crying, "Bird! Bird!" Shari leapt off the bleachers and began running to the circle of horrified onlookers.

Greg started to follow, but stopped when he saw a familiar figure crossing the street at a full run, waving to him.

"Terry!" Greg cried.

Why was his brother coming to the playground? Why wasn't he at his after-school job at the Dairy Freeze?

"Terry? What's happening?" Greg cried.

Terry stopped, gasping for breath, sweat pouring down his bright red forehead. "I . . . ran . . . all . . . the . . . way," he managed to utter.

"Terry, what's wrong?" A sick feeling crept up from Greg's stomach.

As Terry approached, his face held the same

frightened expression as in the photograph Greg had snapped of him.

The same frightened expression. With the same house behind him across the street.

The snapshot had come true. Just as the snapshot of Bird lying on the ground had come true.

Greg's throat suddenly felt as dry as cotton. He realized that his knees were trembling.

"Terry, what *is* it?" he managed to cry.

"It's Dad," Terry said, putting a heavy hand on Greg's shoulder.

"Huh? Dad?"

"You've got to come home, Greg. Dad — he's been in a bad accident."

"An accident?" Greg's head spun. Terry's words weren't making any sense to him.

"In the new car," Terry explained, again placing a heavy hand on Greg's trembling shoulder. "The new car is totaled. Completely totaled."

"Oh," Greg gasped, feeling weak.

Terry squeezed his shoulder. "Come on. Hurry."

Holding the camera tightly in one hand, Greg began running after his brother.

Reaching the street, he turned back to the playground to see what was happening with Bird.

A large crowd was still huddled around Bird, blocking him from sight.

But — what was that dark shadow behind the bleachers? Greg wondered.

Someone — someone all in black — was hiding back there.

Watching Greg?

"Come *on!*" Terry urged.

Greg stared hard at the bleachers. The dark figure pulled back out of sight.

"Come *on*, Greg!"

"I'm coming!" Greg shouted, and followed his brother toward home.

15

The hospital walls were pale green. The uniforms worn by the nurses scurrying through the brightly lit corridors were white. The floor tiles beneath Greg's feet as he hurried with his brother towards their father's room were dark brown with orange specks.

Colors.

All Greg could see were blurs of colors, indistinct shapes.

His sneakers thudded noisily against the hard tile floor. He could barely hear them over the pounding of his heart.

Totaled. The car had been totaled.

Just like in the snapshot.

Greg and Terry turned a corner. The walls in this corridor were pale yellow. Terry's cheeks were red. Two doctors passed by wearing lime-green surgical gowns.

Colors. Only colors.

Greg blinked, tried to see clearly. But it was

all passing by too fast, all too unreal. Even the sharp hospital smell, that unique aroma of rubbing alcohol, stale food, and disinfectant, couldn't make it real for him.

Then the two brothers entered their father's room, and it all became real.

The colors faded. The images became sharp and clear.

Their mother jumped up from the folding chair beside the bed. "Hi, boys." She clenched a wadded-up tissue in her hand. It was obvious that she had been crying. She forced a tight smile on her face, but her eyes were red-rimmed, her cheeks pale and puffy.

Stopping just inside the doorway of the small room, Greg returned his mother's greeting in a soft, choked voice. Then his eyes, focusing clearly now, turned to his father.

Mr. Banks had a mummylike bandage covering his hair. One arm was in a cast. The other lay at his side and had a tube attached just below the wrist, dripping a dark liquid into the arm. The bedsheet was pulled up to his chest.

"Hey — how's it going, guys?" their father asked. His voice sounded fogged in, as if coming from far away.

"Dad — " Terry started.

"He's going to be okay," Mrs. Banks interrupted, seeing the frightened looks on her sons' faces.

"I feel great," Mr. Banks said groggily.

"You don't *look* so great," Greg blurted out, stepping up cautiously to the bed.

"I'm okay. Really," their father insisted. "A few broken bones. That's it." He sighed, then winced from some pain. "I guess I'm lucky."

"You're very lucky," Mrs. Banks agreed quickly.

What's the lucky part? Greg wondered silently to himself. He couldn't take his eyes off the tube stuck into his father's arm.

Again, he thought of the snapshot of the car. It was up in his room at home, tucked into the secret compartment in his headboard.

The snapshot showing the car totaled, the driver's side caved in.

Should he tell them about it?

He couldn't decide.

Would they believe him if he *did* tell them?

"What'd you break, Dad?" Terry asked, sitting down on the radiator in front of the windowsill, shoving his hands into his jeans pockets.

"Your father broke his arm and a few ribs," Mrs. Banks answered quickly. "And he had a slight concussion. The doctors are watching him for internal injuries. But, so far, so good."

"I was lucky," Mr. Banks repeated. He smiled at Greg.

"Dad, I have to tell you about this photo I took," Greg said suddenly, speaking rapidly, his voice trembling with nervousness. "I took a picture of the new car, and — "

"The car is completely wrecked," Mrs. Banks interrupted. Sitting on the edge of the folding chair, she rubbed her fingers, working her wedding ring round and around, something she always did when she was nervous. "I'm glad you boys didn't see it." Her voice caught in her throat. Then she added, "It's a miracle he wasn't hurt any worse."

"This photo — " Greg started again.

"Later," his mother said brusquely. "Okay?" She gave him a meaningful stare.

Greg felt his face grow hot.

This is *important*, he thought.

Then he decided they probably wouldn't believe him, anyway. Who would believe such a crazy story?

"Will we be able to get another new car?" Terry asked.

Mr. Banks nodded carefully. "I have to call the insurance company," he said.

"I'll call them when I get home," Mrs. Banks said. "You don't exactly have a hand free."

Everyone laughed at that, nervous laughter.

"I feel kind of sleepy," Mr. Banks said. His eyes were halfway closed, his voice muffled.

"It's the painkillers the doctors gave you," Mrs. Banks told him. She leaned forward and patted his hand. "Get some sleep. I'll come back in a few hours."

She stood up, still fiddling with her wedding band, and motioned with her head toward the door.

"Bye, Dad," Greg and Terry said in unison.

Their father muttered a reply. They followed their mother out the door.

"What *happened*?" Terry asked as they made their way past a nurses' station, then down the long, pale yellow corridor. "I mean, the accident."

"Some guy ran right through a red light," Mrs. Banks said, her red-rimmed eyes straight ahead. "He plowed right into your father's side of the car. Said his brakes weren't working." She shook her head, tears forming in the corners of her eyes. "I don't know," she said, sighing. "I just don't know what to say. Thank goodness he's going to be okay."

They turned into the green corridor, walking side by side. Several people were waiting patiently for the elevator at the far end of the hall.

Once again, Greg found himself thinking of the snapshots he had taken with the weird camera.

First Michael. Then Terry. Then Bird. Then his father.

All four photos had shown something terrible. Something terrible that hadn't happened yet.

And then all four photos had come true.

Greg felt a chill as the elevator doors opened and the small crowd of people moved forward to squeeze inside.

What was the truth about the camera? he wondered.

Does the camera *show* the future?

Or does it actually *cause* bad things to happen?

16

"Yeah. I know Bird's okay," Greg said into the phone receiver. "I saw him yesterday, remember? He was lucky. Real lucky. He didn't have a concussion or anything."

On the other end of the line — in the house next door — Shari agreed, then repeated her request.

"No, Shari. I really don't want to," Greg replied vehemently.

"Bring it," Shari demanded. "It's *my* birthday."

"I don't want to bring the camera. It's not a good idea. Really," Greg told her.

It was the next weekend. Saturday afternoon. Greg had been nearly out the door, on his way next door to Shari's birthday party, when the phone rang.

"Hi, Greg. Why aren't you on your way to my party?" Shari had asked when he'd run to pick up the receiver.

"Because I'm on the phone with you," Greg had replied dryly.

"Well, bring the camera, okay?"

Greg hadn't looked at the camera, hadn't removed it from its hiding place since his father's accident.

"I don't want to bring it," he insisted, despite Shari's high-pitched demands. "Don't you understand, Shari? I don't want anyone else to get hurt."

"Oh, Greg," she said, talking to him as if he were a three-year-old. "You don't really believe that, do you? You don't really believe that camera can hurt people."

Greg was silent for a moment. "I don't know what I believe," he said finally. "I only know that first, Michael, then, Bird — "

Greg swallowed hard. "And I had a dream, Shari. Last night."

"Huh? What kind of dream?" Shari asked impatiently.

"It was about the camera. I was taking everyone's picture. My whole family — Mom, Dad, and Terry. They were barbecuing. In the back yard. I held up the camera. I kept saying, 'Say Cheese, Say Cheese,' over and over. And when I looked through the viewfinder, they were smiling back at me — but . . . they were skeletons. All of them. Their skin was gone, and — and . . ."

Greg's voice trailed off.

"What a dumb dream," Shari said, laughing.

"But that's why I don't want to bring the camera," Greg insisted. "I think — "

"Bring it, Greg," she interrupted. "It's not your camera, you know. All four of us were in the Coffman house. It belongs to all four of us. Bring it."

"But *why*, Shari?" Greg demanded.

"It'll be a goof, that's all. It takes such weird pictures."

"That's for sure," Greg muttered.

"We don't have anything else to do for my party," Shari told him. "I wanted to rent a video, but my mom says we have to go outdoors. She doesn't want her precious house messed up. So I thought we could take everyone's picture with the weird camera. You know. See what strange things come out."

"Shari, I really don't — "

"Bring it," she ordered. And hung up.

Greg stood for a long time staring at the phone receiver, thinking hard, trying to decide what to do.

Then he replaced the receiver and headed reluctantly up to his room.

With a loud sigh, he pulled the camera from its hiding place in his headboard. "It's Shari's birthday, after all," he said aloud to himself.

His hands were trembling as he picked it up. He realized he was afraid of it.

I shouldn't be doing this, he thought, feeling a heavy knot of dread in the pit of his stomach.

I know I shouldn't be doing this.

17

"How's it going, Bird?" Greg called, making his way across the flagstone patio to Shari's back yard.

"I'm feeling okay," Bird said, slapping his friend a high five. "The only problem is, ever since that ball hit me," Bird continued, frowning, "from time to time I start — *pluuccck cluuuck cluuuuck!* — clucking like a chicken!" He flapped his arms and started strutting across the back yard, clucking at the top of his voice.

"Hey, Bird — go lay an egg!" someone yelled, and everyone laughed.

"Bird's at it again," Michael said, shaking his head. He gave Greg a friendly punch on the shoulder. Michael, his red hair unbrushed as usual, was wearing faded jeans and a flowered Hawaiian sports shirt about three sizes too big for him.

"Where'd you get that shirt?" Greg asked, holding Michael at arm's length by the shoulders to admire it.

"In a cereal box," Bird chimed in, still flapping his arms.

"My grandmother gave it to me," Michael said, frowning.

"He made it in home ec," Bird interrupted. One joke was never enough.

"But why did you *wear* it?" Greg asked.

Michael shrugged. "Everything else was dirty." Bird bent down, picked up a small clump of dirt from the lawn, and rubbed it on the back of Michael's shirt. "Now this one's dirty, too," he declared.

"Hey, you — " Michael reacted with playful anger, grabbing Bird and shoving him into the hedge.

"Did you bring it?"

Hearing Shari's voice, Greg turned towards the house and saw her jogging across the patio in his direction. Her black hair was pulled back in a single braid, and she had on an oversized, silky yellow top that came down over black spandex leggings.

"Did you bring it?" she repeated eagerly. A charm bracelet filled with tiny silver charms — a birthday present — jangled at her wrist.

"Yeah." Greg reluctantly held up the camera.

"Excellent," she declared.

"I really don't want — " Greg started.

"You can take my picture first since it's my birthday," Shari interrupted. "Here. How's this?"

She struck a sophisticated pose, leaning against a tree with her hand behind her head.

Greg obediently raised the camera. "Are you sure you want me to do this, Shari?"

"Yeah. Come on. I want to take everyone's picture."

"But it'll probably come out weird," Greg protested.

"I know," Shari replied impatiently, holding her pose. "That's the fun of it."

"But, Shari — "

"Michael puked on his shirt," he heard Bird telling someone near the hedge.

"I did not!" Michael was screaming.

"You mean it looks like that *naturally*?" Bird asked.

Greg could hear a lot of raucous laughing, all of it at Michael's expense.

"Will you take the picture!" Shari cried, holding on to the slender trunk of the tree.

Greg pointed the lens at her and pressed the button. The camera whirred, and the undeveloped, white square rolled out.

"Hey, are we the only boys invited?" Michael asked, stepping up to Shari.

"Yeah. Just you three," Shari said. "And nine girls."

"Oh, wow." Michael made a face.

"Take Michael's picture next," Shari told Greg.

"No way!" Michael replied quickly, raising his hands as if to shield himself and backing away. "The last time you took my picture with that thing, I fell down the stairs."

Trying to get away, Michael backed right into Nina Blake, one of Shari's friends. She reacted with a squeal of surprise, then gave him a playful shove, and he kept right on backing away.

"Michael, come on. It's *my* party," Shari called.

"What are we going to do? Is this *it*?" Nina demanded from halfway across the yard.

"I thought we'd take everyone's picture and then play a game or something," Shari told her.

"A game?" Bird chimed in. "You mean like Spin the Bottle?"

A few kids laughed.

"Truth or Dare!" Nina suggested.

"Yeah. Truth or Dare!" a couple of other girls called in agreement.

"Oh, no," Greg groaned quietly to himself. Truth or Dare meant a lot of kissing and awkward, embarrassing stunts.

Nine girls and only three boys.

It was going to be *really* embarrassing.

How could Shari *do* this to us? he wondered.

"Well, did it come out?" Shari asked, grabbing his arm. "Let me see."

Greg was so upset about having to play Truth or Dare, he had forgotten about the snapshot developing in his hand. He held it up, and they both examined it.

"Where am I?" Shari asked in surprise. "What were you aiming at? You missed me!"

"Huh?" Greg stared at the snapshot. There was the tree. But no Shari. "Weird! I pointed it right at you. I lined it up carefully," he protested.

"Well, you missed me. I'm not in the shot," Shari replied disgustedly.

"But, Shari — "

"I mean, come *on* — I'm not invisible, Greg. I'm not a vampire or something. I can see my reflection in mirrors. And I do usually show up in photos."

"But, look — " Greg stared hard at the photograph. "There's the tree you were leaning against. You can see the tree trunk clearly. And there's the spot where you were standing."

"But where *am* I?" Shari demanded, jangling her charm bracelet noisily. "Never mind." She grabbed the snapshot from him and tossed it on the grass. "Take another one. Quick."

"Well, okay. But — " Greg was still puzzling over the photo. Why hadn't Shari shown up in it? He bent down, picked it up, and shoved it into his pocket.

"Stand closer this time," she instructed.

Greg moved a few steps closer, carefully centered Shari in the viewfinder, and snapped the picture. A square of film zipped out the front.

Shari walked over and pulled the picture from the camera. "This one better turn out," she said, staring hard at it as the colors began to darken and take form.

"If you really want pictures of everyone, we should get another camera," Greg said, his eyes also locked on the snapshot.

"Hey — I don't *believe* it!" Shari cried.

Again, she was invisible.

The tree photographed clearly, in perfect focus. But Shari was nowhere to be seen.

"You were right. The dumb camera is broken," she said disgustedly, handing the photo to Greg. "Forget it." She turned away from him and called to the others. "Hey, guys — Truth or Dare!"

There were some cheers and some groans.

Shari headed them back to the woods behind her back yard to play. "More privacy," she explained. There was a circular clearing just beyond the trees, a perfect, private place.

The game was just as embarrassing as Greg had imagined. Among the boys, only Bird seemed to be enjoying it. Bird loves dumb stuff like this, Greg thought, with some envy.

Luckily, after little more than half an hour, he heard Mrs. Walker, Shari's mom, calling from the house, summoning them back to cut the birthday cake.

"Aw, too bad," Greg said sarcastically. "Just when the game was getting good."

"We have to get out of the woods, anyway," Bird said, grinning. "Michael's shirt is scaring the squirrels."

Laughing and talking about the game, the kids made their way back to the patio where the pink-and-white birthday cake, candles all lit, was waiting on the round umbrella table.

"I must be a pretty bad mom," Mrs. Walker joked, "allowing you all to go off into the woods by yourselves."

Some of the girls laughed.

Cake knife in her hand, Mrs. Walker looked around. "Where's Shari?"

Everyone turned their eyes to search the back yard. "She was with us in the woods," Nina told Mrs. Walker. "Just a minute ago."

"Hey, Shari!" Bird called, cupping his hands to his mouth as a megaphone. "Earth calling Shari! It's cake time!"

No reply.

No sign of her.

"Did she go in the house?" Greg asked.

Mrs. Walker shook her head. "No. She didn't come by the patio. Is she still in the woods?"

"I'll go check," Bird told her. Calling Shari's name, he ran to the edge of the trees at the back of the yard. Then he disappeared into the trees, still calling.

A few minutes later, Bird emerged, signaling to the others with a shrug.

No sign of her.

They searched the house. The front yard. The woods again.

But Shari had vanished.

Greg sat in the shade with his back against the tree trunk, the camera on the ground at his side, and watched the blue-uniformed policemen.

They covered the back yard and could be seen bending low as they climbed around in the woods. He could hear their voices, but couldn't make out what they were saying. Their faces were intent, bewildered.

More policemen arrived, grim-faced, business-like.

And then, even more dark-uniformed police-men.

Mrs. Walker had called her husband home from a golf game. They sat huddled together on canvas chairs in a corner of the patio. They whispered to each other, their eyes darting across the yard. Holding hands, they looked pale and worried.

Everyone else had left.

On the patio, the table was still set. The birth-day candles had burned all the way down, the blue and red wax melting in hard puddles on the pink-and-white icing, the cake untouched.

"No sign of her," a red-cheeked policeman with a white-blond mustache was telling the Walkers. He pulled off his cap and scratched his head, revealing short, blond hair.

"Did someone . . . take her away?" Mr. Walker asked, still holding his wife's hand.

"No sign of a struggle," the policeman said. "No sign of anything, really."

Mrs. Walker sighed loudly and lowered her head. "I just don't understand it."

There was a long, painful silence.

"We'll keep looking," the policeman said. "I'm sure we'll find . . . something."

He turned and headed toward the woods.

"Oh. Hi." He stopped in front of Greg, staring down at him as if seeing him for the first time. "You still here, son? All the other guests have gone home." He pushed his hair back and replaced his cap.

"Yeah, I know," Greg replied solemnly, lifting the camera into his lap.

"I'm Officer Riddick," he said.

"Yeah, I know," Greg repeated softly.

"How come you didn't go home after we talked with you, like the others?" Riddick asked.

"I'm just upset, I guess," Greg told him. "I mean, Shari's a good friend, you know?" He cleared his throat, which felt dry and tight. "Besides, I live right over there." He gestured with his head to his house next door.

"Well, you might as well go home, son," Riddick said, turning his eyes to the woods with a frown. "This search could take a long time. We haven't found a thing back there yet."

"I know," Greg replied, rubbing his hand against the back of the camera.

And I know that this camera is the reason Shari is missing, he thought, feeling miserable and frightened.

"One minute she was there. The next minute she was gone," the policeman said, studying Greg's face as if looking for answers there.

"Yeah," Greg replied. "It's so weird."

It's weirder than anyone knows, Greg thought.

The camera made her invisible. The camera did it.

First, she vanished from the snapshot.

Then she vanished in real life.

The camera did it to her. I don't know how. But it did.

"Do you have something more to tell me?" Riddick asked, hands resting on his hips, his right hand just above the worn brown holster that carried his pistol. "Did you see something? Something that might give us a clue, help us out? Something you didn't remember to tell me before?"

Should I tell him? Greg wondered.

If I tell him about the camera, he'll ask where I got it. And I'll have to tell him that I got it in the Coffman house. And we'll all get in trouble for breaking in there.

But — big deal. Shari is missing. Gone. Vanished. That's a lot more important.

I should tell him, Greg decided.

But then he hesitated. If I tell him, he won't believe me.

If I tell him, how will it help bring Shari back?

"You look very troubled," Riddick said, squatting down next to Greg in the shade. "What's your name again?"

"Greg, Greg Banks."

"Well, you look very troubled, Greg," the policeman repeated softly. "Why don't you tell me what's bothering you? Why don't you tell me what's on your mind? I think it'll make you feel a lot better."

Greg took a deep breath and glanced up to the patio. Mrs. Walker had covered her face with her hands. Her husband was leaning over her, trying to comfort her.

"Well . . ." Greg started.

"Go ahead, son," Riddick urged softly. "Do you know where Shari is?"

"It's this camera," Greg blurted out. He could suddenly feel the blood throbbing against his temples.

He took a deep breath and then continued. "You see, this camera is weird."

"What do you mean?" Riddick asked quietly.

Greg took another deep breath. "I took Shari's picture. Before. When I first arrived. I took two pictures. And she was invisible. In both of them. See?"

Riddick closed his eyes, then opened them. "No. I don't understand."

"Shari was invisible in the picture. Everything else was there. But she wasn't. She had vanished, see. And, then, later, she vanished for real. The camera — it predicts the future, I guess. Or it makes bad things happen." Greg raised the camera, attempting to hand it to the policeman.

Riddick made no attempt to take it. He just stared hard at Greg, his eyes narrowing, his expression hardening.

Greg felt a sudden stab of fear.

Oh, no, he thought. Why is he looking at me like that?

What is he going to do?

19

Greg continued to hold the camera out to the policeman.

But Riddick quickly climbed to his feet. "The camera makes bad things happen?" His eyes burned into Greg's.

"Yes," Greg told him. "It isn't my camera, see? And every time I take a picture — "

"Son, that's enough," Riddick said gently. He reached down and rested a hand on Greg's trembling shoulder. "I think you're very upset, Greg," he said, his voice almost a whisper. "I don't blame you. This is very upsetting for everyone."

"But it's *true* — " Greg started to insist.

"I'm going to ask that officer over there," Riddick said, pointing, "to take you home now. And I'm going to have him tell your parents that you've been through a very frightening experience."

I *knew* he wouldn't believe me, Greg thought angrily.

How could I have been so stupid?

Now he thinks I'm some kind of a nut case.

Riddick called to a policeman at the side of the house near the hedge.

"No, that's okay," Greg said, quickly pulling himself up, cradling the camera in his hand. "I can make it home okay."

Riddick eyed him suspiciously. "You sure?"

"Yeah. I can walk by myself."

"If you have anything to tell me later," Riddick said, lowering his gaze to the camera, "just call the station, okay?"

"Okay," Greg replied, walking slowly towards the front of the house.

"Don't worry, Greg. We'll do our best," Riddick called after him. "We'll find her. Put the camera away and try to get some rest, okay?"

"Okay," Greg muttered.

He hurried past the Walkers, who were still huddled together under the umbrella on the patio.

Why was I so stupid? he asked himself as he walked home. Why did I expect that policeman to believe such a weird story?

I'm not even sure I believe it myself.

A few minutes later, he pulled open the back screen door and entered his kitchen. "Anybody home?"

No reply.

He headed through the back hall towards the living room. "Anyone home?"

No one.

Terry was at work. His mother must have been visiting his dad at the hospital.

Greg felt bad. He really didn't feel like being alone now. He really wanted to tell them about what had happened to Shari. He really wanted to talk to them.

Still cradling the camera, he climbed the stairs to his room.

He stopped in the doorway, blinked twice, then uttered a cry of horror.

His books were scattered all over the floor. The covers had been pulled off his bed. His desk drawers were all open, their contents strewn around the room. The desk lamp was on its side on the floor. All of his clothes had been pulled from the dresser and his closet and tossed everywhere.

Someone had been in Greg's room — and had turned it upside down!

20

Who would do this? Greg asked himself, staring in horror at his ransacked room.

Who would tear my room apart like this?

He realized that he knew the answer. He knew who would do it, who *had* done it.

Someone looking for the camera.

Someone desperate to get the camera back.

Spidey?

The creepy guy who dressed all in black was living in the Coffman house. Was he the owner of the camera?

Yes, Greg knew, Spidey had done it.

Spidey had been watching Greg, spying on Greg from behind the bleachers at the Little League game.

He knew that Greg had his camera. *And he knew where Greg lived.*

That thought was the most chilling of all.

He knew where Greg lived.

Greg turned away from the chaos in his room,

leaned against the wall of the hallway, and closed his eyes.

He pictured Spidey, the dark figure creeping along so evilly on his spindly legs. He pictured him inside the house, Greg's house. Inside Greg's room.

He was here, thought Greg. He pawed through all my things. He wrecked my room.

Greg stepped back into his room. He felt all mixed up. He felt like shouting angrily and crying for help all at once.

But he was all alone. No one to hear him. No one to help him.

What now? he wondered. What now?

Suddenly, leaning against the doorframe, staring at his ransacked room, he knew what he had to do.

21

"Hey, Bird, it's me."

Greg held the receiver in one hand and wiped the sweat off his forehead with the other. He'd never worked so hard — or so fast — in all his life.

"Did they find Shari?" Bird asked eagerly.

"I haven't heard. I don't think so," Greg said, his eyes surveying his room. Almost back to normal.

He had put everything back, cleaned and straightened. His parents would never guess.

"Listen, Bird, I'm not calling about that," Greg said, speaking rapidly into the phone. "Call Michael for me, okay? Meet me at the playground. By the baseball diamond."

"When? Now?" Bird asked, sounding confused.

"Yeah," Greg told him. "We have to meet. It's important."

"It's almost dinnertime," Bird protested. "I don't know if my parents — "

"It's important," Greg repeated impatiently. "I've got to see you guys. Okay?"

"Well . . . maybe I can sneak out for a few minutes," Bird said, lowering his voice. And then Greg heard him shout to his mother: "It's no one, Ma! I'm talking to no one!"

Boy, *that's* quick thinking! Greg thought sarcastically. He's a worse liar than I am!

And then he heard Bird call to his mom: "I *know* I'm on the phone. But I'm not talking to anyone. It's only Greg."

Thanks a lot, pal, Greg thought.

"I gotta go," Bird said.

"Get Michael, okay?" Greg urged.

"Yeah. Okay. See you." He hung up.

Greg replaced the receiver, then listened for his mother. Silence downstairs. She still wasn't home. She didn't know about Shari, Greg realized. He knew she and his dad were going to be very upset.

Very upset.

Almost as upset as he was.

Thinking about his missing friend, he went to his bedroom window and looked down on her yard next door. It was deserted now.

The policemen had all left. Shari's shaken parents must have gone inside.

A squirrel sat under the wide shade of the big tree, gnawing furiously at an acorn, another acorn at his feet.

In the corner of the window, Greg could see the birthday cake, still sitting forlornly on the deserted table, the places all set, the decorations still standing.

A birthday party for ghosts.

Greg shuddered.

"Shari is alive," he said aloud. "They'll find her. She's alive."

He knew what he had to do now.

Forcing himself away from the window, he hurried to meet his two friends.

22

"No way," Bird said heatedly, leaning against the bleacher bench. "Have you gone totally bananas?"

Swinging the camera by its cord, Greg turned hopefully to Michael. But Michael avoided Greg's stare. "I'm with Bird," he said, his eyes on the camera.

Since it was just about dinnertime, the playground was nearly deserted. A few little kids were on the swings at the other end. Two kids were riding their bikes round and around the soccer field.

"I thought maybe you guys would come with me," Greg said, disappointed. He kicked up a clump of grass with his sneaker. "I have to return this thing," he continued, raising the camera. "I know it's what I have to do. I have to put it back where I found it."

"No way," Bird repeated, shaking his head. "I'm not going back to the Coffman house. Once was enough."

"Chicken?" Greg asked angrily.

"Yeah," Bird quickly admitted.

"You don't have to take it back," Michael argued. He pulled himself up the side of the bleachers, climbed onto the third deck of seats, then lowered himself to the ground.

"What do you mean?" Greg asked impatiently, kicking at the grass.

"Just toss it, Greg," Michael urged, making a throwing motion with one hand. "Heave it. Throw it in the trash somewhere."

"Yeah. Or leave it right here," Bird suggested. He reached for the camera. "Give it to me. I'll hide it under the seats."

"You don't understand," Greg said, swinging the camera out of Bird's reach. "Throwing it away won't do any good."

"Why not?" Bird asked, making another swipe for the camera.

"Spidey'll just come back for it," Greg told him heatedly. "He'll come back to my room looking for it. He'll come after me. I know it."

"But what if we get caught taking it back?" Michael asked.

"Yeah. What if Spidey's there in the Coffman house, and he catches us?" Bird said.

"You don't understand," Greg cried. "He knows where I live! He was in my house. He was in my *room*! He wants his camera back, and — "

"Here. Give it to me," Bird said. "We don't have

to go back to that house. He can find it. Right here."

He grabbed again for the camera.

Greg held tightly to the strap and tried to tug it away.

But Bird grabbed the side of the camera.

"No!" Greg cried out as it flashed. And whirred. A square of film slid out.

"No!" Greg cried to Bird, horrified, staring at the white square as it started to develop. "You took *my* picture!"

His hand trembling, he pulled the snapshot from the camera.

What would it show?

23

"Sorry," Bird said. "I didn't mean to — "

Before he could finish his sentence, a voice interrupted from behind the bleachers. "Hey — what've you got there?"

Greg looked up from the developing snapshot in surprise. Two tough-looking boys stepped out of the shadows, their expressions hard, their eyes on the camera.

He recognized them immediately — Joey Ferris and Mickey Ward — two ninth-graders who hung out together, always swaggering around, acting tough, picking on kids younger than them.

Their specialty was taking kids' bikes, riding off on them, and dumping them somewhere. There was a rumor around school that Mickey had once beaten up a kid so badly that the kid was crippled for life. But Greg believed Mickey made up that rumor and spread it himself.

Both boys were big for their age. Neither of them did very well in school. And even though they were always stealing bikes and skateboards, and terrorizing little kids, and getting into fights, neither of them ever seemed to get into serious trouble.

Joey had short blond hair, slicked straight up, and wore a diamondlike stud in one ear. Mickey had a round, red face full of pimples, stringy black hair down to his shoulders, and was working a toothpick between his teeth. Both boys were wearing heavy metal T-shirts and jeans.

"Hey, I've gotta get home," Bird said quickly, half-stepping, half-dancing away from the bleachers.

"Me, too," Michael said, unable to keep the fear from showing on his face.

Greg tucked the snapshot into his jeans pocket.

"Hey, you found my camera," Joey said, grabbing it out of Greg's hand. His small, gray eyes burned into Greg's as if searching for a reaction. "Thanks, man."

"Give it back, Joey," Greg said with a sigh.

"Yeah. Don't take that camera," Mickey told his friend, a smile spreading over his round face. "It's *mine!*" He wrestled the camera away from Joey.

"Give it back," Greg insisted angrily, reaching out his hand. Then he softened his tone. "Come on, guys. It isn't mine."

"I *know* it isn't yours," Mickey said, grinning. "Because it's *mine!*"

353

"I have to give it back to the owner," Greg told him, trying not to whine, but hearing his voice edge up.

"No, you don't. I'm the owner now," Mickey insisted.

"Haven't you ever heard of finders keepers?" Joey asked, leaning over Greg menacingly. He was about six inches taller than Greg, and a lot more muscular.

"Hey, let him have the thing," Michael whispered in Greg's ear. "You wanted to get rid of it — right?"

"No!" Greg protested.

"What's your problem, Freckle Face?" Joey asked Michael, eyeing Michael up and down.

"No problem," Michael said meekly.

"Hey — say cheese!" Mickey aimed the camera at Joey.

"Don't do it," Bird interrupted, waving his hands frantically.

"Why not?" Joey demanded.

"Because your face will break the camera," Bird said, laughing.

"You're real funny," Joey said sarcastically, narrowing his eyes threateningly, hardening his features. "You want that stupid smile to be permanent?" He raised a big fist.

"I know this kid," Mickey told Joey, pointing at Bird. "Thinks he's hot stuff."

Both boys stared hard at Bird, trying to scare him.

Bird swallowed hard. He took a step back, bumping into the bleachers. "No, I don't," he said softly. "I don't think I'm hot stuff."

"He looks like something I stepped in yesterday," Joey said.

He and Mickey cracked up, laughing high-pitched hyena laughs and slapping each other high fives.

"Listen, guys. I really need the camera back," Greg said, reaching out a hand to take it. "It isn't any good, anyway. It's broken. And it doesn't belong to me."

"Yeah, that's right. It's broken," Michael added, nodding his head.

"Yeah. Right," Mickey said sarcastically. "Let's just see." He raised the camera again and pointed it at Joey.

"Really, guys. I need it back," Greg said desperately.

If they took a picture with the camera, Greg realized, they might discover its secret. That its snapshots showed the future, showed only bad things happening to people. That the camera was evil. Maybe it even *caused* evil.

"Say cheese," Mickey instructed Joey.

"Just snap the stupid thing!" Joey replied impatiently.

No, Greg thought. I can't let this happen. I've got to return the camera to the Coffman house, to Spidey.

Impulsively, Greg leapt forward. With a cry, he snatched the camera away from Mickey's face.

"Hey — " Mickey reacted in surprise.

"Let's *go!*" Greg shouted to Bird and Michael.

And without another word, the three friends turned and began running across the deserted playground towards their homes.

His heart thudding in his chest, Greg gripped the camera tightly and ran as fast as he could, his sneakers pounding over the dry grass.

They're going to catch us, Greg thought, panting loudly now as he raced toward the street. They're going to catch us and pound us. They're going to take back the camera. We're dead meat. Dead meat.

Greg and his friends didn't turn around until they were across the street. Breathing noisily, they looked back — and cried out in relieved surprise.

Joey and Mickey hadn't budged from beside the bleachers. They hadn't chased after them. They were leaning against the bleachers, laughing.

"Catch you later, guys!" Joey called after them.

"Yeah. Later," Mickey repeated.

They both burst out laughing again, as if they had said something hilarious.

"That was close," Michael said, still breathing hard.

"They mean it," Bird said, looking very troubled. "They'll catch us later. We're history."

"Tough talk. They're just a lot of hot air," Greg insisted.

"Oh, yeah?" Michael cried. "Then why did we run like that?"

"Because we're late for dinner," Bird joked. "See you guys. I'm gonna catch it if I don't hurry."

"But the camera — " Greg protested, still gripping it tightly in one hand.

"It's too late," Michael said, nervously raking a hand back through his red hair.

"Yeah. We'll have to do it tomorrow or something," Bird agreed.

"Then you guys will come with me?" Greg asked eagerly.

"Uh . . . I've gotta go," Bird said without answering.

"Me, too," Michael said quickly, avoiding Greg's stare.

All three of them turned their eyes back to the playground. Joey and Mickey had disappeared. Probably off to terrorize some other kids.

"Later," Bird said, slapping Greg on the shoulder as he headed away. The three friends split up, running in different directions across lawns and driveways, heading home.

Greg had run all the way to his front yard before he remembered the snapshot he had shoved into his jeans pocket.

He stopped in the driveway and pulled it out.

The sun was lowering behind the garage. He held the snapshot up close to his face to see it clearly.

"Oh, no!" he cried. "I don't believe it!"

24

"This is *impossible!*" Greg cried aloud, gaping at the snapshot in his trembling hand.

How had Shari gotten into the photo?

It had been taken a few minutes before, in front of the bleachers on the playground.

But there was Shari, standing close beside Greg.

His hand trembling, his mouth hanging open in disbelief, Greg goggled at the photo.

It was very clear, very sharp. There they were on the playground. He could see the baseball diamond in the background.

And there they were. Greg and Shari.

Shari standing so clear, so sharp — right next to him.

And they were both staring straight ahead, their eyes wide, their mouths open, their expressions frozen in horror as a large shadow covered them both.

"Shari?" Greg cried, lowering the snapshot and

darting his eyes over the front yard. "Are you here? Can you hear me?"

He listened.

Silence.

He tried again.

"Shari? Are you here?"

"Greg!" a voice called.

Uttering a startled cry, Greg spun around. "Huh?"

"Greg!" the voice repeated. It took him a while to realize that it was his mother, calling to him from the front door.

"Oh. Hi, Mom." Feeling dazed, he slid the snapshot back into his jeans pocket.

"Where've you been?" his mother asked as he made his way to the door. "I heard about Shari. I've been so upset. I didn't know where you were."

"Sorry, Mom," Greg said, kissing her on the cheek. "I — I should've left a note."

He stepped into the house, feeling strange and out-of-sorts, sad and confused and frightened, all at the same time.

Two days later, on a day of high, gray clouds, the air hot and smoggy, Greg paced back and forth in his room after school.

The house was empty except for him. Terry had gone off a few hours before to his after-school job at the Dairy Freeze. Mrs. Banks had driven to

360

the hospital to pick up Greg's dad, who was finally coming home.

Greg knew he should be happy about his dad's return. But there were still too many things troubling him, tugging at his mind.

Frightening him.

For one thing, Shari still hadn't been found.

The police were completely baffled. Their new theory was that she'd been kidnapped.

Her frantic, grieving parents waited home by the phone. But no kidnappers called to demand a ransom.

There were no clues of any kind.

Nothing to do but wait. And hope.

As the days passed, Greg felt more and more guilty. He was sure Shari hadn't been kidnapped. He knew that somehow, the camera had made her disappear.

But he couldn't tell anyone else what he believed.

No one would believe him. Anyone he tried to tell the story to would think he was crazy.

Cameras can't be evil, after all.

Cameras can't make people fall down stairs. Or crash their cars.

Or vanish from sight.

Cameras can only record what they see.

Greg stared out of his window, pressing his forehead against the glass, looking down on

Shari's back yard. "Shari — where *are* you?" he asked aloud, staring at the tree where she had posed.

The camera was still hidden in the secret compartment in his headboard. Neither Bird nor Michael would agree to help Greg return it to the Coffman house.

Besides, Greg had decided to hold on to it a while longer, in case he needed it as proof.

In case he decided to confide his fears about it to someone.

In case . . .

His other fear was that Spidey would come back, back to Greg's room, back for the camera.

So much to be frightened about.

He pushed himself away from the window. He had spent so much time in the past couple of days staring down at Shari's empty back yard.

Thinking. Thinking.

With a sigh, he reached into the headboard and pulled out two of the snapshots he had hidden in there along with the camera.

The two snapshots were the ones taken the past Saturday at Shari's birthday party. Holding one in each hand, Greg stared at them, hoping he could see something new, something he hadn't noticed before.

But the photos hadn't changed. They still showed her tree, her back yard, green in the sunlight. And no Shari. No one where Shari had been standing. As if the lens had penetrated right through her.

Staring at the photos, Greg let out a cry of anguish.

If only he had never gone into the Coffman house.

If only he had never stolen the camera.

If only he had never taken any photos with it.

If only . . . if only . . . if only . . .

Before he realized what he was doing, he was ripping the two snapshots into tiny pieces.

Panting loudly, his chest heaving, he tore at the snapshots and let the pieces fall to the floor.

When he had ripped them both into tiny shards of paper, he flung himself facedown on his bed and closed his eyes, waiting for his heart to stop pounding, waiting for the heavy feeling of guilt and horror to lift.

Two hours later, the phone by his bed rang.

It was Shari.

25

"Shari — is it really you?" Greg shouted into the phone.

"Yeah. It's me!" She sounded as surprised as he did.

"But how? I mean — " His mind was racing. He didn't know what to say.

"Your guess is as good as mine," Shari told him. And then she said, "Hold on a minute." And he heard her step away from the phone to talk to her mother. "Mom — stop crying already. Mom — it's really me. I'm home."

A few seconds later, she came back on the line. "I've been home for two hours, and Mom's still crying and carrying on."

"I feel like crying, too," Greg admitted. "I — I just can't believe it! Shari, where *were* you?"

The line was silent for a long moment. "I don't know," she answered finally.

"Huh?"

"I really don't. It was just so weird, Greg. One

minute, there I was at my birthday party. The next minute, I was standing in front of my house. And it was two days later. But I don't remember being away. Or being anywhere else. I don't remember anything at all."

"You don't remember going away? Or coming back?" Greg asked.

"No. Nothing," Shari said, her voice trembling.

"Shari, those pictures I took of you — remember? With the weird camera? You were invisible in them — "

"And then I disappeared," she said, finishing his thought.

"Shari, do you think — ?"

"I don't know," she replied quickly. "I — I have to get off now. The police are here. They want to question me. What am I going to tell them? They're going to think I had amnesia or flipped out or something."

"I — I don't know," Greg said, completely bewildered. "We have to talk. The camera — "

"I can't now," she told him. "Maybe tomorrow. Okay?" She called to her mother that she was coming. "Bye, Greg. See you." And then she hung up.

Greg replaced the receiver, but sat on the edge of his bed staring at the phone for a long time.

Shari was back.

She'd been back about two hours.

Two hours. Two hours. Two hours.

He turned his eyes to the clock radio beside the phone.

Just two hours before, he had ripped up the two snapshots of an invisible Shari.

His mind whirred with wild ideas, insane ideas.

Had he brought Shari back by ripping up the photos?

Did this mean that the camera *caused* her to disappear? That the camera *caused* all of the terrible things that showed up in its snapshots?

Greg stared at the phone for a long time, thinking hard.

He knew what he had to do. He had to talk to Shari. And he had to return the camera.

He met Shari on the playground the next afternoon. The sun floated high in a cloudless sky. Eight or nine kids were engaged in a noisy brawl of a soccer game, running one way, then the other across the outfield of the baseball diamond.

"Hey — you look like *you*!" Greg exclaimed as Shari came jogging up to where he stood beside the bleachers. He pinched her arm. "Yeah. It's you, okay."

She didn't smile. "I feel fine," she told him, rubbing her arm. "Just confused. And tired. The police asked me questions for hours. And when they finally went away, my parents started in."

"Sorry," Greg said quietly, staring down at his sneakers.

"I think Mom and Dad believe somehow it's my fault that I disappeared," Shari said, resting her back against the side of the bleachers, shaking her head.

"It's the camera's fault," Greg muttered. He raised his eyes to hers. "The camera is evil."

Shari shrugged. "Maybe. I don't know what to think. I really don't."

He showed her the snapshot, the one showing the two of them on the playground staring in horror as a shadow crept over them.

"How weird," Shari exclaimed, studying it hard.

"I want to take the camera back to the Coffman house," Greg said heatedly. "I can go home and get it now. Will you help me? Will you come with me?"

Shari started to reply, but stopped.

They both saw the dark shadow move, sliding toward them quickly, silently, over the grass.

And then they saw the man dressed all in black, his spindly legs pumping hard as he came at them.

Spidey!

Greg grabbed Shari's hand, frozen in fear.

He and Shari gaped in terror as Spidey's slithering shadow crept over them.

26

Greg had a shudder of recognition. He knew the snapshot had just come true.

As the dark figure of Spidey moved toward them like a black tarantula, Greg pulled Shari's hand. "Run!" he cried in a shrill voice he didn't recognize.

He didn't have to say it. They were both running now, gasping as they ran across the grass toward the street. Their sneakers thudded loudly on the ground as they reached the sidewalk and kept running.

Greg turned to see Spidey closing the gap. "He's catching up!" he managed to cry to Shari, who was a few steps ahead of him.

Spidey, his face still hidden in the shadows of his black baseball cap, moved with startling speed, his long legs kicking high as he pursued them.

"He's going to catch us!" Greg cried, feeling as

if his chest were about to burst. "*He's* . . . too
. . . fast!"

Spidey moved even closer, his shadow scuttling
over the grass.

Closer.

When the car horn honked, Greg screamed.

He and Shari stopped short.

The horn blasted out again.

Greg turned to see a familiar young man inside
a small hatchback. It was Jerry Norman, who
lived across the street. Jerry lowered his car window. "Is this man chasing you?" he asked excitedly. Without waiting for an answer, he backed
the car towards Spidey. "I'm calling the cops,
mister!"

Spidey didn't reply. Instead, he turned and
darted across the street.

"I'm warning you — " Jerry called after him.

But Spidey had disappeared behind a tall hedge.

"Are you kids okay?" Greg's neighbor demanded.

"Yeah. Fine," Greg managed to reply, still
breathing hard, his chest heaving.

"We're okay. Thanks, Jerry," Shari said.

"I've seen that guy around the neighborhood,"
the young man said, staring through the windshield at the tall hedge. "Never thought he was
dangerous. You kids want me to call the police?"

"No. It's okay," Greg replied.

As soon as I give him back his camera, he'll stop chasing us, Greg thought.

"Well, be careful — okay?" Jerry said. "You need a lift home or anything?" He studied their faces as if trying to determine how frightened and upset they were.

Greg and Shari both shook their heads. "We'll be okay," Greg said. "Thanks."

Jerry warned them once again to be careful, then drove off, his tires squealing as he turned the corner.

"That was close," Shari said, her eyes on the hedge. "Why was Spidey chasing us?"

"He thought I had the camera. He wants it back," Greg told her. "Meet me tomorrow, okay? In front of the Coffman house. Help me put it back?"

Shari stared at him without replying, her expression thoughtful, wary.

"We're going to be in danger — all of us — until we put that camera back," Greg insisted.

"Okay," Shari said quietly. "Tomorrow."

27

Something scurried through the tall weeds of the unmowed front lawn. "What *was* that?" Shari cried, whispering even though no one else was in sight. "It was too big to be a squirrel."

She lingered behind Greg, who stopped to look up at the Coffman house. "Maybe it was a racoon or something," Greg told her. He gripped the camera tightly in both hands.

It was a little after three o'clock the next afternoon, a hazy, overcast day. Mountains of dark clouds threatening rain were rolling across the sky, stretching behind the house, casting it in shadow.

"It's going to storm," Shari said, staying close behind Greg. "Let's get this over with and go home."

"Good idea," he said, glancing up at the heavy sky.

Thunder rumbled in the distance, a low roar.

The old trees that dotted the front yard whispered and shook.

"We can't just run inside," Greg told her, watching the sky darken. "First we have to make sure Spidey isn't there."

Making their way quickly through the tall grass and weeds, they stopped at the living room window and peered in. Thunder rumbled, low and long, in the distance. Greg thought he saw another creature scuttle through the weeds around the corner of the house.

"It's too dark in there. I can't see a thing," Shari complained.

"Let's check out the basement," Greg suggested. "That's where Spidey hangs out, remember?"

The sky darkened to an eerie gray-green as they made their way to the back of the house and dropped to their knees to peer down through the basement windows at ground level.

Squinting through the dust-covered windowpanes they could see the makeshift, plywood table Spidey had made, the wardrobe against the wall, its doors still open, the colorful, old clothing spilling out, the empty frozen food boxes scattered on the floor.

"No sign of him," Greg whispered, cradling the camera in his arm as if it might try to escape from him if he didn't hold it tightly. "Let's get moving."

"Are — are you sure?" Shari stammered. She

wanted to be brave. But the thought that she had disappeared for two days — completely *vanished*, most likely because of the camera — that frightening thought lingered in her mind.

Michael and Bird were chicken, she thought. But maybe they were the smart ones.

She wished this were over. All over.

A few seconds later, Greg and Shari pushed open the front door. They stepped into the darkness of the front hall. And stopped.

And listened.

And then they both jumped at the sound of the loud, sudden crash directly behind them.

28

Shari was the first to regain her voice. "It's just the door!" she cried. "The wind — "

A gust of wind had made the front door slam.

"Let's get this over with," Greg whispered, badly shaken.

"We never should've broken into this house in the first place," Shari whispered as they made their way on tiptoe, step by creaking step, down the dark hallway toward the basement stairs.

"It's a little late for that," Greg replied sharply.

Pulling open the door to the basement steps, he stopped again. "What's that banging sound upstairs?"

Shari's features tightened in fear as she heard it, too, a repeated, almost rhythmic banging.

"Shutters?" Greg suggested.

"Yeah," she quickly agreed, breathing a sigh of relief. "A lot of the shutters are loose, remember?"

The entire house seemed to groan.

Thunder rumbled outside, closer now.

They stepped onto the landing, then waited for their eyes to adjust to the darkness.

"Couldn't we just leave the camera up here, and run?" Shari asked, more of a plea than a question.

"No. I want to put it back," Greg insisted.

"But, Greg — " She tugged at his arm as he started down the stairs.

"No!" He pulled out of her grasp. "He was in my *room*, Shari! He tore everything apart, looking for it. I want him to find it where it belongs. If he doesn't find it, he'll come back to my house. I *know* he will!"

"Okay, okay. Let's just hurry."

It was brighter in the basement, gray light seeping down from the four ground-level windows. Outside, the wind swirled and pushed against the windowpanes. A pale flash of lightning made shadows flicker against the basement wall. The old house groaned as if unhappy about the storm.

"What was *that*? Footsteps?" Shari stopped halfway across the basement and listened.

"It's just the house," Greg insisted. But his quivering voice revealed that he was as frightened as his companion, and he stopped to listen, too.

Bang. Bang. Bang.

The shutter high above them continued its rhythmic pounding.

"Where did you find the camera, anyway?" Shari whispered, following Greg to the far wall across from the enormous furnace with its cob-webbed ducts sprouting up like pale tree limbs.

"Over here," Greg told her. He stepped up to the worktable and reached for the vise clamped on the edge. "When I turned the vise, a door opened up. Some kind of hidden shelf. That's where the camera — "

He cranked the handle of the vise.

Once again, the door to the secret shelf popped open.

"Good," he whispered excitedly. He flashed Shari a smile.

He shoved the camera onto the shelf, tucking the carrying strap under it. Then he pushed the door closed. "We're out of here."

He felt so much better. So relieved. So much *lighter*.

The house groaned and creaked. Greg didn't care.

Another flash of lightning, brighter this time, like a camera flash, sent shadows flickering on the wall.

"Come on," he whispered. But Shari was already ahead of him, making her way carefully over the food cartons strewn everywhere, hurrying towards the steps.

They were halfway up the stairs, Greg one step behind Shari, when, above them, Spidey stepped silently into view on the landing, blocking their escape.

29

Greg blinked and shook his head, as if he could shake away the image of the figure that stared darkly down at him.

"No!" Shari cried out, and fell back against Greg.

He grabbed for the railing, forgetting that it had fallen under Michael's weight during their first unfortunate visit to the house. Luckily, Shari regained her balance before toppling them both down the stairs.

Lightning flashed behind them, sending a flash of white light across the stairway. But the unmoving figure on the landing above them remained shrouded in darkness.

"Let us go!" Greg finally managed to cry, finding his voice.

"Yeah. We returned your camera!" Shari added, sounding shrill and frightened.

Spidey didn't reply. Instead, he took a step towards them, onto the first step. And then he descended another step.

Nearly stumbling again, Greg and Shari backed down to the basement floor.

The wooden stairs squeaked in protest as the dark figure stepped slowly, steadily, down. As he reached the basement floor, a crackling bolt of lightning cast a blue light over him, and Greg and Shari saw his face for the first time.

In the brief flash of color, they saw that he was old, older than they had imagined. That his eyes were small and round like dark marbles. That his mouth was small, too, pursed in a tight, menacing grimace.

"We returned the camera," Shari said, staring in fear as Spidey crept closer. "Can't we go now? Please?"

"Let me see," Spidey said. His voice was younger than his face, warmer than his eyes. "Come."

They hesitated. But he gave them no choice.

Ushering them back across the cluttered floor to the worktable, he wrapped his large, spidery hand over the vise and turned the handle. The door opened. He pulled out the camera and held it close to his face to examine it.

"You shouldn't have taken it," he told them, speaking softly, turning the camera in his hands.

"We're sorry," Shari said quickly.

"Can we go now?" Greg asked, edging towards the stairs.

"It's not an ordinary camera," Spidey said, raising his small eyes to them.

"We know," Greg blurted out. "The pictures it took. They — "

Spidey's eyes grew wide, his expression angry. "You took pictures with it?"

"Just a few," Greg told him, wishing he had kept his mouth shut. "They didn't come out. Really."

"You know about the camera, then," Spidey said, moving quickly to the center of the floor.

Was he trying to block their escape? Greg wondered.

"It's broken or something," Greg said uncertainly, shoving his hands into his jeans pockets.

"It's not broken," the tall, dark figure said softly. "It's evil." He motioned toward the low plywood table. "Sit there."

Shari and Greg exchanged glances. Then, reluctantly, they sat down on the edge of the board, sitting stiffly, nervously, their eyes darting towards the stairway, towards escape.

"The camera is evil," Spidey repeated, standing over them, holding the camera in both hands. "I should know. I helped to create it."

"You're an inventor?" Greg asked, glancing at Shari, who was nervously tugging at a strand of her black hair.

"I'm a scientist," Spidey replied. "Or, I should say, I *was* a scientist. My name is Fredericks. Dr. Fritz Fredericks." He transferred the camera from one hand to the other. "My lab partner invented this camera. It was his pride and joy. More than that, it would have made him a fortune. *Would* have, I say." He paused, a thoughtful expression sinking over his face.

"What happened to him? Did he die?" Shari asked, still fiddling with the strand of hair.

Dr. Fredericks snickered. "No. Worse. I stole the invention from him. I stole the plans and the camera. I was evil, you see. I was young and greedy. So very greedy. And I wasn't above stealing to make my fortune."

He paused, eyeing them both as if waiting for them to say something, to offer their disapproval of him, perhaps. But when Greg and Shari remained silent, staring up at him from the low plywood table, he continued his story.

"When I stole the camera, it caught my partner by surprise. Unfortunately, from then on, all of the surprises were mine." A strange, sad smile twisted across his aged face. "My partner, you see, was much more evil than I was."

Dr. Fredericks coughed into his hand, then began to pace in front of Greg and Shari as he talked, speaking softly, slowly, as if remembering the story for the first time in a long while.

"My partner was a *true* evil one. He dabbled in

the dark arts. I should correct myself. He didn't just dabble. He was quite a master of it all."

He held up the camera, waving it above his head, then lowering it. "My partner put a curse on the camera. If he couldn't profit from it, he wanted to make sure that I never would, either. And so he put a curse on it."

He turned his gaze on Greg, leaning over him. "Do you know about how some primitive peoples fear the camera? They fear the camera because they believe that if it takes their picture, it will steal their soul." He patted the camera. "Well, this camera really *does* steal souls."

Staring up at the camera, Greg shuddered.

The camera had stolen Shari away.

Would it have stolen *all* of their souls?

"People have died because of this camera," Dr. Fredericks said, uttering a slow, sad sigh. "People close to me. That is how I came to learn of the curse, to learn of the camera's evil. And then I learned something just as frightening — the camera cannot be destroyed."

He coughed, cleared his throat noisily, and began to pace in front of them again. "And so I vowed to keep the camera a secret. To keep it away from people so it cannot do its evil. I lost my job. My family. I lost everything because of it. But I am determined to keep the camera where it can do no harm."

He stopped pacing with his back towards them.

He stood silently, shoulders hunched, lost in thought.

Greg quickly climbed to his feet and motioned for Shari to do the same. "Well . . . uh . . . I guess it's good we returned it," he said hesitantly. "Sorry we caused so much trouble."

"Yeah, we're very sorry," Shari repeated sincerely. "Guess it's back in the right hands."

"Good-bye," Greg said, starting towards the steps. "It's getting late, and we — "

"No!" Dr. Fredericks shouted, startling them both. He moved quickly to block the way. "I'm afraid you can't go. You know too much."

30

"I can never let you leave," Dr. Fredericks said, his face flickering in the blue glow of a lightning flash. He crossed his bony arms in front of his black sweatshirt.

"But we won't tell anyone," Greg said, his voice rising until the words became a plea. "Really."

"Your secret is good with us," Shari insisted, her frightened eyes on Greg.

Dr. Fredericks stared at them menacingly, but didn't reply.

"You can trust us," Greg said, his voice quivering. He cast a frightened glance at Shari.

"Besides," Shari said, "even if we *did* tell anyone, who would believe us?"

"Enough talk," Dr. Fredericks snapped. "It won't do you any good. I've worked too long and too hard to keep the camera a secret."

A rush of wind pushed against the windows, sending up a low howl. The wind carried a drumroll of rain. The sky through the basement windows was as black as night.

"You — can't keep us here *forever!*" Shari cried, unable to keep the growing terror from her voice.

The rain pounded against the windows now, a steady downpour.

Dr. Fredericks drew himself up straight, seemed to grow taller. His tiny eyes burned into Shari's. "I'm so sorry," he said, his voice a whisper of regret. "So sorry. But I have no choice."

He took another step towards them.

Greg and Shari exchanged frightened glances. From where they stood, in front of the low plywood table in the center of the basement, the steps seemed a hundred miles away.

"Wh-what are you going to do?" Greg cried, shouting over a burst of thunder that rattled the basement windows.

"Please — !" Shari begged. "Don't — !"

Dr. Fredericks moved forward with surprising speed. Holding the camera in one hand, he grabbed Greg's shoulder with the other.

"No!" Greg screamed. "Let go!"

"Let go of him!" Shari screamed.

She suddenly realized that both of Dr. Frederick's hands were occupied.

This may be my only chance, she thought.

She took a deep breath and lunged forward.

Dr. Fredericks' eyes bulged, and he cried out

in surprise as Shari grabbed the camera with both hands and pulled it away from him. He made a frantic grab for the camera, and Greg burst free.

Before the desperate man could take another step, Shari raised the camera to her eye and pointed the lens at him.

"Please — no! Don't push the button!" the old man cried.

He lurched forward, his eyes wild, and grabbed the camera with both hands.

Greg stared in horror as Shari and Dr. Fredericks grappled, both holding onto the camera, each trying desperately to wrestle it away from the other.

FLASH!

The bright burst of light startled them all.

Shari grabbed the camera. "Run!" she screamed.

31

The basement became a whirring blur of grays and blacks as Greg hurtled himself towards the stairs.

He and Shari ran side by side, slipping over the food cartons, jumping over tin cans and empty bottles.

Rain thundered against the windows. The wind howled, pushing against the glass. They could hear Dr. Fredericks' anguished screams behind them.

"Did it take our picture or his?" Shari asked.

"I don't know. Just *hurry!*" Greg screamed.

The old man was howling like a wounded animal, his cries competing with the rain and wind pushing at the windows.

The stairs weren't that far away. But it seemed to take forever to reach them.

Forever.

Forever, Greg thought. Dr. Fredericks wanted to keep Shari and him down there *forever*.

Panting loudly, they both reached the dark stairway. A deafening clap of thunder made them stop and turn around.

"Huh?" Greg cried aloud.

To his shock, Dr. Fredericks hadn't chased after them.

And his anguished cries had stopped.

The basement was silent.

"What's going on?" Shari cried breathlessly.

Squinting back into the darkness, it took Greg a while to realize that the dark, rumpled form lying on the floor in front of the worktable was Dr. Fredericks.

"What happened?" Shari cried, her chest heaving as she struggled to catch her breath. Still clinging to the camera strap, she gaped in surprise at the old man's still body, sprawled on its back on the floor.

"I don't know," Greg replied in a breathless whisper.

Reluctantly, Greg started back towards Dr. Fredericks. Following close behind, Shari uttered a low cry of horror when she clearly saw the fallen man's face.

Eyes bulged out, the mouth open in a twisted O of terror, the face stared up at them. Frozen. Dead.

Dr. Fredericks was dead.

"What — *happened*?" Shari finally managed to say, swallowing hard, forcing herself to turn away from the ghastly, tortured face.

"I think he died of fright," Greg replied, squeezing her shoulder and not even realizing it.

"Huh? Fright?"

"He knew better than anyone what the camera could do," Greg said. "When you snapped his picture, I think . . . I think it scared him to *death*!"

"I only wanted to throw him off-guard," Shari cried. "I only wanted to give us a chance to escape. I didn't think — "

"The picture," Greg interrupted. "Let's see the picture."

Shari raised the camera. The photo was still half-inside the camera. Greg pulled it out with a trembling hand. He held it up so they could both see it.

"Wow," he exclaimed quietly. "Wow."

The photo showed Dr. Fredericks lying on the floor, his eyes bulging, his mouth frozen open in horror.

Dr. Fredericks' fright, Greg realized — the fright that had killed him — was there, frozen on film, frozen on his face.

The camera had claimed another victim. This time, forever.

"What do we do now?" Shari asked, staring down at the figure sprawled at their feet.

"First, I'm putting this camera back," Greg said, taking it from her and shoving it back on its shelf. He turned the vise handle, and the door to the secret compartment closed.

Greg breathed a sigh of relief. Hiding the dreadful camera away made him feel so much better.

"Now, let's go home and call the police," he said.

Two days later, a cool, bright day with a gentle breeze rustling the trees, the four friends stopped at the curb, leaning on their bikes, and stared up at the Coffman house. Even in bright sunlight, the old trees that surrounded the house covered it in shade.

"So you didn't tell the police about the camera?" Bird asked, staring up at the dark, empty front window.

"No. They wouldn't believe it," Greg told him. "Besides, the camera should stay locked up forever. *Forever!* I hope no one ever finds out about it."

"We told the police we ran into the house to get out of the rain," Shari added. "And we said we started to explore while we waited for the storm to blow over. And we found the body in the basement."

"What did Spidey die of?" Michael asked, gazing up at the house.

"The police said it was heart failure," Greg told him. "But we know the truth."

"Wow. I can't believe one old camera could do so much evil," Bird said.

"I believe it," Greg said quietly.

"Let's get out of here," Michael urged. He raised his sneakers to the pedals and started to roll away. "This place really creeps me out."

The other three followed, pedaling away in thoughtful silence.

They had turned the corner and were heading up the next block when two figures emerged from the back door of the Coffman house. Joey Ferris and Mickey Ward stepped over the weed-choked lawn onto the driveway.

"Those jerks aren't too bright," Joey told his companion. "They never even saw us the other day. Never saw us watching them through the basement window."

Mickey laughed. "Yeah. They're jerks."

"They couldn't hide this camera from *us*. No way, man," Joey said. He raised the camera and examined it.

"Take my picture," Mickey demanded. "Come on. Let's try it out."

"Yeah. Okay." Joey raised the viewfinder to his eye. "Say cheese."

A click. A flash. A whirring sound.

Joey pulled the snapshot from the camera, and both boys eagerly huddled around it, waiting to see what developed.

About the Author

R.L. STINE is the author of over three dozen best-selling thrillers and mysteries for young people. Recent titles for teenagers include *I Saw You That Night!*, *Call Waiting*, *Halloween Night II*, *The Dead Girlfriend*, and *The Baby-sitter III*, all published by Scholastic. He is also the author of the *Fear Street* series.

Bob lives in New York City with his wife, Jane, and his fifteen-year-old son, Matt.